"Learn how to unleash more of your true potential for greater success! This powerful book gives you the recipe for high achievement."

—Brian Tracy
Author, *The 100 Absolutely Unbreakable Laws of Business Success*

"I have attended over 50 time management seminars in my time by industry gurus, and many of them were of some use. But NONE has provided the depth of control of my time and life as Time Control has. I was amazed at how effective I became after just three weeks personally using Vince's tools in *The 26-Hour Day*. We proudly recommend *The 26-Hour Day* to all of our members and their clients."

—J. Stephen Lanning
Executive Director
National Association of Business Coaches (NABC)
www.MyNABC.org

"In television production, time is money. The best way to save money is to control your time. *The 26-Hour Day* has freed me to concentrate on the all-important creative aspects of producing a television series."

—James C. Hart
Co-Executive Producer / Director, *Chicago Hope* and *CSI*
Producer / Director, *LA Law*
Producer, *Hill Street Blues*

"Vince Panella's Time Control systems and techniques in the *The 26-Hour Day* are an absolute necessity for personal and business growth in the 21st Century. His simple idea of 'just 5 minutes a day' improved my productivity immediately."

—Gary Curry
President, ORBA Financial Management Company

"Vince Panella's Time Control strategies in *The 26-Hour Day* have helped me tremendously increase my time management and subsequently grow my business. As a business owner for over sixteen years, I stay extremely busy and need techniques which are simple to implement and worth my time investment. I have discovered that Vince's strategies continue to meet my needs and challenge me to continual improvement."

—Irene Cox
   Houston small business owner

"A number of *The 26-Hour Day*'s tutorials are invaluable. They are clear, simple and concise, giving easy means to create additional time in every day. From knowing what I want, to improving my sleep, to cutting down on simple distractions, I accomplish more and more every day. The lessons learned and applied have helped and will continue to help in limitless ways."

—Dr. Kevin Worry
   Canadian physician

The 26-HOUR DAY

How to Gain at Least Two Hours a Day with Time Control

By

Vince Panella

CAREER
PRESS

Franklin Lakes, NJ

Copyright © 2002 by Vince Panella

The 26-Hour Day
Edited by Kristen Mohn
Typeset by Eileen Dow Munson
Cover design by Johnson Design
Printed in the U.S.A. by Book-mart Press

To order this title, please call toll-free 1-800-CAREER-1 (NJ and Canada: 201-848-0310) to order using VISA or MasterCard, or for further information on books from Career Press.

The Career Press, Inc., 3 Tice Road, PO Box 687
Franklin Lakes, NJ 07417
www.careerpress.com

Library of Congress Cataloging-in-Publication Data

Panella, Vince.
    The 26-hour day : how to gain at least two hours a day with time control / by Vince Panella.
        p. cm.
    Includes index.
        ISBN 1-56414-580-8 (pbk.)
        1. Time management. I. Title: Twenty-four-hour day. II. Title.

HD69.T54 P36 2001
650.1—dc21

                                                                                   2001026621

For Vicki, Tony, and Nicky—
You inspire me to make the most
of my time every day.

My final editing for this book
comes during and in the aftermath of
the worst attacks and tragedy
suffered in American history. I'll
never forget, as I pray you never
will, the many thousands of innocent
and brave lives lost on
September 11, 2001 in
New York, Washington D.C.,
and Pennsylvania.

CONTENTS

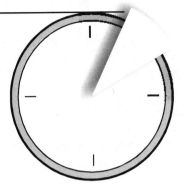

PREFACE

So, you'd like to learn more about time management?

Sorry. You're reading the wrong book.

Instead, what I'd like to teach you is Success-Centered Time Management, a concept I've created and taught since 1982 in more than 25 different countries around the world. It's a concept that enabled me to graduate with distinction from the United States Naval Academy and complete a successful eight-year career as a naval officer and aviator. It's the same concept that allowed me to work as a college professor for three years, then go on to become a corporate founder and president by the age of 30. And most importantly, it's the same concept that has helped me teach hundreds of thousands of people around the world how to be more successful in the their lives by means of their time.

My purpose in writing this book is not to amaze you with impressive, but complex, behavioral and time management tools that only work for a precious few. Instead, you will learn skills that you can put to immediate use, regardless of who you are and what business or personal situation you're in.

In this book's lessons, the key to my approach is stressing the following:

Complete this sentence: Knowledge is _____.

If you answered "power," I absolutely disagree with you.

We've been taught all our lives that knowledge is power. Here is an example of why this thinking doesn't work. Let's say I gave you a simple 10-page booklet with the secrets of life: how to have abundant health and energy, how to achieve financial freedom, how to grow incredible relationships, and how to live in eternal peace. The booklet would be written so that it speaks very personally to you, so that you completely understand each word and are capable of fulfilling all of its promises. You take the booklet, you read and understand it, but then put it on your bookshelf and never act on the secrets in order to bring their promises to your life. Would you call this power? I wouldn't. You have the knowledge to change your life, but without *action*, it's powerless!

I believe that knowledge is potential power or potential energy. With knowledge, you have the ability to create great power in your and others' lives. But you must act in order to spark that power. True power is the application or use of what you already know.

As a college professor, I encountered some of the most brilliant people I've ever met. Having earned their doctorates, many had experienced formal education on a higher level than I ever planned on achieving. But for all their knowledge, it was sad to see how little of it was applied to their personal lives.

We are all familiar with the stories of someone who dropped out of high school, only to become successful in business because they learned a simple concept and kept on applying and modifying it. Or others who live very simple lives and aren't very financially prosperous, but who live a life filled with joy and wonderful relationships because each day they learn and apply the knowledge of peace, love, and acceptance.

Please don't get me wrong—I believe education is very important. But instead of our goal being the pursuit of knowledge, I believe we should pursue the growth and continuous application of our knowledge.

Another way of looking at this is that most of us *know* that exercise and eating right are important to a healthy and happy life, yet over 60 percent of our country is out of shape. Most of us *know* that sleep and rest are important to our mental sharpness and productivity, yet over 50 percent of us are chronically sleep deprived. Behaviors, not knowledge, drive most of our actions! That's why I want to focus on positively shifting your behaviors in time.

Consequently, my approach in this book is to not only teach you new skills, but also to get you to apply them in order to create the life you desire. You will most likely have heard many of the skills in this book before, but my goal is to successfully teach you the skills to apply the knowledge in powerfully unique combinations.

The key to moving knowledge into action in order to create true power is using *tools*—simple, repeatable skill steps that bring consistent results. The purpose of this book is to give you knowledge in ways that will massively leverage your time, teach you simple tools to bring those consistent results to life, then motivate the heck out of you to use the tools to create the extra time you desire.

In closing, I'd like to share with you a simple roadmap to the success of gaining more time. Frequent *repetition* of positive skill tools leads to *consistency*, creating habit. *Consistency* leads to *discipline,* creating the strength to overcome most obstacles and distractions. And *discipline* leads to *success,* creating control of most of your habits and behaviors, your time, and ultimately, your destiny.

An Introduction to Time Control

Success-Centered Time Management versus Time Management

So what, exactly, is the difference between Success-Centered Time Management and traditional time management? The best way to recognize the difference is by walking you through a couple of questions.

First, do you think your life would benefit both at work and home if you were more *organized* in your time?

That's the focus of time management. Not bad—*if* you organize the right things and consistently act on your plans.

Now, do you think your life would benefit much more if you concentrated your improvement on your *behaviors*, your motivation, and your focus within the time you have and then assisted that with a few organizational skills?

That's the unique and very powerful focus of Success-Centered Time Management—the key being your behaviors. You see, over the last 19 years of research, testing, and teaching, I've come to the conclusion that—*time management does not work*!

As a result of my studies conducted around the world, I've discovered that when people are taught time management by traditional organizational methods, 80 to 90 percent fall right back into old habits and behaviors within one month. In other words, when we're taught a tool to save us time, such as how to use a "to do" list or a day planner, most of us will find an excuse *not* to use this beneficial tool within just a few weeks despite being convinced that this new tool will work and despite being motivated by a sharp trainer. Has this ever happened to you?

Through my own early experiences with time management methods, I discovered, quite accidentally, that the fortunate 10 to 20 percent of people that were taught and found success with time management tools had a common background. All had some basis or education in skills that focused on their habits and behaviors within the realm of time. It was my experience that, when I was 14 years old, I began to realize a passion for studying the foundational skills needed for mastering time. It took Jerry Lucas, an NBA player who co-authored *The Memory Book* (Ballantine Books), to spark this destiny. Throughout the following years of study, practice, and testing, I improved this set of skills and its combination with traditional time management skills. This was the birth of Success-Centered Time Management.

What Is Time Control?

Gain control of yourself,
And you can fully control your time.
Control your time,
And you control your destiny. (SM)

Time Control is the program that brings Success-Centered Time Management to life by helping you build a solid foundation in the critical behavioral skills needed to conquer time. It will help you build a base to conquer your time-stealing habits and gain control of yourself. The program then mixes in the most effective and simple-to-use time management skills I've found in my near 20 years of experience. This combination of focusing *first* on behavioral-based success skills, *then* mixing effective and simple time management skills gives you control of your destiny.

I define destiny as the chain reaction of consistent thoughts and actions that take your life in a particular direction. It's simply the summation of what you think and do on a daily basis over time. I feel that destiny is less of a destination and more of a direction, and that we have absolute control over the direction in which we point our lives.

3 Categories to Gain More Time

I have found that there are only three main categories of required action in order to gain more time in your day:

1. Reduce your Distractions and Time Wasters
2. Improve your Action Systems
3. Increase your Human Performance

Number one is fairly obvious. In this category, as you remove or reduce things in your life that "steal" time and do not move you toward your goals and vision, you increase the total amount of productive time available to you. By improving in this category, most people can usually gain one to four hours a day.

Examples of reducing distractions and time wasters include reducing telephone and personal interruptions, controlling socializing, reducing procrastination, streamlining or eliminating wasteful meetings, controlling the television and time surfing the Web, and reducing paperwork. Gaining clarity and focus, as well as setting and frequently reviewing goals, can help immensely in this category.

Day planners and "to do" lists can also help reduce distractions and time wasters. But *beware*! Day planners and "to do" lists are *only* as good as the information you put into them. No matter how organized you are, if you fill your day with events and tasks that do not take you toward your goals and clear vision, then you are still wasting your time. You're just doing so with flair.

Improving your action systems can add precious hours to your day. In this category, you increase your total daily time as you reduce the time needed to perform your daily functions. Even better—if you can find ways to massively increase your results for the same or even less effort, you will grow your time by leaps and bounds! The amount of time you gain from this category can vary greatly from a few minutes a day to exponential numbers.

Examples of improving your action systems include reducing the time you need for exercise while actually increasing your results, reducing housework, and reducing the time allotted for events at work. In business, two of my favorite action systems to improve on are sales and small business marketing. Through incredible mentors, I have found systems that greatly accelerate time in sales and marketing by focusing on simplicity and better than average returns on time, effort, and cost expended.

The last category in gaining more time in your day is increasing your human performance. By focusing on increasing your human alertness, energy, motivation, and focus, you can easily add two to four hours to your day.

Examples of increasing your human performance include getting adequate sleep (this will give most of us two more hours a day), exercise, and mental rest. Eating a proper diet and reducing stress also increase how well you perform in the time you have. Simply increasing your motivation can also add several hours to your day.

These three categories all work together to give you more time in your day. Improve in any one category, and you will grow your time linearly. Be careful, though. If you improve in one area, but are destructive in another, your efforts could cancel each other out. By this, I mean if you are organized, have and use a day planner, and try not to waste time, *but* you average less than seven hours of sleep a night and drink caffeine products to get through the day, your efforts are canceling out their effectiveness. You're shooting yourself in the foot!

However, if you improve in all three categories—even just a little bit, you will grow your time geometrically as the improvements reinforce each other. A small improvement in all three categories could easily add several hours to your day. Increase your improvement aggressively in each category, and you can drastically change your destiny.

The Time Control Modules

You'll notice that between the Introduction and Conclusion of this book, there aren't any chapters—there are 13 modules. A chapter is something you read before moving on to the next chapter. This is fine if your goal is to only gain knowledge. A module, however, is something you actually work on and apply action to before moving on to the next module. Modules are about knowledge *and* action!

Repetition leads to consistency; consistency leads to discipline; and discipline leads to success. Repetition of a positive, time-accelerating skill or technique leads to consistency or habit in about three weeks. All 13 Time Control modules in this book are designed to be individually studied, and more importantly, applied for three to four weeks before moving on to the next module. Through this module method, you'll ingrain positive habits into your behaviors before adding something new—a true formula for increased power and control in your life.

Before we dive into the modules, I think it's important to share with you how they're put together and arranged and the best way to use them to maximize your time-building benefit from this book.

This book contains 13 Time Control modules. I consider these particular modules to be the foundation and cornerstone of my entire Time Control program. Each module contains two sections, the module text and the module worksheets. The module text is the coaching guide where you walk through the module's background, relevance, and case histories, and are taught, step-by-step, how to apply its techniques and tools to your life. Application of each module's tools is the key to your success in this program, and the worksheets are your guides to application. All applicable worksheets mentioned in the module text are contained in a section called "Put Your Knowledge Into Action" at the end of each module.

The order of these 13 modules is specifically designed to give you maximum yield in the shortest amount of time—working together to create powerful behavioral changes for you to add at least two to four more enriched hours to each of your days. Each successive module will add a new dimension and strength to your success in time, either leveraging additional daily minutes or hours, or building your behavioral strength to keep the time you've gained to date.

Let's take a quick look at the modules to give you a taste of what's in store for you.

Module 1
For Starters...Clarity!

Do you know where you are in your life? Do you know where you want to be? This module can help! Learn how to create and apply your *Clarity*—the most critical, yet overlooked and underutilized, first step in building personal and business success in time!

Module 2
The Continual Success Improvement Formula

Learn a simple, four-step formula that will empower you to constantly achieve and improve your success in time at both work and home.

Module 3
Bit by Bit

The simple, amazing power of five minutes! Learn how just five minutes a day can change your destiny and help you accomplish what you thought impossible. Includes "The War Board," a tool to greatly accelerate your learning and application of any chosen field of study.

Module 4
Gain 2 More Hours a Day Through the Power of Sleep

Almost all of us want more, but few take it seriously. This module shows you how the lack of adequate sleep is the reason for 90 percent of our problems in time. It then teaches you how sleep can help you gain several more productive, creative, focused hours each day; reduce your stress levels immensely; gain a tremendous boost in day-long energy; and spend more enjoyable time with those you love.

Module 5
The Power and Purpose of Behavioral Goals

Learn the awesome power and purpose of goals, then discover the guidelines of behavioral-based goal setting for fulfilling any goal. Includes a powerful, step-by-step Goal Setting Workshop.

Module 6
Reducing Distractions

Learn the 13 leading time wasters in our lives and gain skills to reduce them. The exercises in this module will easily help you gain, on average, over an hour extra at both work and home.

Module 7
Motivation Control

Learn and practice powerful tools to increase both short and long term motivation in all life's situations: from presentations to meetings with clients to selling to going to work everyday to improving your health and relationships.

Module 8
Increasing Your Energy Level

The less than 6 percent time solution! Learn how to maximize your diet, exercise, and rest to maintain a peak level of energy all day.

Module 9
Removing Stress From Your Life

Discover the dynamics of stress and how it affects your control of time; then learn specific ways to remove it from your life. Includes our famous Sword and Shield Technique.

Module 10
Controlling Your Values, Beliefs, and Character

Uncover the time dynamics of your values, beliefs, and character; master the proven value of initiative; then design your own Daily Corps Values as a front-line of defense for daily decision-making.

Module 11
Winning the War Against Procrastination

Learn the powerful dynamics of procrastination and the tools to permanently defeat it. Includes a special behavior-changing Time Warp visualization that will positively change your life.

Module 12
Moments: The Secret of Life

Discover how the meaning, depth, and enjoyment of your life is centered around individual moments and learn how to accumulate a fulfilling, rich bank account of these defining points in your life.

Module 13
Maximizing Any Experience

Gain 20/20 hindsight for your life ahead of time through a simple tool allowing you to take control over things you have influence over prior to an event or experience.

How to Get the Most Out of This Book

Unfortunately, most of us who read self-help books usually gain from them intellectual stimulation and some short-term motivation, but little direct and long-lasting benefit. Why? We tend to quickly read through improvement books, taking little time to actually try the exercises they contain and only half-heartedly testing the suggestions for change.

This type of studying pattern will give you knowledge and allow you to read a multitude of self-help books over a short period of time, but it will not give you power. And it will not bring about lasting positive change.

As a great example of this: recently, I was a guest on a Houston business radio talk show. The last caller of the morning called in to see how she could reduce her constant feeling of overwhelm at both work and home. When I suggested that she try my Time Control tool of creating and using Clarity for herself, she replied that she already had read Stephen Covey's books and had even "purchased his mugs and t-shirts." I had to laugh. She was setting the perfect example of how to gain knowledge but not power. Books, and especially mugs and t-shirts, don't bring about desired change!

If you want to go from knowledge to power, and if you want to bring about measurable, positive, and lasting change, then you have to break your existing pattern of study. You'll have to commit to focusing on action and testing over knowledge.

It is for this exact purpose that I've designed this book. You see, I'm more of a coach than a teacher. A coach focuses on action while a teacher focuses on knowledge. Don't get me wrong, I believe knowledge is important. Without knowledge, you can't take effective action. But I focus on action, knowing this is by far where you should dedicate the majority of your time to achieve success.

You have two options in going through this book. You can jump right into working Module 1, and then progress through each successive module every three to four weeks following completion of each module's concluding action plan. Or you can read through the entire book first to get an overview of how all the modules work together, and then work through each module individually.

Either way, when you begin working on a module to ingrain its lessons into your positive habits, do the following to maximize the learning and habit-formation of each module:

▶ Spend a few days reading the module text to gain knowledge of the new Time Control technique.

▶ Spend a few days completing any included worksheets for the module.

▶ Apply the module's action plan for the remainder of the month as instructed.

▸   Review the module's "60-Second Power Summary" as
    necessary to reinforce the material and gain new insight into
    each lesson.

Going through each module as described above will take you from
knowledge to power. Although this book should take you about a year to
complete, the amount of time you'll need to expend on learning and applying these modules on a daily basis is minimal. Even if you only invest a few
minutes a day, five days a week on working through these modules, you'll
still benefit from significant improvement on your time control.

A quick and final note about the module worksheets. Because you'll
need to work through many of these worksheets more than once over
time, feel free to photocopy the worksheets for your own personal use.
This way you can write on your copies and keep the worksheets in your
book clean for future use.

MODULE

FOR STARTERS... CLARITY!

All successful people who have full control of their time start with the basis of Clarity—a very clear and detailed vision of their future!

In a *balanced* and *detailed* plan, which may include business, career, home-life, relationships, health, wealth, service, and personal growth, they start with the foundational questions of "Where am I now?" and "Where do I want to be?" then passionately, aggressively, and continuously attack with the questions of "How can I get there?" and "What are the 'wins' along the way?"

Simply put—Clarity is the most critical, yet most overlooked and underutilized, first step toward improving your time.

Where Am I Now?

Clarity is the map to get you to your destiny, the direction in which you want your life to point. Knowing the answer to the question "Where am I now?" tells you where you are on your map to start your journey. The more precisely and detailed you know where you are in whatever areas of your life you want to improve, the more accurate you'll be when you're starting from your life's map.

Can you imagine how hard it would be to begin a journey without knowing where you're starting from?

To answer "Where am I now?" simply take a snapshot of your life at this very moment in the specific areas you want to improve (business, career, home-life, relationships, health, wealth, service, and personal growth) and list the details you see from that picture. I've provided worksheets at the end of this module to help you in this extremely important process.

In business, this means knowing where you currently spend your time, energy, and capital on a daily basis and what results they're yielding. It means knowing all of your gross income and your expenditures, then comparing all that to your current sales, marketing, and distribution systems. It also means knowing your current employee work force and how you're taking care of them.

At work, this means evaluating your current position and company, your salary or commission structure, how you're currently performing in your job, what your current efforts bring in value to your company, how much time you put in, how much you enjoy your work, and whether or not others appreciate what you do.

At home, this means knowing how much time you're currently spending with your loved ones and how you're using that time. It also means knowing how much leisure and personal time you allow yourself and being aware of your family's current savings, investments, and debt status.

In your health, it means knowing how much and what type of exercise you do, what you eat, how much restful sleep you get, how you handle stress, and how much mental recharging you allow yourself.

You can answer the other areas in a similar way.

You don't have to answer "Where am I now?" for all of the areas, just the ones you want to improve at this time. You can always go back later and work on other categories when you're ready.

How much detail and effort should you put into answering "Where am I now?" is up to you, but understand that the more exact you are in knowing your location on your life's map, the better and easier it is to begin your journey in the right direction. Don't be a perfectionist, though. Get a good, detailed answer, then move on. Give yourself no more than an hour to answer this question, and then it's on to the next critical question to define your Clarity.

Where Do I Want to Be?

Now answer the question "Where do I want to be?" This is your destination on your life's map in about *two to three years from now*, and it's the most important question in your Clarity. The more precisely and detailed you answer this question for the areas you want to improve, the better your chances are of actually getting there.

Again, imagine how hard a journey would be if you didn't know exactly where you wanted to *go*. You would be absolutely stunned by how few people and businesses actually have a clear vision (Clarity) of where they would like to be!

To make this process easier, imagine precisely what your life, business, or situation will look when you can say you've "made it" in a particular category of your life in a perfect two to three years. Now take a snapshot of the image you see and list as many details as you can. I suggest choosing a two to three-year future point for your Clarity. Why? This will give you plenty of time to take action in order to bring about the future vision you desire. But it also isn't so far in the future that if you don't start taking some action now, and a little every day, that you'll be able to reach your vision. It's the perfect middle ground! This two to three year goal maximizes your motivation by keeping an attainable, yet challenging future vision consistently in front of you.

Let's look at some areas to apply this critical question.

In business, answering "Where do I want to be?" means knowing, at the very least, how much you want your business to be worth; what the salaries will be of you and your employees; knowing exactly how many employees and the type of personnel structure make up your company; your needed gross revenues to satisfy all of your needs and growth desires; where this revenue must come from; and how much time you want to work each day.

At work, this means detailing what position you want; the company or industry you want to work in; the salary you desire or how much you'd like to make from commissions; how much time you want put in on a daily or weekly basis; and how much you want to enjoy your job.

At home, this means detailing how much time you want to spend with your loved ones; exactly how you'd like to use that time; how much leisure and personal time you'd like for yourself; how much you'd like to have in savings and investments; and how much you want to reduce your debt.

And in your health, this means detailing what you'd like to look and feel like; how much energy you'd like to have; how healthy you'd like to be; how much sleep you'd like to get each night; and how much mental rest you'd like to have each day.

Don't let this exercise overwhelm you! Pretend that you have a piece of clay, which represents your future, and you now have free reign to mold it into any future you'd like to have. Be creative, and most of all, have fun doing this. Once again, don't be a perfectionist. Get a good, detailed list of your desired future, and try to do so in an hour of solid effort. You can always add to your Clarity as you move forward in your journey to success.

Having just answered "Where do I want to be?" you now know exactly where you want to go on your life's map in two to three years. You know where you are, and you know where you want to go. Once you know these two critical elements, life becomes so much more easy and clear.

So few people have taken the little effort required to define where they are and where they want to be in any detail. Think about it, though. How can anyone expect to have any chance of achieving his or her success unless they define that success in detail? No wonder so many of us are frustrated and overwhelmed.

How can you get more time in your life unless you know how you use your time right now, exactly how much more you want, and exactly what you want to use it for? Get Clarity!

How can you successfully grow your business unless you know the health of your business right now and exactly where you want it to be in the future? Get Clarity!

How can you improve your home life and relationships unless you know what you're doing right now and where exactly you want your home life and relationships to be in the future? Get Clarity!

And how can you be more healthy and have more energy unless you know where you stand right now and exactly what being in better health and having more energy means for you in the future? Again, get Clarity!

Your Clarity Support Questions

The next two questions "How can I get there?" and "What are the 'wins' along the way?" are used to help you get from where you are now to where you want to be.

Probably for the first time in your life you have a detailed and clear vision of what you'd like your future to be in a few years. Now answer, "How can I get there?" Brainstorm all the ways you can think of to help you successfully complete your journey. What steps can you take? Who can you go to for advice or assistance? What skills can you learn and apply that would be of help?

You don't have to make this list perfect, and it will probably never be all-inclusive, just concentrate on making it the best you can and realize that you can always add to it as you grow in your life's journey. You'll surprise yourself at how much you have accumulated that you've completely forgotten about through the years. Your books and tapes do absolutely no good if they just sit around and collect dust.

I want you to view this list as your Clarity resource guide. Add to it, edit it, and refer to it when making plans to move forward toward your Clarity. Next Module, when you start learning the Continual Success Improvement Formula, you'll begin referring to this list often in a structured plan.

The last question to answer for your Clarity is "What are the 'wins' along the way?" Look at your journey from where you are now to where you want to be, and pick several midpoints along the way. These will be celebration points in your journey to measure your growth and keep you motivated. Then write next to each point specifically how you'd like to celebrate that achievement. As human beings, we absolutely love a sense of accomplishment. I want you to consistently feel a sense of accomplishment in your journey and to realize that the journey itself, your growth, is every bit as important as your actual destination. You don't have to answer this Clarity question for every item you have for your future clear vision, just those that are most important to you.

Using Your Clarity

This exercise is probably one of the biggest ways to massively increase the amount of time you have. Why? From now on, I want you to compare everything you do to the map you've created in your Clarity. If what you're doing or have scheduled in your planner or "to do" list is not helping you move toward your Clarity, it's a waste of time! By only acting, to the best of your ability and control, on things that move you toward your clear future vision, you'll massively leverage your time to work for you. This will easily add hours to your day, improving all three categories of gaining more time! Beware of trying to run yourself into the ground, however. Proper sleep, exercise, mental rest, and having fun are some of the very best things you can do to keep yourself at your peak in order to consistently and progressively move toward your Clarity.

You need to review and compare to your schedule your answers to the Clarity question "Where do I want to be?" at least five days each week to gain this leverage. The business days of the week work best, and reviewing in the morning to make sure the rest of your day is in alignment with your Clarity is preferred. It should only take you a few minutes of your morning to do this, but the power it generates to make the most of your precious time is astronomical.

Also, about once a week, ask yourself "Where am I now?" to check your progress and go through your answers to the support questions "How can I get there?" and "What are the 'wins' along the way?" This will continually keep you positioned to create and act on opportunities to accelerate your progress toward achieving your future vision. This weekly review should, again, only take you a few minutes, and weekends are great for this.

Finally, you can and will change your Clarity. It is not in stone, and as your future unfolds, you will in all likelihood, adjust where you'd like to be. Go for it! I evaluate my Clarity on a quarterly basis, sometimes making no changes, and other times making major adjustments. Just sit down every three months or so and go through your Clarity questions once again. Then simply make any changes you feel are needed or desired.

60-Second Power Summary

▶   Your Clarity is a detailed and balanced vision of the future you want in two to three years.

▶   It includes the areas of business, career, home-life, relationships, health, wealth, service, and personal growth that are important to you.

▶   "Where am I now?" helps you see your starting point in achieving more time and success.

▶   "Where do I want to be?" is the most critical Clarity question and helps you identify the specific elements of the life you want in two to three years.

▶ "How can I get there?" helps you create a Clarity resource guide.

▶ "What are the 'wins' along the way?" helps you stay motivated as you progress toward your future vision.

▶ Review "Where do I want to be?" at least five mornings a week and compare it to your schedule.

▶ Review the other Clarity questions once a week.

▶ Revisit your Clarity every three months for possible updating.

Put Your Knowledge Into Action

The focus for the first part of this module's action plan is step-by-step instruction for the Clarity worksheets to create the critical, balanced, and clear vision you'll need for your personal and business success. Even if you already have a clear vision for yourself, the thought-provoking questions will challenge you to ensure your Clarity is as specific and detailed as it can be. I'll also make sure your clear vision is balanced to include your time commitment to your business or career, your personal and family relationships, and your personal recharging and health.

Please don't take creating your Clarity lightly. It is the cornerstone of your Time Control training and will play a part in almost every one of this book's modules.

Here is how to put the Clarity module into action:

1. Make copies of your Clarity worksheets. There are four of them, with the titles "Where am I now?" "Where do I want to be?" "How can I get there?" and "What are the 'wins' along the way?"

2. Pick one day and complete the worksheet "Where am I now?" As explained earlier, take a snapshot of your business and personal lives as they are today. Now simply go through these areas and record the details of what you see. It should take no more than an hour to do this. If adding hours to your day is important to you, I know you can make the time to perform this critical action plan for your success.

Following are some thought-provoking questions listed in different categories to give you guidance as you complete your worksheet. You need only use the categories that apply to your life.

You also don't have to answer every question in the categories you do choose, just the ones that apply to your situation and your comfort zone. You want your Clarity to have detail, but you also don't want it to be too cumbersome and something you find too big to review daily. There are quite a few questions in each category to choose from, and I don't come close to using all of them in my own personal Clarity. All of the questions are listed to spark your imagination and give you choice. Find your own personal mix and balance! If you find it more comfortable, start simple and add more detail to your Clarity in the future as you see fit.

Your Business

▶ What is your gross income (annual, quarterly, monthly—you decide)?

▶ Where does your income come from? List your income streams.

▶ List approximately how much income you receive from each income stream.

▶ How many clients do you have?

▶ What are your fixed expenses?

▶ What's an estimate of your variable expenses?

▶ How much do you pay in taxes?

▶ How much business debt do you have?

▶ How many employees do you have?

▶ What is your payroll for each employee?

▶ What employee benefit packages do you have?

▶ How much do you pay yourself?

▶ What are the profits for your business?

▶ Are you building any equity in your business?

▶ If so, how much annually?

▶ What kind of business support equipment do you have?

▶ How much time do you spend at work?

▶ How much time do your employees put in?

▶ How do you market?

▶ How many new marketing strategies do you test on a monthly basis?

▶ Do you have systems in place to continually improve your marketing?

▶ How often do you study marketing material?

▶ What are your formalized referral policies?

▶ How do you follow-up with your clients and prospects?

▶ How do you educate your clients to the benefits of doing business with you?

▶ What guarantees do you offer?

▶ What strategic alliance relationships are you in?

▶ In what ways do you maximize the back-end of your business?

▶ How do you make doing business with you enjoyable and fun for your clients?

▶ How much do you enjoy your business?

Your Career

▶ What position are you in?

▶ What company do you work for?

▶ What is your salary?

▶ What are your employee benefit packages?

▶ What part of the country or world do you work?

▶ How educated, trained, or qualified are you for your job?

▶ How much do you enjoy your relationships with your peers, your employees, and your supervisors or boss?

▶ How strong are your leadership skills?

▶ How strong are your team skills?

▶ How long do you work each day on average?

▶ How long do you work each week on average?

▶ How much do you enjoy your job and career?

Personal

▶ How much time do you spend with your family on a daily basis?

▶ How do you spend that time with them?

▶ How much do you enjoy your personal relationships?

▶ How much sleep do you get each night?

▶ How much and what kind of exercise do you do each week?

▶ How healthy is your diet?

▶ How much personal time do you get each day?

▶ How many and what kind of sports and recreational activities do you allow yourself each week?

▶ How often do you go on vacation and where?

▶ How much do you have in investments or savings?

▶ How much debt do you carry?

▶ How happy are you with your life?

Again, answer the questions that apply to your life, situation, and desires. Don't go overboard, though, and keep looking for that simple balance. Avoid being a perfectionist, and just answer the questions so that you understand your current situation. And keep this within the approximate one-hour time limit to complete.

So few businesses and individuals have any clue as to where they are and where they want to go. No wonder so many businesses fail and so many people are overwhelmed by their lives! Make sure this doesn't happen to you.

3.   Pick another day and complete the worksheet "Where do I want to be?" This is your most important worksheet, and you'll use your answers to "Where am I now?" to complete it. Envision exactly where you'd like to be in about two years or so down the road and take a snapshot of your business and personal lives. Now, simply go through these areas again and record the details of what you see.

Remember, this is where you would *like* to be and *want* to be in the future. It's your chance to take the clay that represents your future and mold it into anything you'd like it to be. Don't be afraid to reach. What's the worst that can happen if you do? If you are afraid of failure and don't reach at all, I can predict with certainty that you will fail.

Again, take no more than an hour to complete this. The idea is to list what you want and create good detail, but you don't want to get frozen in perfectionism and over-analyze. Remember, if you make it too long, you'll probably avoid reviewing it on a frequent, routine basis. And it's your consistent review that will bring you success!

Here are additional thought-provoking questions to give you guidance in the categories you choose.

Your Business

▶   What do you want your gross income to be (annual, quarterly, monthly—you decide)?

▶   Where do you want your income streams to come from?

▶   How much income do you want to receive from each income stream?

▶   How many clients do you want?

▶   What fixed expenses would you like to have?

▶   What would you like to keep your variable expenses to?

▶   How much do you want to pay in taxes?

▶   What do you want your business debt to be?

▶   How many employees do you want?

▶   How much do you want to pay each employee?

▶   What employee benefit packages do you want?

▶   How much do you want to pay yourself?

▶   What do you want your business profits to be?

▶   How much equity do you want to build annually?

▶   What kind of business support equipment do you want?

▶   How much time do you want to spend at work?

▶   How much time do you want your employees to put in?

▶ How many new marketing strategies would you like to test on a monthly basis?

▶ Do you want systems in place to continually improve your marketing?

▶ How often would you like to study marketing material?

▶ Do you want formalized referral policies? (how many)

▶ Do you want to improve your follow-up with your clients and prospects?

▶ Do you want to improve how you educate your clients to the benefits of doing business with you?

▶ Do you want to continually improve the guarantees you offer?

▶ Do you want more strategic alliance relationships? How many?

▶ Do you want to continually maximize the back-end of your business?

▶ How do you want to make doing business with you more enjoyable and fun for your clients?

▶ How much more do you want to enjoy your business?

Your Career

▶ What position do you want to be in?

▶ What company do you want to work for?

▶ What salary do you want?

▶ If you work on commission, how much do you want to make?

▶ What employee benefit packages do you want?

▶ What part of the country or world do you want to work?

▶ How much more educated, trained, or qualified do you want to be for your job?

▶ How much do you want to enjoy your relationships with your peers, your employees, and your supervisors or boss?

▶ How strong do you want your leadership skills to be?

▶ How strong do you want your team skills to be?

▶ How long do you want to work each day on average?

▶ How long do you want to work each week on average?

▶ How much do you want to enjoy your job and career?

Personal

▶ How much time do you want to spend with your family on a daily basis?

▶ How do you want to spend that time with them?

▶ How much sleep do you want each night? If you're not sure, take the time to study the Sleep Module. For most of us, the peak time is about eight hours a night.

▶ How much and what kind of exercise do you want to do each week?

▶ How healthy do you want your diet to be?

▶ How much personal time do you want each day? I recommend 30 minutes minimum.

▶ How many and what kind of sports and recreational activities do you want to do each week?

▶ How often do you want to go on vacation and where?

▶ How much do you want in investments or savings?

▶ How much debt do you want?

▶ How happy do you want your life to be?

You don't have to stick to the questions that have been provided. If you think of other questions or areas for input to your clear future vision, by all means, use them. Each of us is different and has varying situations and desires. These questions are just guidance and can't possibly cover every important area of everyone's lives. Go with your gut instincts!

This process takes a little time, but is so easy to do. I guarantee you the exponential, positive impact it will have on your business or career and personal life is absolutely worth your investment in time and energy.

4. Take another day and answer the question "How can I get there?" Steps 2 and 3 are the most intensive and take the longest. They are the cornerstone questions of your Clarity. This question, as well as "What are the 'wins' along the way?" are support questions used to help you get to your clear future vision.

In about one hour or less, simply brainstorm all of the ways at your disposal to help you get to your Clarity. The purpose of this is to keep you from taking for granted all of the incredible resources you already have or can easily obtain to help you achieve your Clarity.

▶ What ways can you think of to help you successfully complete your journey?

▶ Whom can you go to for advice or assistance?

▶ Who are your mentors?

▶ Who could be your mentor?

▶ What skills can you learn and apply that would be of help?

▶ What resources do you have at your disposal right now?

▶ List all of the business and career training material that you own.

▶ List all of your self-help and business tapes and books.

▶ List training material or programs that you may want to obtain or go to in the future.

5. The last worksheet in this module asks you to answer the question "What are the 'wins' along the way?" Like the other worksheets, this shouldn't take you more than an hour to accomplish.

You don't have to pick mid-points for every listed input to your Clarity, just the most important ones. List not only what the mid-point is, but also how you'd like to celebrate it. This will give you sub-goals to shoot for, making your elephant easier to eat—one bite at a time.

6. Clean up your Clarity and place it in a format that is easy for you to review. You can have it in a folder on your desk; write it in your day planner; put it on 3 x 5 index cards and tape them to your bathroom mirror; record it on tape to listen to in your car; or my favorite, put it in Microsoft PowerPoint or another computer slide show format.

7. Now for the most important part of your action plan. Review and compare. Creating your Clarity means absolutely nothing if you don't use it!

Concentrating on this over the next three or four weeks to build positive behavioral change, compare *everything* you do to the map you've created in your Clarity. If what you're doing or have scheduled in your planner or "to do" list is not helping you move toward your Clarity, then it's a waste of time! By only acting on things that move you toward your Clarity, you'll massively leverage your time to work for you.

Then, about once a week, ask yourself "Where am I now?" to check your progress and go through your answers to the support questions "How can I get there?" and "What are the 'wins' along the way?" This weekly review should only take you a few minutes, and weekends are perfect.

You'll be rewarded from this module's action plan based on how much effort you put into it. If you half-heartedly or hurriedly go through the steps, you'll only scratch the surface of possibilities for increased control of your time. Take it seriously, though, and the future is yours.

And the final thought to conclude this critical first Time Control module is to not jump ahead to Module 2 (unless you're reading through the book first to get an overview of its material) until you first spend a few days to create your Clarity and then spend another three to four weeks ingraining your five mornings a week review into habit. This process sounds *so* simple. But I've worked with thousands and thousands of people with this very tool to know that getting yourself to consistently and frequently review and compare your Clarity to your schedule takes a little work. Behavioral change takes time. Invest in yourself, and give yourself this month to make reviewing your Clarity a solid habit and gift to your time control.

For Starters...Clarity! Worksheet 1

Where am I now?

Take a snapshot of your business and personal lives right now and take notes on what you see in the critical areas of your life.

_____

_____

_____

_____

_____

_____

_____

_____

_____

_____

_____

_____

_____

_____

_____

_____

_____

_____

_____

_____

_____

_____

_____

_____

_____

_____

_____

_____

_____

For Starters...Clarity! Worksheet 2

Where do I want to be?

Go into the future you desire about two to three years and take notes on what you want to see in the critical areas of your life.

_____

_____

_____

_____

_____

_____

_____

_____

_____

_____

_____

_____

_____

_____

_____

_____

_____

_____

_____

_____

_____

_____

_____

_____

For Starters...Clarity! Worksheet 3

How can I get there?

Brainstorm all of the ways you have at your disposal to help you get to your Clarity.

_____

_____

_____

_____

_____

_____

_____

_____

_____

_____

_____

_____

_____

_____

_____

_____

_____

_____

_____

_____

_____

_____

For Starters...Clarity! Worksheet 4

What are the "wins" along the way?

Look at your journey from where you are now to where you want to be, and pick several mid-points along the way. These will be celebration points in your journey to measure your growth and keep you motivated.

_____

_____

_____

_____

_____

_____

_____

_____

_____

_____

_____

_____

_____

_____

_____

_____

_____

_____

_____

_____

_____

_____

_____

_____

MODULE

THE CONTINUAL SUCCESS IMPROVEMENT FORMULA

Continual Success Improvement

Once you have Clarity, gaining more control of your time becomes a simple process of staying on the path of your chosen success journey. Reducing your distractions and time wasters, improving your action systems, and increasing your human performance will all help you stay on track and reach your destination much faster.

One incredible tool that can help you in all three categories of improving your time and staying on your Clarity's path is the Continual Success Improvement Formula. This formula is a simple, four-step process that allows you to consistently and progressively improve any part of your life, business, or career.

If you apply this disarmingly simple formula toward reducing distractions and time wasters, you'll see your productive and available time continually grow as you gain more focus and waste less time each day. If you apply it toward improving your action systems, you'll leverage your time by not only improving how you perform an action system, but also by continually seeking better actions systems that require less effort and time and produce far greater yield. And if you apply it toward increasing your human performance, you'll consistently get more done in less time with more energy, motivation, and focus.

The Continual Success Improvement Formula is based on an industrial and statistical formula from W. Edwards Deming, an American economist and statistician who is given credit for engineering Japan's modern industrial success over the last 50 years.

W. Edwards Deming

To fully understand the power and impact of this simple formula, you must first know its history and that of its creator, W. Edwards Deming.

Deming was trained as an economist and statistician in the early part of the 20th century and used his expertise during World War II to assist the United States government in its effort to improve the quality of war materials. During this time, he came to the understanding that focusing on quality and measurable constant improvement were critical to the long-term health of any industry.

Following the war, Dr. Deming tried to share his concepts with American industry, but ran into a virtual brick wall, as the entire U.S. industry spurned his ideas of quality and focused solely on quantity and production numbers. In the years after World War II, the United States was the only highly industrialized country that still had its factories intact. As the world demand for U.S. products surged rapidly, American companies struggled to keep up with demand and shifted their focus almost completely to quantity over quality.

Following World War I, the world learned an important lesson that would land Dr. Deming in Japan. In World War I, following defeat to the Allies, Germany was so economically oppressed by the stringent peace accords that the seeds were planted for a madman with unbelievably radical ideas to come to power. An economically desperate people allowed Adolf Hitler to take control of their struggling country.

Following Axis defeat in World War II, the Allies wanted to make sure that a similar economic situation would be prevented from happening again in Germany and Japan. In 1945, a 200-person reconstruction team led by General Douglas MacArthur was sent to Japan to rebuild their infrastructure and economy. One of the members of this team was W. Edwards Deming.

The Japanese business industry opened their arms, and, most importantly, their minds, to Dr. Deming's philosophy of quality and constant measurable improvement. For the next 40 years, while U.S. industry slowly declined focusing on quantity and production, Japanese industry steadily grew and improved with a quality mindset.

What does this mean to you now?

Dr. Deming and his simple formula for constant improvement, are directly responsible for the wave of Japanese produced automobiles and electronics that have a dominant market share today! Do you or anyone you know drive a Japanese produced or designed car, truck or motorcycle? Do you, or anyone you know, own a Japanese produced or designed radio, stereo, television, or computer? If you answered yes—why were those purchases made? Probably because they were dependable, affordable, and could be expected to last a long time. In other words—quality!

The Formula

I first came across Dr. Deming's formula for constant improvement when I was a Total Quality Leadership instructor for the Navy. Although Deming's quality concepts were originally intended to continually improve action systems within industry, the military began to adapt it to its success in the early 1990s.

When I first learned this formula and began to apply it to naval systems, I had already accumulated over 10 years of experience in creating the Success-Centered Time Management concept. I soon wondered if this simple formula could accelerate an individual's success in gaining control of their time. I was amazed at how quickly it produced results for myself, so I began to test it on others. Time after time, I had similar success! Over the last nine years, I have continued to adapt Deming's industry formula to the Continual Success Improvement Formula for individual improvement in time.

So, what's the formula?

It's very simple—PDCA.

1. Plan
2. Do
3. Check
4. Act

1. Plan a change.

Start by answering the question "What can I improve?" Use your Clarity from the previous module to help you decide. If you haven't completed the Clarity worksheets yet, stop reading this module right now and please take the time to go back and complete the critical steps of creating your Clarity. It will help save you so much time! Otherwise, you could end up trying to randomly improve things in your life that aren't fully helping you move toward your desired destiny—simply because you haven't taken the time and effort to fully define it.

Look at your Clarity worksheets titled "Where do I want to be?" and "How can I get there?" The effort you put into these worksheets should provide you with a list of things to improve, moving you forward to the future you desire. Don't get overwhelmed if you have a lot of choices. Just choose what you think is the most critical element or would help you make the biggest progress. Once you are into the cycle of improving on this critical area, you'll be able to pick the next most critical element and begin to work on it. Continue this process at a comfortable yet consistent pace, and you'll constantly see progress in the most important areas of your life. This can only lead to constantly improved control of your time. Now that you have something that you'd like to improve, answer the question "How can I improve it?"

You can do this one of two ways. First, you can brainstorm ways to improve, choosing steps that look like they'll give you the most improvement. I highly recommend a second way, however. Use role models! Put some effort into finding someone who has already improved in the area you are seeking to improve in. Where can you look? Ask mentors, family, friends, and close business relationships if they have experience in the area you are looking to improve. If they do, ask for their advice and recommendations in setting up a plan for improvement. You can also look to professionals, books, tapes, seminars, and workshops. Specifically use these resources to help you create a plan of action to improve in your chosen area.

Role models are better than brainstorming because they help save you the time and pain of trial and error. They allow you to learn from others' successes, failures, strengths, and weaknesses. As Admiral Hyman G. Rickover, the Father of the U.S. Nuclear Navy, pointed out, "All of us must become better informed. It is necessary for us to learn from others' mistakes. You will not live long enough to make them all yourself."

No matter what your current situation is and no matter what area of your life you'd like to improve, somebody somewhere has faced it before, successfully improved upon it, and documented their success in a media form you can gain access to if you look hard enough. Actively seek and use these role models to your advantage in gaining more time!

2. Do it!

Once you've chosen something to improve, and through brainstorming or role models you've come up with a plan, *do it*! Follow the steps of your plan. Don't get frozen in perfectionism by trying to make your plan perfect. Execute and move on to the next step in the PDCA loop.

This step is where a lot of people get hung up. As human beings, we're prone to our comfort zones. If something, no matter how beneficial it may be in the long run, moves us away from our areas of comfort, we're subject to being frozen by inaction. Your brain might come up with all kinds of reasons and excuses of why not to take action. Your fear of the pain of doing something new might try to dominate your actions. Once you start an improvement and take the first steps, each step becomes easier to take.

Get focused on your Clarity and remember *why* you want to make this improvement. What will be the costs in your life if you don't improve in this area? What will be the wonderful rewards if you improve just a little bit in your chosen area continuously over time? Know that you cannot possibly add more hours to your day unless you take *action*.

3. Check your results.

4. Act on what you learn.

Find ways to measure your progress in the area you're trying to improve, then act on that information. These last two steps work hand-in-hand and are the critical parts of the formula. They are best explained together.

If you don't find ways to measure your progress, how are you going to know if your plan is working? By measuring your success frequently, you'll gain knowledge that will help you decide if you should continue with your current plan, tweak it to make it even better, or seek an entirely different approach that brings faster, stronger, and more consistent results for less effort and cost.

Your measurement device can be very simple. As a matter of fact, it can just be a question you ask yourself each night to see how you've progressed or improved in your chosen area that day. I would suggest you log your measurements so you can really see if your plan is moving you forward. Nothing needs to be fancy. Simplicity is actually preferred. Worksheets are included with this module to walk you through the formula step-by-step, as well as a sample measurement log sheet for you to adapt to your plans.

Even though we don't like to admit it, our actions are driven by our behaviors. Measuring your progress in your improvement plan will help you see how, and to what extent, your current behaviors are influencing your actions. Once armed with this knowledge, you can focus on how to improve your plan to best overcome negative behaviors distracting you from your progress and promote the positive behaviors needed to bring you success in your chosen area.

After you make significant progress and "succeed" in your chosen area of improvement, don't forget this area of your life or business as you move on to other areas to improve. Constantly keep your eyes and mind open for new ideas and go back to the area you've already improved on a regular basis and ask, "How can I make it even better?" Then simply go back through the Continual Success Improvement Formula again.

Don't overwhelm yourself. Remember that this is a tool to help create more time. Don't let the process of going through the formula's steps become a time waster by becoming overzealous and a perfectionist. Keep it simple and have fun.

Your Compounding Success

I want you to fully realize the leverage you create once you start improving any area of your life or business on a consistent basis—even if you only take tiny steps forward each time.

If you improve any one area of your life or business by 1/2 percent five days a week, you'll improve by "over" 2 1/2 percent each week and "over" 10 percent each month. Why "over"? Because in reality, you are improving not 1/2 percent on where you started from, but 1/2 percent on the *total* of where you started from *plus* all of the improvements you've made from the beginning. This is called compounding interest. Most of the time you hear about compounding interest in relation to finance, but if you grasp its power in your own success, it will help you gain more time in your life.

If you compound your success in any one specific area at this tiny, but consistent rate of only 1/2 percent a day for just five days a week, in just one year you'll have improved in that area by over 300 percent from where you started. If you continue at this simple, continual pace, you can expect to improve by over 1,000 percent in two years, over 3,000 percent in three years, and over an astounding 10,000 percent from where you started in just four years!

How much time, effort, and energy does improving your free time, your business, your career, your relationships, your health, or your financial security by half a percent a day take? It can be as little as five minutes a day! One new thought, one new phone call, one simple sentence spoken, one tiny shift in what you do now, or one step in a new way of doing something, can easily improve any area by at least 1/2 percent. Add the effects of these small improvements together through time and you experience the exponential power of continual success improvement.

How is this possible? Most people never try to consistently grow over time. They grow by spurts, and do this even less frequently as they get older.

Have you ever improved, no matter how little, any area of your life or business for five days a week for at least a year? If you have, congratulations —I'm sure you experienced the power and dramatic growth of continual success. Did you keep at it or translate this lesson over to other areas of your life to improve?

If you've never experienced this growth before or fully exploited its power in all areas of your life and business, you have so much more room and capability to grow and improve than you've ever given yourself credit for. Your mind is an incredible gift. Give it a chance to work positively for you rather than on automatic "get by on life" mode or hindered by self-created bad habits and behaviors.

Many people won't think it's possible to grow 100 times in any area in four years no matter what kind of improvement rate you have, let alone a mere 1/2 percent a day. All you have to do to see that this is really possible is to look at a child's physical and mental development between 1 and 5 years old. The ability to walk, run, jump, draw, write, talk, sing, and think, all improve by at least 100 times in this short four-year period.

Another time many of us have seen a similar growth in four years is in college. Many of us started college near age 18 and walked across the stage to receive our diploma around age 22. In this four-year period, most of us grew exponentially in our academic knowledge, our social maturity, and our ability to support ourselves financially.

You can achieve this geometric growth rate in any part of your life or business, going beyond two to four more hours added to your day compared to now, by simply consistently and diligently applying the Continual Success Improvement Formula.

Applying the Formula for Your Success

The theory sounds nice, but I know you would like to see how it applies to real-life situations.

To better help you leverage your time, the following is provided as direction on how to apply the Continual Success Improvement Formula specifically to improving your business marketing, your career, your family relationships, and your energy level.

Your Business Marketing

Innovation and marketing are two of the most critical elements of any business. One of your continual focuses should be to find marketing systems to incorporate into your business that require less time, effort, and capital and produce far greater sales than you have now. Having this mindset will add days—not just hours—to your business week as you break free from the struggle of doing the same old things and producing the same old results as you've always done.

I counsel small and medium-size businesses every week on how to produce more time. One of the first steps I always start with after helping them find their Clarity is getting them to apply the Continual Success Improvement Formula to their marketing mindset. A great deal of marketing systems exist that are easier to implement, faster producing, greater yielding, and cheaper to run, but extremely few businesses take the time and effort to find them! Because of human behaviors, almost every business stays with the same systems similar to their competitors. The ones that break out of this mode are almost assured of being within the 5 percent of businesses that succeed.

You've decided to improve your marketing, so what's the next step? Find answers to "How can I improve my marketing." I suggest finding role models to help in this area. Seek successful business owners that are willing to share their strategies or just observe how they market from a customer's point of view. Pick up marketing books or tapes and begin formulating a plan that will move you forward.

A few areas I can suggest from my experience and research that if you start continually improving now will significantly improve your marketing are:

▶ Developing and aggressively promoting your business's niche and advantages.

▶ Trapping customer contact and buying pattern information, then concentrating your marketing efforts more on your current customers.

▶ Educating and frequently following-up with your customers.

▶ Implementing and testing structured referral policies.

▶ Understanding and using the lifetime value of your customers.

▶ Shifting from institutional advertising to direct response advertising.

▶ Following any direct response or mailing campaign with phone calls as much as possible.

▶ Getting other businesses to host your business's products or services for a profit split.

▶ Seeking other businesses that have a product or service your customers could use and hosting them for a profit split.

Before you execute your plan, decide how you're going to test your marketing results. Now take action and begin your plan! Test your plan on a small scale before sinking any large amount of capital, time, or energy into it. If you see improvement, expand your efforts and continue testing to find even better ways to grow your marketing. If your test doesn't produce significant improvement, learn from the knowledge you gain and apply it to finding a better plan.

This attitude and application of continual growth will set you far apart from your competitors.

Your Career

To gain more time at work, increase your productivity, and improve your ultimate earning potential, you want to focus on your current skill position and future employment desires.

First, define your current skill position. In other words, what is your company paying you to do? You may have several roles within your company, so be sure to define all of them. Have you been hired to provide leadership, supervise and manage others, provide a service to customers, contribute to building a product, perform sales, or provide company administrative or technical support?

Once your skill position is defined, write down in detail the vision of how you'd ultimately like your position to be. Sounds like Clarity, doesn't it? Well, it is! Define the skill level you'd like to have and how exactly you'd like to be performing that skill. Define exactly how you'd like to be spending your work time and with what attitude. If you need help defining your vision, you can seek assistance from your supervisor, a mentor, or senior peers in your company.

As an example, let's look at the skill of performing sales for your company. If you could be the "perfect" salesperson for your company, what would you be doing differently from now? Could you sell more, in less time, with less stress to you? Could you change your sales approach to focus more on the needs and desires of your customers? Could you get your customers to appreciate your company's products or services more? Could you work the same, or even fewer, hours than you do now and achieve greater results?

Creating this vision and answering similar questions, no matter what position you have, will give you a list of specific areas you can choose to improve to help your career. Now apply the Continual Success Improvement Formula, beginning with the most critical areas first.

As you're working on improving your current skill position for your company, you also want to define your future employment desires. Here goes that Clarity again!

Do you want to remain in your current position, do you want to grow into another position in the same company, or do you want to eventually be working for another company in an entirely different position?

Once you've defined this vision, you can begin applying the Continual Success Improvement Formula toward moving in that direction. This may include getting a degree, taking specific courses, gaining experience in a certain area, networking, or self-study.

At the same time, you're improving yourself and helping your company by getting better and better at your current skill position, you can be taking the steps necessary to move forward in your chosen career—no matter what it is.

While most employees are just trying to get by and are only focused on the end of the workday and TGIF, you'll be taking the small but consistent steps that will help you become the very best you can be in your chosen profession. Where do you think this will take you in your career?

Family Relationships

You can improve the amount of time you put toward your family or loved ones as well as the quality of these relationships by applying the Continual Success Improvement Formula.

Your first step is to get Clarity in this area. What relationships do you want to improve, how do you define "improvement," how much more time would you like to spend in these relationships, and how would you like to spend that time?

Now define what specific steps you can take to reach your answers. To seek help, look to role models: others you respect, books, tapes, magazines, or seminars.

From my experience as a husband and father of two boys and having closely observed my parents, married for almost 50 years, here are some areas to consider improving to add more joy to your most important relationships:

▶ Find ways to laugh together every day.
▶ Find ways to reduce your dependency on television.
▶ Keep a family gratitude journal.
▶ Find ways to incorporate your loved ones into your exercise time.

▸ Find out your main distractions at home, and work on reducing them.

▸ Learn to cherish your relationships and make them a *priority*.

▸ Find ways to become more fit, energetic, and motivated, so that you're not dead tired and grouchy when you're with the ones you love.

▸ Observe the patterns of you and your loved ones when you have an argument, and learn to work more peacefully within these patterns.

▸ Give your loved ones freedom to be alone at least 30 minutes every day.

▸ Try to change your loved ones less and work on your acceptance skills more.

By getting just a little better at least five days a week, you'll begin to see incredible growth in your relationships. Unlike most people caught up in life, you'll no longer allow yourself to take the most important people in your life for granted.

Your Energy Level

In the Introduction, I introduced how increasing your human performance can massively add more time to your day. The Continual Success Improvement Formula can greatly help you improve in this critical area of your life to gain the energy you desire.

For your plan, think about what areas in your life you can improve upon to add more energy to your day. Could you eat healthier, exercise more, use more sleep, use more mental rest and recharging? The role models you can use to help you devise your plan's steps can be your doctor, friends, books, tapes, videos, or other health experts.

To help you get started with your plan, the following are some specific areas that can help you increase your energy:

▸ Find ways to get between seven and eight hours of sleep a night minimum.

▸ Find ways to add more fruits and vegetables to your diet.

▸ Drink more water.

▸ Find ways to reduce heavy, fatty meals that will drain your energy level within just one hour of eating them and continue to do so for several hours.

▸ Find ways to add consistent, enjoyable exercise to your lifestyle.

▸ Find ways to give yourself at least 30 minutes a day of mental recharging.

Consistently and frequently improving your energy will give you a decisive advantage to handling daily stress, reducing distractions, staying motivated, and maintaining focus on your Clarity.

60-Second Power Summary

▸ Plan. Do. Check. Act.

   1. Plan a change.

   2. Do it!

   3. Check your results.

   4. Act on what you learn.

▸ A 1/2 percent improvement applied 5 days a week will improve you:

▸ 300 percent in one year.

▸ 1,000 percent in two years.

▸ 3,000 percent in three years.

▸ 10,000 percent in four years.

Put Your Knowledge Into Action

Your action plan for this module is first to complete your Clarity worksheets if you haven't already. Then use the knowledge you gain from the "Where do I want to be?" and "How can I get there?" worksheets and begin applying the Continual Success Improvement Formula worksheets to the critical areas of your life or business. Try to take at least some small steps forward in your chosen plans at least five days a week. Keep this simple, make it fun, and for the next few weeks begin taking the first small steps to make this formula a permanent part of your life's success.

The Continual Success Improvement Formula Worksheet 1

Plan a Change

Area to Improve:

_____

_____

_____

_____

_____

Steps to Improve It (can you use Role Models?):

_____

_____

_____

_____

_____

Do It!

What can you do to get motivated and started?

_____

_____

_____

_____

_____

How can you stay on track with your plan?

_____

_____

_____

_____

_____

_____

The Continual Success Improvement Formula Worksheet 1 page 2

Check Your Results

How can you measure and keep track of your progress?

_____

_____

_____

_____

_____

_____

How often do you want to measure your progress?

_____

_____

_____

_____

_____

Act on What You Learn!

What have you learned from your measurements?

_____

_____

_____

_____

_____

How can you act on this information?

_____

_____

_____

_____

_____

_____

The Continual Success Improvement Formula Worksheet 2

Progress Measurement Log

Date: _____

Your Daily Goal or Plan Step:

_____

_____

_____

Did you meet your goal? _____

If "no" then why:

_____

_____

_____

How can you improve tomorrow?

_____

_____

_____

Date: _____

Your Daily Goal or Plan Step:

_____

_____

_____

Did you meet your goal? _____

If "no" then why:

_____

_____

_____

How can you improve tomorrow?

_____

_____

_____

MODULE

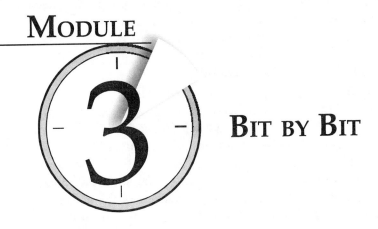

BIT BY BIT

The Amazing Power of Five Minutes!

Five minutes a day sounds likes so little time, yet it can bring you success in endeavors you think impossible. It can improve your health; it can spark your relationships; it can exponentially grow your business; and it can launch your career.

Simply put—five minutes a day can materialize your Clarity. Impossible, you say?

Remember the lesson of compounding success from the previous module. Improve any area of your life by just 1/2 percent, five days a week, and you can expect to see exponential growth in that area—at least 300 percent in one year, 1,000 percent in two years, and 10,000 percent in four years. In most cases, that 1/2 percent improvement takes less than five minutes a day!

If five minutes a day is so simple, why doesn't everyone reap its powerful rewards? The answer is easy—human behavior. Sometimes the easiest things are the hardest to put into action because of our established habits and self-imposed limitations.

Shattering the Paradigm

I want to put the incredible power of five minutes into perspective for you. The paradigm you need to shift in order to achieve success is that you can't do much in just five minutes. But applied over time, five minutes a day can have a drastic impact in what you can accomplish and learn.

When I'm teaching this topic before an extended audience, I always ask a series of questions that help lead people to their own conclusions about what five minutes a day can do for them. I start with a show of hands of those in the audience who would like to speak another language. I then ask for a show of hands of those that presently speak a second language and distinguish what different languages are represented. I'll then pick a few multi-lingual people out at random and ask them to participate candidly with the following premise:

If I wanted to learn to speak their particular language and had basic direction and instruction (a language primer book, tapes, software, etc.), how much could I learn if I spent only five minutes a day over the next week studying? The answers are always similar. I might learn a few words or phrases for languages with a similar alphabet structure to English (Spanish, French, and German, for example) or learn a few characters and perhaps a few words for those languages with different alphabets (Arabic, Russian, Chinese, Japanese, etc.). The point is, I wouldn't progress very far no matter what the language is.

I then pose this question: if I were to continue at this pace, studying just five minutes a day for at least five days a week, how much could I learn over the next year, three years, five, 10, or 20 years? The answers vary slightly, but most agree that I would gain a competent, if not higher, level of proficiency and become more and more comfortable speaking the language through time. I certainly would gain a high enough level to enjoy a foreign trip or improve any foreign business relations.

I posed these questions to language instructors and had similar results. Fluency would be very difficult to master at this pace, but competency would definitely not be.

In a similar fashion to how I asked about languages, I develop the same scenario for learning how to play any musical instrument. At five minutes a day over one week, almost everyone that knows how to play an instrument agrees that I would learn just enough to sound quite awful. But something wonderful happens when I ask them to project how I could play if I applied this same tool over the next three to five years, or even longer. All agree I could learn to play socially very well. Every musical instructor I've polled agrees—anyone can learn to play for their own enjoyment if they practice a little almost every day.

What do you think? If just five minutes a day for five days a week can give you the power to learn a new language or play a musical instrument over time, what else can it change in *your* life?

The most important area I've used this tool is in my family relationships. Every day (to the best of my human ability—but at least five days a week) I take a few minutes and ask myself what is one small thing I can do or say to my wife and two sons that would grow our relationships even more. Many times the ideas that hit me are very simple—a heartfelt "I love you," a tickle attack, playing my boys' favorite games, or just a pleasant talk. The idea I shoot for is to come up with something small above and

beyond normal. This keeps me from taking the most important relationships in my life for granted. Through the years the consistent small bits of
love and caring add up to be every bit as important as the large commit-
ments.

Another way my family uses this tool is by keeping a simple gratitude
journal that takes us just five minutes to complete. Each night my wife, my
two boys, and I list at least two things we are grateful for that day. Sometimes the gratitude is deep and profound and other times they focus on the
simple pleasures of life. When we are done, we read over a gratitude listing
from the past to remember our constant blessings. This simple act has grown
us closer together as a family and has produced volumes of family memories to cherish.

For the last 19 years I've applied this concept of five minutes a day to my
studying of human behaviors in time. A little every day, making sure, at the
very least, I studied about time for just five minutes, I've built my concept of
Success-Centered Time Management and created my Time Control program. What could you learn if you studied one area of interest for at least
five minutes a day, five days a week, for the next 19 years? The effort is not
difficult at all—being patient in your growth is the true challenge.

Some of the greatest action systems to improve on in order to accelerate
your time in business are improving your marketing and sales strategies.
Using the power of five minutes has helped me grow exponentially in
these areas.

Five days a week for only five minutes each day I use a learning system
I created called the War Board to grow in both knowledge and application in the vital business area of marketing. Whereas most businesses are
fortunate if they have five to 10 active marketing systems in place, I have
over 80 active tools at the time of this writing. I am constantly adding new
tools to test, merging effective tools when possible, and deleting ineffec-
tive tools. All of this in only five minutes a day!

The final area of my life I want to share with you where I have reaped
the tremendous benefits of five minutes a day is in the process of focusing
my day and the review of my goals. Each morning when I awake, as I'm
showering and getting dressed, I power up my day through a series of motivational questions that help me focus on what I'm grateful for, what I'm
committed to, what I'm excited about, and what I most want to achieve
that day. Then I mentally review my most treasured and sought after values to ensure I meet the day's challenges on my terms. This takes all of five
minutes and the rewards are unbelievable!

At least five days each week, usually as I'm eating breakfast, I also review my Clarity and short and long-term goals. Guess how long this takes?
The powerful blinders this creates to the daily distractions I'll soon face
over the next 15 hours keeps me steadily on track to successfully achieve
all of my goals.

The power of five minutes works for me, but I want to show you that it works for others equally as well. The best example to share with you is a client who is president of a 750-million-dollar financial management company. His name is Gary Curry, and he's president of ORBA Financial Management Company out of Sacramento, California. The power of five minutes a day is one of the single most important tools he uses to lead his company to success in the 21st century. It forces him to focus on what is truly important and to take action in these areas at least a little every day. He has been so thrilled with this tool's success in his life that he has chosen to endorse it publicly.

The Tool: Bit by Bit

Let's talk about the tool itself. It is called Bit by Bit. Why call it Bit by Bit? Do you remember the old joke, "How do you eat an elephant?" with the punch line, "One bite at a time"? The same concept applies here. The elephant, in relation to time, is the task or goal that seems impossible because of its shear size. Your "one bite at time" weapon is the simple power of consistently applying five minutes a day, five days a week—bit by bit—to your eventual success.

Bit by Bit is extremely easy to understand and do:

1. Choose an area of your life you wish to improve or a goal you would like to accomplish. Your Clarity and the plans you developed in the previous module with the Continual Success Improvement Formula are perfect places to start.

2. Now simply apply five concentrated minutes a day, at least five days each week, to your growth in this area or toward your chosen goal's completion.

That's it! Just make sure the area you choose to improve is in line with your Clarity. Otherwise, it's a creative waste of time, which is exactly what you don't need and are looking to eliminate in your life.

Using the Continual Success Improvement Formula in conjunction with Bit by Bit is an awesome combination. Bit by Bit gives you the power to find the half of a percent improvement a day that continual improvement needs for fuel. The testing, or "Check/Act" steps of the Continual Success Improvement Formula make sure you maximize your five minute efforts to their fullest potential, accelerating your growth and accomplishments even faster.

How aggressive should you be in adding Bit by Bit to your business and home life?

Use the KISS Principle as your guide—Keep It Short and Simple. Start with just a few areas as you begin to create the habit of applying Bit by Bit at least five days a week. If you overwhelm yourself with too many areas to apply the tool at once, you run a high risk of creating excuses not to act at least five days each week. This could lead to frustration and eventual abandonment of this great time-building tool.

Start simple—a few areas at most in the beginning. As you create the habits to build the discipline you need, you can slowly add more areas to work on if you desire. If at any time you ever feel overwhelmed, pull back and simplify until you're ready to try again.

Always remember—Keep It Short and Simple, and you will rarely go wrong.

Put Bit by Bit to Work for You

Using the examples mentioned above and through the areas you have chosen to improve with your application of the Continual Success Improvement Formula, you should have a few good ideas of where to apply Bit by Bit to your life. Just in case you're a little stuck or would like a few more ideas of where to apply Bit by Bit, here is a categorized brainstorm of more possibilities.

Your Family Relationships

▶ Improving your relationship with your spouse or significant other.
▶ Improving your relationship with your children.
▶ Improving your relationship with your parents.
▶ Improving your relationship with your siblings.
▶ Improving your relationship with your grandparents.
▶ Improving your relationship with your in-laws.
▶ Improving your relationship with your friends.

Your Health

▶ Adding a little exercise to your life (be sure to consult your doctor about any exercise program you want to start).
▶ Finding new ways to make exercise more fun and enjoyable.
▶ Learning how to make smarter diet decisions.
▶ Learning how sleep impacts your health (and your time).
▶ Growing your knowledge base on your general health.
▶ Learning about a health issue that impacts you specifically.
▶ Finding ways to reduce your stress.
▶· Finding ways to mentally recharge.

Your Personal Growth

▶ Growing spiritually.

▶ Reviewing your goals.

▶ Focusing your day ahead.

▶ Learning a new language.

▶ Learning to play a musical instrument.

▶ Learning and improving a sport (what would this do to your golf game?).

▶ Learning new cooking techniques.

▶ Improving your garden.

▶ Studying any area of academic interest.

▶ Learning or improving any desired skill.

Your Finances

▶ Learning how to reduce and eliminate credit debt.

▶ Educating yourself on saving and investing.

▶ Learning how to protect your loved ones.

▶ Learning how to protect your estate.

▶ Learning the power of compounding interest.

▶ Learning the power of dollar-cost-averaging.

Your Career

▶ Improving your current skill position.

▶ Learning others' skill positions (cross-training).

▶ Growing in your future desired skill position.

▶ Improving your education.

▶ Improving your leadership and managerial skills.

▶ Improving your teamwork skills.

▶ Improving your relationships with your employees.

▶ Improving your relationships with your peers.

▶ Improving your relationships with your supervisors.

Your Business

▶ Improving your marketing.

▶ Improving your sales force.

▶ Improving your production (higher quality, less cost, faster, less waste, etc.).

▶ Adding innovation.

▸ Improving your client relationships.

▸ Improving your employee relationships.

▸ Improving your vendor relationships.

▸ Improving your administrative systems.

▸ Improving your operations.

▸ Improving your distribution.

▸ Improving your safety.

▸ Improving teamwork.

The idea of lists above is not to overwhelm you, but to *excite* you with the possibilities. Can you possibly improve all the areas above with Bit by Bit at the same time? Absolutely not! You'd go insane.

Just pick a few of the most important areas to you now and work on them until you've completed the desired improvement or until improving in that area is a strong, disciplined habit. Then add more, slowly.

Keys to Success

Bit by Bit is easy to understand and carry out, but consistently sticking with your commitment can sometimes be a challenge. Your behavioral tendency for excuses will be your worst enemy to reaping the rewards of five minutes a day.

Unfortunately, today we live in a society dominated by the instant, miracle-pill mentality. We want results, and we want them *now*! Cutting corners is almost expected to achieve success.

I've heard a radio commercial recently that epitomizes this sabotaging trend. The advertisement was for a miracle, fat-absorbing diet pill that claimed you would not only lose weight through its use, but also sculpt your body without exercise. What blows my mind are the millions of people who will throw their money and energy at this scam rather than follow the all-too-simple advice of eating smarter and exercising more.

You need to avoid the trap of thinking that if your energy doesn't pro-duce instant results and gratification, then it isn't worthwhile. You *must* have a long-term outlook to stay focused with Bit by Bit and harvest its rewards in your life.

Know that a little effort consistently added up over time will bring you success.

Small drops added together will eventually fill a large swimming pool. But what happens when you only add a couple of drops a week? Evaporation!

Consistency is the key factor to Bit by Bit's success. No matter what area of your life you apply the power of five minutes, you must consistently work on it at least five days a week. Just remember 5 x 5 for your success. Any effort less than five days a week will bring you status quo at best.

In the beginning stages of creating the habit and discipline of using Bit by Bit in a new area of your life, I highly suggest you use one of several ways to track your consistency. You can choose the method that is best suited to your style and circumstances, but if you come up with a better way for yourself, by all means, use it.

1. Mark your progress on a calendar, crossing out the days you apply Bit by Bit and visually inspecting each week to make sure you're staying on track.

2. Track your progress on a simple spreadsheet, comparing how many days you've applied Bit by Bit since you started to your total number of days. As long as this ratio is at least 5:7 you're on track.

3. Use what I call the +1/-2 Method. Obtain a small jar or bowl and a source of two different color marbles, beads, coins, etc., with one color representing positive improvement and the other negative. Place the jar or bowl where you will see it daily; your desk is a great location. For every day you use Bit by Bit, place one positive color into the jar or bowl. For every day you do not use Bit by Bit, remove two positive colors. If you go below zero, place negative colors as necessary into the jar or bowl. The opposite is true as well. If you have negative colors in the jar or bowl and you start making positive progress, take away one negative color for each day of progress until you go above zero again, then start adding positive colors.

   You should only have one color in the jar or bowl at any one time. The idea is simply one step forward for progress and two steps backward for non-progress. If you used Bit by Bit for five straight days, you would add five positive colors to your jar or bowl. If you took the next two days off, you would then subtract four (2 x 2 days) positive colors, leaving one positive color for your total week's progress. With this method, you'll be able to tell at a glance if you're making positive or negative overall progress just by observing the color in your jar or bowl.

In all methods above, if you fail to meet your five days a week goal, don't beat yourself up. Ask yourself why you think you fell short, and what you can do to improve the next week. Then take action on your answers!

Here are a few more key areas to remember:

When teaching Bit by Bit, I've often been asked how can you get much of anything accomplished in just five minutes. The argument being that it takes some people five minutes just to get settled into doing anything. The answer is simple. Don't accept anything but at least five concentrated and productive minutes from yourself for this tool, anything less, and you'll be cheating yourself. The second part of my answer is that as you begin to work on something consistently, it becomes easy to transition from one project to another. You tend to keep whatever you're working on readily available.

Two very interesting things happen as you use Bit by Bit. First, once you get started working on your project, you'll find that many times you'll work on it past the five-minute mark, increasing your progress simply due to momentum. Second, because you're working on your project area on a very consistent basis, you'll mentally review and actually progress on your growth throughout the day between your five-minute sessions. This is when incredible growth begins to take seed.

Finding the Time

The last excuse you should ever have for not applying the incredible benefits of Bit by Bit to your life is not having enough time. On average, each of us has 200 five-minute, awake increments throughout the day to use as we see fit. All you need is one of them, only 1/2 percent, to make full use of Bit by Bit. Half of a percent—hmmm, that number sounds strangely familiar. When you realize that for every 30 minutes of primetime television programming, 10 minutes are reserved for commercials, you really have no excuse.

As an example, I use a small jar filled with 200 nickels to represent our available five-minute increments in a day. When you pull one nickel out and compare it to what's left, you realize how little commitment Bit by Bit asks you to make each day to move you toward success. To help focus and inspire you to use the power of five minutes, place a nickel where it can be easily seen in your car, your bathroom, on your nightstand, on your desk, or anywhere else you'd like to apply the power of Bit by Bit.

Accelerate Your Growth With the War Board

The purpose of the War Board is to greatly accelerate your learning and application of a chosen field of study. Through a large corkboard and a stack of 3 x 5 index cards, you'll consistently develop a strategic visual display of your growth—and Bit by Bit will be its heart and soul.

First, decide what area you would like to use your War Board to improve. As I explained earlier, I use mine for marketing. I have clients who use their War Board for variety of different areas. I consult a manager who uses one for her leadership development, several sales staffs that use them for their sales development and strategies, several consultants that use one for general business growth, and dentists that use them for their practices' optimization and customer satisfaction.

These are just a few areas to apply the War Board. In business, you could also use them to define your Clarity, project development, customer service, employee training, safety, innovation, morale development, company values, logistics, increasing general productivity, etc. At home you could use a War Board for improving relationships, academic study skills, sports development, and service projects, to name just a few.

Once you know what area to apply the War Board, obtain a corkboard, a stack of 3 x 5 index cards, and a supply of pushpins. I personally use and recommend a 3' x 4' board for business projects. Home applications might be better served with a smaller board. Place your War Board in an area you will readily see and be able to update it on almost a daily basis. If you use it in a business setting with a group, place it in a conference room or office where you conduct your strategic planning meetings and can easily review and update your progress during these meetings.

Now for the power of the War Board—using Bit by Bit, applying at least five minutes a day, five days a week to your progress, study in your selected area. I study my marketing mentor, Jay Abraham, and other marketing gurus through a tape library and a collection of newsletters and books. You can listen to or watch tapes; study reference books, magazines or newsletters; go to seminars; browse the Internet; or talk to role models or mentors.

When studying media (books, tapes, videos, etc.), go through the source one time just to get a feel for the material. Then go through a second time with the focus being to dissect the material slowly and thoroughly. Go through just long enough until you find an idea or technique that could improve your chosen area of study. Many times this will only be a couple of minutes into the tape or even a few paragraphs into your reading material.

Now place the idea or technique onto the front of a 3 x 5 card (the blank side). You may have to summarize the idea to fit on one side of the card. In my experience, if you can't place an idea on the front of a 3 x 5 card, it's probably too complex to use for your success. On the back of the card write how *you* plan to utilize the idea or technique to improve your business or your life. The front of the card is for the idea; the back is for the action. Finally, commit to taking the action you've listed on the card and pin it onto your War Board. When studying at a seminar or learning from a role model or mentor, you won't have the privilege of working at this slow pace. Take notes on the front of your index cards and later go back to fill in the action steps on the back at your own pace.

At least once a week, review your War Board to make sure you are taking the actions you've listed. As your index card base grows, you can merge cards that are similar to conserve space on your board. When you find a technique that is not effective, or one which you consistently procrastinate in performing its action, remove it from your board. You only want items on your board that you *use* and bring you positive *results*. If you ever find ideas or techniques that you like, but are not appropriate right now, create a reserve pile for future consideration in a special section on your board or somewhere close to it.

Working at this slow, dissecting pace, it sometimes takes me a couple of weeks to go through one tape. A book can take a year. Most people listen to self-help tapes or read books very quickly. At this pace, the vast majority of the benefits that source could provide are never realized. By far, the vast majority of people trying to improve this way get the motivation from their self-help material but rarely get the long-term change they desired.

Moving slowly and thoroughly, Bit by Bit will allow you to squeeze every benefit you could want from a learning source. You won't end up using every idea in a source, but you will try the majority—discarding many, but finding gems that will change your life forever.

60-Second Power Summary

▶ Bit by Bit tool.

  ▷ Five minutes a day for five days a week.

▶ Use KISS Principle as your guide.

▶ Consistency is the key factor to Bit by Bit's success.

▶ Measure your progress.

  ▷ Calendar.

  ▷ Spreadsheet with at least a 5:7 (0.7) ratio.

  ▷ +1/-2 Method.

▶ Use the War Board to greatly accelerate your learning and application of a chosen field of study.

  ▷ Corkboard, 3 x 5 index cards, and pushpins.

  ▷ Apply Bit by Bit.

  ▷ Front of 3 x 5 card is for the idea; the back is for the action.

  ▷ Review weekly.

Put Your Knowledge Into Action

No worksheets are necessary for Bit by Bit's action plan. Your Clarity worksheets and the Continual Success Improvement Formula worksheets will give you the direction you need. Before moving on to the next module, take the next few weeks to begin ingraining Bit by Bit into your life at both work and home. Take a few days to decide and commit to a couple of areas at work and home to apply this tool. Then spend the next three weeks focusing on applying action to your choices at least five minutes a day at least five days a week.

MODULE

GAIN 2 MORE HOURS A DAY THROUGH THE POWER OF SLEEP

Lack of adequate sleep is the reason for 90 percent of the problems many of us experience in gaining more control of our time. If you average less than seven and a half hours of sleep a night, improving your sleep habits, just making one simple lifestyle change, can easily help you gain several more productive, creative, focused hours a day; reduce your stress levels immensely; gain a tremendous boost in day-long energy; and enjoyably spend more time with those you love.

Sleep. Almost all of us want more, but few take it seriously enough to do what it takes to add more to our lives. Once again our habits and behaviors get in the way.

Sleep is something that seems to get in the way of our success. It takes away from the things we "need" and "want" to do in our hectic and overstressed lives. To get more time in our days, we cut back on how much sleep we allow ourselves. "We'll be fine," we say. "We must sacrifice to get to the top," has become the new creed of our culture. And what better place to sacrifice for our success than sleep.

Nothing could be further from the truth!

America's Top Health Problem

What is lack of sleep costing us as a society?

According to a 1997 CNN online article ("Lack of sleep America's top health problem, doctors say," March 17), more and more research is showing that sleep deprivation is reaching epidemic proportions in America and could now be our country's number-one health problem.

Some of our most terrible man-made disasters were at least partly caused by actions or inactions from lack of sleep. Investigations show that the Space Shuttle "Challenger" disaster, the Chernobyl nuclear reactor meltdown, and the Exxon "Valdez" oil spill are all linked to workers suffering from severe sleep deprivation.

In the research for his book *Power Sleep*(Billard Books), Dr. James Maas of Cornell University discovered that 50 percent of American adults, over 100 million, are chronically sleep deprived; 31 percent of all drivers have fallen asleep while driving at least once; and that at least 100,000 accidents and 1,500 fatalities per year are due to people falling asleep while driving.

What is this national problem costing us financially? The National Commission on Sleep Disorders estimates that sleep deprivation costs $150 billion a year in stress-related disorders and reduced workplace productivity. That's about $500 for every single man, woman, and child in America each year!

Our country's high school and college students are suffering just as much, if not more than working adults. A study at Cornell and Stanford Universities showed that only 1 percent of students report being fully alert all day long. The study found that most students are sleep deprived, being moody, lethargic, unprepared, or unable to learn because of their poor sleep habits. Most also experience a loss of memory, concentration, communication, and critical thinking skills from lack of sleep.

Many other studies support these claims. One report shows that 30 percent of high school and college students fall asleep in class at least once a week. And Dr. James Maas' research shows that on national average students are getting 4 hours less sleep a night than they need to be fully alert all day long! Is it any wonder why many of our youth are having problems learning?

Our nation's leadership is at least partly to blame for the reckless message that sleep isn't needed to succeed. Through their example, prominent national figures are consistently sending Americans the wrong message about work and sleep. Former President Clinton claims he ran the country just fine on 5 to 6 hours of sleep a night. This poor habit is listed clinically as severe sleep deprivation.

Our most recent 2000 Presidential campaign was no different. President Bush's campaign managers released press releases that he was making sure he got a good night's sleep before his critical debates with former Vice President Al Gore. If it is headline news when President Bush gets a good night's sleep, what does this infer that his night-to-night sleep habits are?

All of the above facts are chilling. What makes it even more disturbing is that the vast majority of devastation caused by lack of sleep is self-created by our personal choices and behaviors.

Shattering the Sleep Myth

A 1995 Gallup poll sponsored by the National Sleep Foundation sheds some interesting light on our society's myth on sleep. The survey showed that 25 percent of adults believe they cannot be successful and get enough sleep and that 20 percent feel that less sleep gives them more time to work.

True, cutting back on sleep may allow you to physically spend more time at work and spend more time with your family. But at what cost?

If at work you're between 25 and 50 percent less productive and creative, make between 25 and 50 percent more mistakes, and are sick at least 30 percent more often, is it worth it? If at home you're more moody, irritable, tired, and sick when you're with the ones you love most, again, is it worth it?

New research shows that on average, adults need between eight and nine hours of sleep every night to properly recharge from the day's stresses to our bodies and minds. Many of us can properly recharge with seven to eight hours of sleep, but others may require as much as nine or 10. Almost nobody can get by with less than seven hours of sleep a night without paying a significant cost in performance.

Our youth require even more rest to properly recuperate. According to Dr. Maas, adolescents and young adults need about 10 hours of sleep each night to be fully alert all day. The sad truth is that most average just six hours of sleep!

Over the counter and prescription drugs, caffeine, and sugar are no substitutes for lost sleep. Stanford University's Dr. Dale Edgar says that drugs to help you stay awake may buy you only a little more time, can be easily abused, and cause severe side effects. "When the drug wears off you have a drug crash," he says. "In other words, you have much more sleepiness than if there had been nothing at all." On the subject of caffeine, he says, "There is considerable tolerance to these drugs. You end up having to take more and more and more over time." On drinking a little alcohol before bed to try to unwind and sleep better, Dr. Edgar points out, "It'll help you get to sleep quick, but when the alcohol wears off in just a couple of hours, you'll have this rebound wakefulness right after the effect."

As a matter of fact, the harmful effects of lack of sleep add up with every missed hour of proper sleep! According to every sleep authority I've studied over the last 15 years of personal sleep research, lost sleep accumulates over time as a sleep debt. The only way to repay this debt is through proper sleep.

For most of us a normal 16-hour day requires eight hours of sleep to cancel the day's debt. Anything less and we begin to build a sleep debt. If we get extra sleep above and beyond what we need each day, we can reduce or eliminate this debt. So if you need eight hours of sleep each night and you go five weekdays in a row at just six hours a night, you'll have accumulated a sleep debt of 10 hours. You may sleep extra during the weekend to recoup some, but more than likely you'll go into the next week with a debt still in place. Add this up over years, and your sleep debt could be so severe that it could take four to six weeks of concentrated effort to repay your sleep debt!

It's because of this large sleep debt and the fact that our bodies will adapt somewhat to the lifestyles we subject them to that most people who are sleep deprived claim they actually feel worse when they get near eight hours of sleep. When you subject yourself to less than optimal sleep, you slowly begin to accept your decreased performance, creativity and energy as normal. This why you think you can "get by" on little sleep. You're subtly brainwashing yourself away from your true abilities! You do "get by" but you become a mere shadow of the productive, creative self you should be.

If you have a large sleep debt, I guarantee you'll feel worse the first few times you do get adequate sleep. Even though you're doing something good for your body, it's spent so much time in the harmful lifestyle you led that it goes in shock to a degree until it can adapt again.

Imagine if you were addicted to drugs or alcohol. How would you feel if you went cold turkey and just abruptly stopped putting those harmful substances in your body? Horrible, right? You're doing something that's good for you, but it will take some time to get past the withdrawal symptoms. The same goes for sleep if you have a large sleep debt.

How Sleep Deprivation Affects Your Time

When you build any sleep debt, no matter how small, you begin to suffer from sleep deprivation. The severity of the effects of sleep deprivation depends on how large your sleep debt is.

The following time-specific effects of sleep deprivation will impact your control of time:

1. Wasted education and training.

Much of the time, money, and effort you and others put into your education is wasted because your ability to remember and apply what you've learned is severely diminished. Most high school and college students who are sleep deprived will drop at least one letter grade due to lack of concentration and ability to recall and reason. When they pull "all-nighters" before exams the effects become even worse. Working adults trying to improve themselves at seminars or through self-education will waste hours and hours listening to or reading material due to a highly reduced ability to absorb and apply their knowledge.

2. Reduced productivity and performance.

Just one hour of sleep debt can degrade your productivity by 25 percent! A larger sleep debt can drop your performance even further up to 50 percent and in severe cases even more. In all cases, your cognitive thinking, information recall and reaction time are reduced and you experience a deterioration of the ability to make good decisions about complex information. What do you think this does to your ability to control your time?

3. Daytime drowsiness.

You will feel groggy and foggy throughout the day. Your chances of dozing off at work or in class or even behind the wheel greatly increase. Your creativity and ability to listen effectively also suffer. For those in sales or other listening-intensive fields, this can cause you to miss critical verbal and nonverbal signals in communication. Sales are easily lost and mistakes are easily made.

4. Increased moodiness and irritability.

One of the first things to go when you become sleep deprived is your emotional control. You'll be more prone to mood swings and be provoked to anger much faster. This does affect work but impacts you at home to an even higher degree. After working hard through the day to just get by, you're more apt to take out your frustrations on those you love most. And it's your children who'll suffer the most.

5. Increased stress, anxiety, and a loss of coping skills.

Normal day-to-day stress will hit you even harder, increasing your anxiety and decreasing your confidence in your abilities. You'll feel more and more overwhelmed as you increase your sleep debt. This will impact the risks you're willing to take and could keep you from trying to grow or move out of a situation you're not happy with.

6. Laziness.

As your sleep debt increases, you'll become more and more lethargic, just going through the motions at work and home to "get by" rather than trying to improve. Employees will have increased difficulty accepting responsibility and taking ownership of challenges. Owners and executives will increasingly decrease their concerns about growth and improvement of their business. And parents will help their children's growth less and less. How many times have you crashed on the couch or zoned in front of a television because you were "beat" instead of talking to your kids, reading to them, or helping them with their homework?

7. Loss of income.

Because of the effects above, sleep deprivation could easily cause you to lose income on a personal and business level. Due to poor performance and increased mistakes, you could lose sales opportunities or even get fired. In America alone, businesses lose an average of $150 billion a year due to employee and management sleep deprivation. How much time must be spent to recover from these losses?

8. Increased illness.

When you're sleep deprived, your body's immune system is not given the time to recharge properly. A minor sleep debt will decrease your immune system about 30 percent, increasing your chances of catching colds or the flu. What does it cost you in time every time you're sick?

Several years ago I caught a cold and went through a two-week period of not following my own advice on the importance of proper sleep. I got caught up in several seminar projects, and because of my own poor sleep choices allowed my cold to develop into pneumonia. I was bed-ridden and fully out of commission for two weeks and took another month to finally develop my strength and energy back to normal. I'm a living testimony to how sleep affects your immune system and ultimately your time.

9. Loss of life.

Even a minor case of sleep deprivation can cause a fatal accident involving you, your family or innocent bystanders. The loss of judgement caused by a high sleep debt has caused some parents to leave their babies in hot cars for hours.

One report I've seen was about a middle-income, computer programmer who was so sleep deprived that one day he forgot to drop off his young baby at daycare on the way to work. When he returned to his car that afternoon, his child had passed away from severe heat exhaustion. Recently in Houston, a three-year-old girl was left in a daycare van to suffer the same horrible fate. The probability that sleep deprivation was involved is very high.

And it doesn't take much sleep debt for your judgement to be affected. I consider myself to have very good sleep habits, but I'm human just like everybody else. Every couple of months I'll allow myself to slip below my minimum of seven hours of sleep at night. Recently, after getting a very rare five hours of sleep and going three hours into sleep debt, I made a left turn into oncoming traffic at a divided road with my wife and two young boys in the car with me. I caught my error right away, but had traffic conditions been slightly different I could easily have faced a head-on accident.

When you're sleep deprived you're also susceptible to micro sleeps. These are unpredictable, uncontrollable burst of sleep that last only a few seconds. The more sleep debt you've accumulated, the higher your odds of experiencing micro sleeps. I once worked with a Naval pilot who experienced a micro sleep behind the stick of an aircraft at an altitude of only a few hundred feet. Luckily no one was hurt, but his career ended quickly. At 70 mph on a freeway or even on a slower, busy street, just a few seconds of micro sleep is all it takes to cause a fatal crash.

Let Sleep Massively Leverage Your Time!

By reducing your sleep debt, lowering or eliminating the effects of sleep deprivation, you'll begin to greatly improve your awareness, productivity, creativity, emotional control, analytical thinking, energy level, and general health. But I want you to see proven numbers to absolutely convince you of the importance of sleep.

According to the Henry Ford Hospital Sleep Research Center in Detroit, the nation's top sleep research center, if most adults sleep just one hour longer than they do now they would boost their awareness by 25 percent. If you're severely sleep deprived and add even more time to your sleep, you could see an even larger increase—up to 50 percent.

What does this mean to you?

If you average seven hours of sleep a night and your optimum sleep amount is eight hours, just putting your head on your pillow for one more hour each night will give you a 25 percent increase to your productivity and creativity. Over the course of a 16-hour day, this means you'll gain an extra four hours a day. Now you're human, so you'll waste some of that newfound time, but you will gain two to three more productive, enjoyable hours to apply toward work and home.

In business you'll be able to pay a lot more attention in important staff and client meetings, picking up key points you'd miss if you were still sleep deprived. You'll be able to listen to your clients better, being more perceptive to their needs and desires, and form creative solutions to their problems or needs on a much higher level. You'll be able to complete assignments and tasks faster and with fewer mistakes. And rather than just getting by, you'll have the increased energy, enthusiasm, and creativity to add innovation to your job or in key business areas such as marketing. That's how you'll add hours to your workday!

At home you'll have a large increase in energy and reduced irritability and mood swings. This means you'll vastly increase the quality of time you spend with those you love most and have more energy to do the things that give you personal enjoyment.

The Four Habits of Highly Effective Sleepers

There are four basic habits to add to your life if you want to massively leverage your time and eliminate the harmful effects of sleep deprivation.

1. Get optimum amount of sleep every night.

The first thing you need to do is find out just how much sleep you need to be fully alert all day long. Remember the average adult needs about eight hours a night, while many others need even more.

To find out your optimum sleep level, I suggest you apply the Continual Success Improvement Formula. If you are severely sleep deprived, I suggest you work through this formula slowly and methodically to reduce the withdrawal symptoms from adding healthful sleep to your current harmful lifestyle. The plan I want you to follow is to go to bed 30 minutes earlier than you do now for the next week. Add 15 to 30 minutes to your sleep each week thereafter until you feel alert throughout the day. In the sleep log provided with this module, track your sleep amount and how you feel throughout the day. Keep this process simple, adding a little at a time until you find your optimum sleep level.

Once you establish your optimum sleep level, commit to getting it every night as much as possible. Use the behavior-shifting Push-Pull Principle worksheet provided with this module to build motivation in establishing this critical habit.

Keep in mind that if you are severely sleep deprived and have a high sleep debt, your required optimum sleep level will eventually drop a little after you've eliminated your sleep debt. You will know when this happens because you'll begin to consistently wake up a little before your alarm. Simply adjust your bedtime as necessary to adapt to your new optimum sleep level.

2. Establish a regular sleep schedule.

To synchronize your biological energy clock and reduce the total amount of optimum sleep your body requires, go to bed and get up near the same time every day. This includes weekends.

British sleep researchers and a team from Harvard Medical School concluded from a joint study that altering your sleep schedule by just a few hours will cause you to experience the sleep deprivation effects of mood swings, increased anxiety and depression.

Personally, I'm not perfect in this habit, but I work hard to go to bed and get up within a range of a couple of hours. I usually go to bed between 11 p.m. and 1 a.m. and get up between 7 and 9 a.m. Although it means I have a slightly larger optimum sleep need than if I stuck to a tighter schedule, I enjoy living a life where I can stay up late on occasion and enjoy sleeping in.

As a human it's difficult to expect yourself to be as programmed as a robot. Just make sure you always shoot for reaching your optimal sleep amount each night and stick to a schedule as best as you can through the week, keeping in mind the closer you keep to a schedule the better your sleep benefits will be.

3. Get continuous sleep.

To maximize the full rejuvenating effects of optimal sleep, sleep in one continuous block of time as much as possible. Naps can help you reduce your sleep debt but cannot give you the full mental recovery that deeper REM sleep cycles can generate from longer, sustained rest. Although putting you in a sleep debt, in the short run six hours of good, solid sleep will subject you to fewer sleep deprivation effects than eight total hours of poor, fragmented sleep.

4. Make up for lost sleep.

If you have gone years building up a significant sleep debt and are severely sleep deprived, make up your debt slowly and consistently using the plan I described earlier to reduce withdrawal symptoms. As I told you earlier, it might take a few months to repay all of the sleep debt damage your lifestyle has caused you up until now. You can begin reducing and eventually eliminating this dangerous trend tonight if you truly want more control of your time.

As you are reducing your established sleep debt or are already optimized, make up any new sleep debt you incur as soon as possible. Go to bed earlier, sleep in later, or combine the two to get sleep above and beyond your optimum sleep level to eliminate the sleep debt. You don't have to make it all up at once. A little at a time is better than nothing.

Keep in mind that burning yourself out during the week and only reducing your sleep debt by crashing on the weekends creates a dangerous, roller coaster lifestyle. For five out of seven days you'll experience the effects of sleep deprivation; then your prolonged sleep during the weekend will make it difficult to go to bed at a decent time Sunday night. You'll go into work Monday morning behind the power curve, setting the cycle up again. Making up your sleep debt only on the weekends is the equivalent of being a weekend warrior, exercising only on Saturdays and Sundays.

Naps can be very helpful in reducing your sleep debt but should not be your primary choice over sleeping a little longer at night. The rule on naps is simple: keep them short. Fifteen to 30 minutes can greatly boost your alertness and productivity for the rest of the day. During this short time you may not actually fall asleep but could very probably drift in and out of a meditative state.

The reason you don't want to sleep any longer than 30 minutes is to prevent you from drifting into deep sleep, the first main phase of your sleep cycle. If you allow yourself to cross into deep sleep, you'll be groggy and difficult to wake, feeling worse than before your nap.

If you have a severe sleep debt from only getting a few hours of sleep the night before, you can attempt to nap for one or two full sleep cycles to recover. One sleep cycle would be about an hour and a half, and two cycles would total near three hours. If you choose to recover some sleep debt in this fashion, realize that you won't be fully alert for about one hour after waking from your extended nap. Be careful to avoid a prolonged full sleep cycle nap in the latter part of the day. This could keep you from being ready to retire at your normal bedtime, planting the seeds for sleep debt all over again.

How to Gain More Sleep and Reduce Your Sleep Debt

Now that you understand the four important habits to establish in your life to optimize the benefits of sleep, here are some strategies to help you maximize your sleep.

1. Relax and reduce your stress.

Anything you do to alleviate your daily stress will help you sleep better each night. Make sure you work hard to give yourself some personal time everyday to unwind. Even just 15 to 30 minutes will do you wonders.

Make sure you create buffer time between any work or studying you're doing and bedtime. One of the worst things you can do is work or study right up to the time you put your head on your pillow for the night. Your mind hasn't unwound, and you stand a very good chance of waking in the middle of the night with restless thoughts about work or school or having restless dreams about the same.

Give yourself at least 15 to 30 minutes to do anything relaxing as a buffer. Watching a little television, enjoyable reading, listening to music, or just sitting quietly are all good choices.

If you still tend to wake up in the middle of the night with ideas or worries, place a pen and paper by your bedside. When you awake during the night record your ideas or note your concerns on paper and let go, knowing you don't have to worry about forgetting your new thoughts or concerns. Making them your prisoner on paper makes it much easier to relax and fall back to sleep.

2. Keep your mind active during the day.

Experiencing a large volume of boredom during the day can make it harder to go to sleep at night. The biggest area to keep an eye on is how much television you watch at night. Relaxing is important, but collapsing in front of a television for hours and hours before you go to bed could make transitioning to sleep more difficult. You're the ultimate judge on how much boredom impacts your sleep ability. Just be aware of the possible effects and use your best judgement.

3. Exercise on a regular basis throughout the week.

Research shows that when you exercise on a frequent basis, you produce chemicals that help you relax and sleep more peacefully at night. Even light exercise is beneficial. Just walking a few days a week will produce beneficial side effects for your sleep.

4. Keep an eye on your diet.

Eating healthy can substantially help your sleep ability. However, the biggest dietary factors are what you eat or drink the hours just before going to bed. A late, heavy dinner or a large nighttime snack can make you feel bloated and full while you try to drift asleep. Worse, after you do eventually fall asleep, you stand a good chance of waking up in the middle of the night with unwanted energy from your digested food.

As much as possible, reduce your caffeine and alcohol intake close to your bedtime. Caffeine is an obvious stimulant, making it difficult to drift asleep. Alcohol is deceptive. It forces you into a quick, deep sleep but then makes it difficult to transition properly through your natural sleep cycles. You'll stand a good chance of waking up in the middle of the night mentally wired.

5. Create a peaceful sleeping atmosphere.

Make your bedroom or sleep area as relaxing and comfortable as possible. Use the big three as a rule: make your room comfortably quiet, dark, and cool when you go to sleep. Try to avoid watching television in bed and never use your bed as a place of work or study.

6. Value sleep and use common sense.

This last strategy is the easiest to remember and probably the most valuable. Learn to value sleep, never forgetting the dangerous and time-stealing effects of sleep deprivation and the wonderful body and mind rejuvenating processes that take place when you sleep enough. Use common sense, knowing better than anyone else what works best for you in your particular situation, to do what it takes to get your optimum sleep amount.

If You Have a True Sleep Disorder

If, after going through these suggestions, you think that you may have a bigger problem causing your sleep deprivation than just lifestyle choices, I suggest you seriously consider that you may be suffering from a true sleep disorder.

Treat this very seriously because its cumulative effects to both your own and others' lives could be devastating. I suggest you see your doctor for advice. Every day you delay could be adding hours to your already critical sleep debt.

A great source on general sleep disorders that you may want to consider as a reference is *Power Sleep* (Billard Books) by Dr. James Maas. The entire second half of his book is dedicated to sleep disorders.

60-Second Power Summary

▶ Lack of adequate sleep is the reason for 90 percent of the problems many of us experience in gaining more control of our time.

▶ Time-specific Effects of Sleep Deprivation

   1. Wasted education and training.

   2. Reduced productivity and performance.

3. Daytime drowsiness.
4. Increased moodiness and irritability.
5. Increased stress, anxiety, and loss of coping skills.
6. Laziness.
7. Loss of income.
8. Increased illness.
9. Loss of life.

▸ If most adults sleep just one hour longer than they do now they can boost their productivity and creativity by 25 percent.
▸ The Four Habits of Highly Effective Sleepers
   1. Get optimum amount of sleep every night.
   2. Establish a regular sleep schedule.
   3. Get continuous sleep.
   4. Make up for lost sleep.

▸ Naps should be short (15-30 minutes).
▸ Better Sleep Strategies
   1. Relax and reduce your stress.
   2. Keep your mind active during the day.
   3. Exercise on a regular basis throughout the week.
   4. Keep an eye on your diet.
   5. Create a peaceful sleeping atmosphere.
   6. Value sleep and use common sense.

Put Your Knowledge Into Action

Your action plan for this module is simple:
▸ Work on reducing or eliminating any sleep debt you may have.
▸ Establish the four habits of highly effective sleepers into your life.
▸ Use the listed sleep strategies to maximize your sleep each day.

A couple of worksheets are provided to help you out.

The first encompasses a behavior-changing motivation tool called the Push-Pull Principle. The Push-Pull Principle, designed from elements of Neuro Linguistic Programming (NLP) and Sigmund Freud's Pain-Pleasure Principle, is designed to generate the powerful purpose and incredible motivation necessary to create a positive habit or behavior change in your life.

Two of the biggest motivators we have in life are the avoidance of pain and the pursuit of pleasure. Most of the time when we're trying to effect change in our lives, we focus on either the costs of not changing—the pain— or on the rewards of changing—the pleasure. Rarely do we ever focus on both sides at the same time.

The pain motivator is best seen as a "push" away from negative or non-beneficial behavior. The pleasure motivator is best described as a "pull" toward a positive behavior. When you focus on either the pain or pleasure motivator by itself, you tend to build a natural resistance to it in the opposite direction.

When someone tells you not to do something, like the pain motivator, a small (sometimes a large) force wants you to rebel and go ahead and do it anyway. A similar force takes place when someone tells you to do something because it's good for you; a part of you wants to rebel and not do it. If you have a strong enough reason why you want to change, and your pain or pleasure motivator is strong enough, you might defeat your rebellious tendencies and create the change in behavior you desire.

There's an easier and much more powerful way to change than focusing on either the pain or pleasure motivators alone—The Push-Pull Principle— focusing on both the pain and pleasure motivators at the same time, working in unison toward a common direction and goal.

How the Push-Pull Principle works is fairly simple. Let's say your goal for a positive change is to move forward 10 feet. If I represent only the rewards of change, the pleasure motivator, and try to "pull" you forward, you'll have a natural tendency to lean backwards and resist. If I don't "pull" you hard enough, you'll never reach your goal. If I only represent the costs of not changing, the pain motivator, and try to "push" you forward, you'll likewise have a tendency to lean backward and resist. Again, if I don't "push" you hard enough, you'll never reach your goal. What happens if I combine the two motivators at the same time?

If I "pull" you forward toward your goal and have someone else "push" you from behind in the same direction, it's much harder for you to create enough resistance not to move the 10 feet to your positive change! That's the power of the Push-Pull Principle! By focusing on both the costs of not changing and the rewards of changing, you create the drive and motivation to succeed at a higher level.

The Push-Pull Principle worksheet first gets you to commit to paper a positive change you desire. This action, in and of itself, is very powerful. You'll then create the Push by brainstorming the costs of not changing on emotional, financial, physical, social, and spiritual levels. You may not have an answer for every area, but at least consider them.

So if you don't bring about the change you desire:

▸ What will it cost you emotionally? How will your self-confidence and self-esteem be affected?

▶ What will it cost you financially? How much money will you lose or what financial opportunities will you miss or not be able to take advantage of?

▶ What will it cost you physically? What will your stress level, your immunity to sickness, and your energy level be?

▶ What will it cost you socially? How will not changing affect your relationships with your family, your friends, your clients, your employees, and your peers?

▶ What will it cost you spiritually? This is a very personal and private area, but address how not changing will affect your relationship with your Creator.

Now it's time to create the Pull by brainstorming the rewards of positively changing on the same emotional, financial, physical, social, and spiritual levels as before. Again, you may not have an answer for every area, but at least consider them.

So when you successfully bring about the change you desire:

▶ What will your emotional rewards be? How much will you increase your self-confidence and self-esteem?

▶ What will your financial rewards be? How much money will you gain or save or what financial opportunities might you be able to take advantage of?

▶ What will your physical rewards be? How much more energy will you have, how much younger will you feel, how much will you reduce your stress level, and how much improved will your overall health be?

▶ What will your social rewards be? How much more improved and joyous will your relationships with your family, friends, clients, employees, or your peers be?

▶ What will your spiritual rewards be?

The more personally painful you list your costs, and the more personally enjoyable you list your rewards, the stronger this tool will be and the greater your chances of succeeding in your change.

Once you've completed your Push-Pull Principle worksheet, simply review it as necessary to create and reinforce the positive change you desire. In the beginning, review your worksheet on a daily basis, but as you establish your new habit, you can reduce your frequency as desired. Once established, if your new positive habit weakens any, simply resume reviewing your worksheet on an increased basis as reinforcement.

Keep in mind when you review your worksheet that you want to be emotional and feel the costs of not changing, and mentally experience the rewards of changing. Your behaviors are fueled by your emotions. Quickly reading through your worksheet in a logical fashion has the same effect as not reading it at all.

The Push-Pull Principle will be used from time to time throughout the modules, and it will be a cornerstone of our behavioral-based goal setting session next module, but in this module, it obviously focuses on sleep. You are specifically going to use it to help commit to gaining more control of your time by eliminating your sleep debt and establishing positive sleep habits.

The second worksheet included with this module is a simple sleep log. If you have any significant sleep debt or poor sleep habits, use the Continual Success Improvement Formula with the plan on sleep improvement already provided. Use the sleep log worksheet to record and check your progress, then simply act on what you learn.

If you're already getting your optimal sleep routinely, feel free to jump ahead to the next module. However, and the odds are this applies to you, if you are not getting your optimal sleep (about eight or more hours for most of us), spend the next three to four weeks working on establishing solid, positive sleep habits. You should also continue applying the lessons and tools you've established over the three previous modules.

Positive Sleep Motivation Worksheet

(Push-Pull Principle)

I am totally committed to gaining more control of my time by elimi-nating my sleep debt and establishing positive sleep habits.

Push:

The *costs* if I do not achieve this goal. (emotional, financial, physical, social, spiritual)

_____

_____

_____

_____

_____

_____

_____

_____

_____

_____

Pull:

The *rewards* when I achieve this goal. (emotional, financial, physical, social, spiritual)

_____

_____

_____

_____

_____

_____

_____

_____

_____

_____

Sleep Log

Week:	Mon	Tue	Wed	Thu	Fri	Sat	Sun
Sleep Goal							
Actual sleep you got							
Was sleep restful? (y/n)							
Did you have energy throughout day? (y/n)							
Did you need a nap? (y/n)							
How long did you nap?							
Did it energize you for rest of day? (y/n)							
* Apply PDCA to continually improve!							

Week:	Mon	Tue	Wed	Thu	Fri	Sat	Sun
Sleep Goal							
Actual sleep you got							
Was sleep restful? (y/n)							
Did you have energy throughout day? (y/n)							
Did you need a nap? (y/n)							
How long did you nap?							
Did it energize you for rest of day? (y/n)							
* Apply PDCA to continually improve!							

Week:	Mon	Tue	Wed	Thu	Fri	Sat	Sun
Sleep Goal							
Actual sleep you got							
Was sleep restful? (y/n)							
Did you have energy throughout day? (y/n)							
Did you need a nap? (y/n)							
How long did you nap?							
Did it energize you for rest of day? (y/n)							
* Apply PDCA to continually improve!							

MODULE

THE POWER AND PURPOSE OF GOALS – A BEHAVIORAL APPROACH

I'll start with this premise: Setting goals works!

One of the best historical studies I've found on goals is a ringing testimony to their amazing power. In 1953, Yale University conducted a survey on the graduating class. They discovered that only 3 percent of the graduates had clear, written goals as they entered the world beyond college.

Twenty years later, the class of 1953 was surveyed again to see the impact goals had over time. Many areas of life were covered in the survey, and on average, the 3 percent who originally had clearly defined, written goals were happier, healthier, and had stronger relationships than their counterparts. Many of these survey areas were somewhat subjective in nature, but one area of the survey was absolutely, statistically convincing. Over the 20 years, the original 3 percent with goals amassed a combined net worth greater than the remaining 97 percent combined!

The Awesome Power of Goals

I absolutely believe the power created by setting positive goals and purposely trying to achieve them creates a force that is impossible to stop. The key words to keep in mind here are "positive" and "purposely." As long as you create clear goals that are aligned with your value system and take consistent steps no matter how small toward their achievement, you will gain success in time through goals. This force will move you in all the directions you wish to go in life even if you don't fully achieve every goal you set.

If goals are so easy and bring such consistent success to those who wield them in their lives, why don't more people use them? The answer is simple—human behavior!

Most of us are afraid to set goals. We're so afraid that if we clearly define what we truly want out of life and then commit to making it come true—we might fail. Failure. Pain. For most of us, failure is one of the most painful things in life we can possibly face. Most of us are behaviorally conditioned from childhood to avoid risks that might be painful. Unfortunately, most of our possible goals are seen as these risks, and we avoid pursuing them to avoid possible pain. To escape failure.

As we discussed last module in the Push-Pull Principle, the avoidance of pain is one of the greatest motivators in our lives. Although we may not be satisfied with our lives, many of us are comfortable. Too comfortable. Too comfortable to face perceived risks and go after our goals. Too comfortable to face failure.

I want you to think about something, though. What is the worst thing that can happen to you if you define your goals and commit to achieving them? You don't quite achieve them as you'd hoped? Would you agree that in the worst case, you approach your goals, and more than likely reach just slightly under them?

How close do you come to your dreams and possible goals if you stay afraid of risks and never define and pursue them? I guarantee you failure if you never try! If you stay too comfortable, you have no one to blame for your lack of success in any area of your life you want to improve upon but yourself. Your relationships, your finances, your health, your time—it's all up to you.

To me the only true failure in life is not to give it direction and purpose. To not set your sights on things that are important to you and pursue them through goals. In my eyes you only fail if you don't try!

Behavioral-based goals will help point and keep you on track toward a chosen direction in your life—a chosen destiny. No matter how simple or how grand. That is the true power of goals. The power to massively leverage your time.

The Purpose of Goals in Time

Goals are extremely powerful tools and will bring you success if you understand their true purpose in life. When wielded unwisely, however, goals do have the capacity to cause harm and actually steal time in our lives. Goals can have a simple purpose and their power can be harnessed in a balanced way to ensure your success in life.

The force created from setting positive goals and committing to their achievement is very real although it may seem to have the power of magic. It's simply the result of a powerful behavioral principle called focus. The basic purpose of goals is to create the blueprints of the direction or destiny you want your life to follow. Behavioral goals then go further to build the blinders necessary to greatly reduce the daily distractions that will try to deter you from your chosen path.

The more often you review your clearly defined goals, creating focus, and the more passionate you are in going after your goals, creating motivation and purpose, the stronger your blinders will be. This will allow fewer distractions to hinder your progress and greatly increase your chances of achieving your goals successfully.

Where you must be careful, though, is in balancing your goals. Understand that goals are more about the process of growing in life and less about the end result of achievement. True success comes from growing stronger as a human being, not in the accumulation of milestone achievements.

I'm sure you've heard others described as being "goal-oriented." This can be dangerous. I've seen people wield the power of goals to reach great achievements, but it came at a great expense to themselves and others. Because they weren't balanced in their goals, some have created so-called success in careers or business at the expense of their families or their health. In the end, with the accumulation of money and power in one hand, some have lost what was most important to them—unrecoverable time with those they love most.

Don't be deterred by this! Having balanced goals that allow you to succeed in your career or business, in your relationships, in your health, and anything else that is important to you in time, is simple and easy—as long as you apply it. The answer is your Clarity.

By using your Clarity to create a balanced set of behavioral-based goals, you'll ensure that your blinders keep you focused on all of the important things in your life. You'll be able to quickly tell if one area is dominating another important area and make adjustments as needed to keep your balance.

The Secrets of Behavioral-Based Goals

Goals are wonderful time accelerators and will work, but only if you review them frequently and commit to their achievement—focus and purpose.

Having goals just in your head or going through extensive goal-setting workshops only to let your written goals collect dust will bring you limited results at best. Having clear, detailed, written goals that you review only once a week may move you forward in your chosen directions, but how much more fulfilled and successful could you be if you spent just another 20 minutes throughout the week building strong blinders to the distractions you'll face on the six other days you don't review? Even if you consider yourself successful in your goals, a very short, simple behavioral change could leapfrog your expectations.

A great example of this is an attorney I met who was strongly into self-improvement techniques and total quality. One of his top goals was to make $15,000 a day from his practice and financial investments. Lofty goals, but he was determined. He worked hard through the goal-oriented material he had studied in the past and created a binder with hundreds of detailed goal worksheets, mission statements and guiding principles.

This guy had clearly defined, written goals! Too much so, as a matter of fact. He had spent so much time creating in great detail the goals he wanted that he made them too complex to easily review. It was no wonder that he was frustrated because he had not moved significantly forward toward his goals' completion. When I asked him to simply tell me his mission statement, he couldn't even paraphrase it. He had to look it up in the middle of his vast goal binder.

The problem was that this attorney only reviewed his goals once a month because of their complexity. His daily routine was then dominated by distractions the remaining days of the month.

The solution to his distress was, in a behavioral sense, very easy to achieve. By simplifying his goals and reviewing them daily, in other words at least five days each week, he completely supercharged his success. One small change—one large result!

So the first secret of behavioral-based goals is the power of frequent review, the power of creating focus. To truly reinforce the blinders to the barrage of daily distractions you face, review your goals, at least your short-term goals, at least five days a week. Sounds like Bit by Bit could really help in creating focus. Remember, all you need to do is improve your goal accomplishment by 1/2 percent a day for five days each week and you'll exponentially grow your success by hundreds to thousands of percent.

The second secret of behavioral-based goals is the motivation and action-building technique of creating purpose. Goals are about action, moving forward in a chosen direction in your life. Never forget that purpose is stronger than outcome in promoting this action. Why you are pursuing a goal determines everything about how successful you'll be in achieving that goal.

If I were to ask you if you wanted a million dollars, how would you answer? Most of us would say, "sure!" To determine if this were a true goal for you or just a want or desire, I would then ask you to tell me why you wanted that much money. I would ask for your purpose. How you answered that question would tell me a lot about how close you could come in attaining that money into your life.

If you couldn't answer the question in detail and with passion, in other words the best answers you could come up with are things like "it would be cool to have that money," "I could quit my job," or "life would be more fun," I would say the odds are against you in ever having that kind of money in your life. However, if you could have detailed any passionate reasons why you wanted that money, your purpose could easily be strong enough to open your eyes to opportunities and move you to action in creating that wealth.

What kind of reasons would create a strong purpose? Detailed and passionate reasons such as all of the emotional, financial, physical, social, and spiritual costs in your life if you don't build a million-dollar wealth. Detailed and passionate reasons such as all of the emotional, financial, physical, social, and spiritual rewards in your life that a million dollars will help bring you. Is this starting to sound familiar?

There is absolutely nothing we cannot achieve if we have strong enough purpose. Purpose creates the motivation for action and action leads to the accomplishment of our goals.

A Driving Purpose to Your Goals

So, what's the best way to create strong enough purpose to fulfill your goals? Easy! Through the simple power of the Push-Pull Principle. As a quick review to last module, the Push-Pull Principle is a simple behavioral tool designed to generate the powerful purpose and incredible motivation necessary to create a positive behavior in your life. The positive behavior we want to create in this case is action toward your chosen goals.

Working through the Push-Pull Principle will help you generate the costs in your life, or the "push" away from an undesired outcome, on an emotional, financial, physical, social, and spiritual level if you don't reach your goal. Likewise, the tool will then help you generate all of the rewards in your life, or the "pull" toward a desired outcome, on the same emotional, financial, physical, social, and spiritual levels when you fulfill your goal.

Applying the Push-Pull Principle toward your important short-term goals will help you create the purpose necessary for motivated action. If you have difficulty coming up with the Push or Pull for a particular goal, that goal may be more of a "want" and not something you are ready or willing to commit to for the extent of its fulfillment.

Once you create the Push and Pull for a desired goal, the true power of having "purpose" comes in your review of the costs and rewards for that goal on a frequent basis. Remember, our behaviors are fueled by our emotions. The more passionate and emotional you are in reviewing your Push-Pull's costs and rewards, the more you'll be driven to motivated action. Don't be logical; be emotional in the purpose for your goals and you'll generate unbelievable drive toward their fulfillment.

Guidelines to Your Goals

You now understand the simple secrets of behavioral-based goals—focus and purpose. Here are some guidelines of how to effectively define the goals you're choosing to pursue to assist you as you approach the goal-setting workshop at the end of this module.

Throughout this module, the importance of having clearly defined and written goals has been alluded to. The importance of having your goals written down is based in commitment. When you write down your goals, you're taking the first step toward their fulfillment. Easy enough. Take a pen or pencil or use your computer to get your goals down on paper or to your computer monitor for easy review.

Getting your goals clearly defined is only slightly harder than writing them down. Your Clarity is a great help in this. When you're brainstorming your goals in the upcoming goal-setting workshop, just make sure they have the following elements:

▶ Specific

▶ Measurable

▶ Realistic but not limiting

▶ Time-specific

Specific and measurable simply mean you want to monitor your progress toward a goal and be able to tell when you reach it. The more concrete and specific your goals, the better your chances of finding opportunities and taking action to achieving them.

A great example of writing specific measurable goals is having a goal to be rich. How clear is this goal? Do you think it's specific and measurable enough? What exactly is "rich" to you? Is it all about money or does it include health, love, peace, and happiness? If money is a part of it, exactly how much would you need to be "rich"? Be specific in how it pertains to your life and situation! The same goes for being healthier, happier, or more successful in your career or business ventures. The more specific your goal and the easier you make it to measure its progress, the better.

Another element to make sure you include in your goal definition is making it realistic but not limiting. By "realistic" I mean certain things in life require a certain amount of time to accomplish. Not factoring this timeline into your goal could lead to frustration and possible abandonment of that goal. Becoming a doctor, a pilot, a gourmet cook, an engineer, a successful business owner, or any of hundreds of other professions takes a certain amount of time to learn and grow experience. Be tenacious in your focus and purpose but have patience in your progress.

Being realistic is an important element to your goals but being "not limiting" is even more important. If you use your Clarity to create your goals then you shouldn't have much of a problem here. Because your Clarity is based on what you "want" for your future, limitations are severely reduced.

Don't limit yourself to what you can accomplish! You can practically be or do anything you want if you have a strong enough focus and purpose. Countless testimonies exist as to what the human spirit can create. Relationship success, financial and business success, overcoming hardships and health challenges, physical breakthroughs—we all know of others who inspire us through their goal accomplishments. Know that the biggest obstacle standing before you and the fulfillment of your goals and dreams is yourself—your own self-imposed limitations. Don't be afraid, and don't limit what you want.

The last element to make sure you include in creating a clearly defined goal is a deadline—being time-specific. The following workshop will automatically help you establish deadlines for your goals. Why are deadlines important? Deadlines help tell you how much energy to put toward action in your goals and when. Having a time commitment to a goal creates the positive pressure necessary to further help push you into action in the direction of your goals—your chosen destiny.

Let's say your goal is to run a marathon. If you don't give yourself a date to be ready, how do you know how to best create and pace your training? If you choose a specific race to enter in the future, it will be much easier to prepare and build your progress.

My pastor is an incredible example of this. He had never run more than a mile at time in his life through his mid-30s. One day he decided to try running and practically died running a mile and a half through his neighborhood. He was attracted to running, nonetheless, and soon made a goal to run a local Houston marathon. By giving himself a realistic deadline for his running ability, he not only completed the marathon with ease, but he also enjoyed the entire process. Last year, only a few years after almost collapsing in that first run in his neighborhood, he competed in an international "Iron Man" competition. With no breaks over a continuous 14-hour period, he swam three miles, biked 120 miles, then ran 26 miles. The power of deadlines—the power of goals!

Keep in mind that deadlines are simply guidelines to action and should not create negative pressure. Even though I've fulfilled every one of my goals using my behavioral-based system, I have not always met my deadlines. When I've past deadlines for some of my goals, I simply re-evaluated my purpose and tested different approaches to meet my goals as quickly as possible. I didn't beat myself up or consider myself a failure for going past a deadline. I got excited and I got motivated!

The Workshop: Put Your Goal-Setting Skills Into Action!

It is time to learn my behavioral-based goal-setting workshop. The process is easy and will probably take you about three hours total to complete the first time you walk through it. If you prefer, you can even break up this time into different segments rather than working through all at once.

If you moaned when I mentioned three hours, I ask you how long does it typically take you to go to a movie? Around three hours, at least, when you consider travel time. If we're talking about seeing *Titanic*, even longer!

All you need is the time you spend going to one movie. If it's too much, then you aren't really ready to pursue your dreams and goals—it's all up to you!

There are 12 worksheets that walk you through the workshop and help you define your goals and create your purpose for your top short-term goals. I strongly suggest you copy them and use them to follow along with the workshop explanation.

This workshop focuses on three main categories of goal setting: Personal Goals, Financial Goals, and Material Goals. You can change the categories as you see fit, but I've found that these three areas cover every goal in life and business that I've ever pursued. Place your goals in the category where *you* best think they fit. There is no right or wrong category to place one of your goals.

The Personal Goals category is a great place to put your relationship and self-development goals. Improving your relationships with those you love, improving your business relationships, improving your health, learning a new skill, gaining an education, improving parts of your business, owning a business, traveling, improving your career, growing spiritually, improving in sports, and writing a book are just a few of the almost limitless goals that would fit well in this category.

The Financial Goals category is fairly self-explanatory. Anything to do with money or finances can go here. Making a certain salary, saving for retirement, improving your financial education, eliminating credit debt, saving for college, saving for a down payment for a home, obtaining revenue and profit levels for a business, reaching certain sales levels, and making donations to church or charities, all fit nicely into this area of the workshop.

The final category I've created for this workshop, Material Goals, is great for all of the toys, amenities, and physical items you would like to have in your or others' lives. Improvements to your home or business, owning a particular home, living in a certain part of the country or world, clothes, electronic entertainment or business equipment, having someone cut your lawn, having someone clean your house, collectibles, and vehicles, are just a few goals you could place into this category.

The Steps

1. Relax.

The first thing you want to do is create a relaxing and creative atmosphere for your goal-setting session. Having the phone ring or being interrupted by others in your home or office every few minutes will stifle your ability to list your goals and generate their purpose effectively.

Set a "do not disturb" time aside and, if possible, put on music that inspires you.

I recognize that it may be difficult to find three undisturbed, continuous hours to put toward this workshop at first. Don't sweat it! Break up the workshop into one-hour or 30-minute sections until you finish. Be consistent, though, and refuse to start something you won't finish in a week or so.

Make sure you are ready to be creative and have fun in this process. If you see this workshop as work and not as the incredible experience it should be, then you'll more than likely see pursuing your dreams and desires as a chore. Goals perceived as work rarely come true.

Please put a high value on this workshop experience. Valuing the importance of this workshop and treating it accordingly will pay off huge future dividends. Again, it's up to you. It's your life and your future. You'll definitely reap what you sow in this workshop.

2. Brainstorm your Personal Goals.

Using the Personal Goals worksheet with the subtitle "Brainstorm/ Deadlines," brainstorm all of the personal goals you would like to fulfill for about five minutes. Be creative! This is your canvas to create the future you desire. Make sure it is in alignment with your Clarity, too. Your clear future vision of where you want your life to be in two to three years has obvious impact on your short and medium-range goals, but it also acts as a springboard for extended longer-term goals.

Don't worry about deadlines at this point, just get down on paper your dreams and desires. Just write down enough for each goal so that you know what it is; then move on. You can always go back later and fill in more detail.

Don't worry about how you'll accomplish a goal; just worry about if you want it. If you want it bad enough and later create a strong purpose for its fulfillment, you can have any goal you desire.

Do not let self-imposed limitations come into play while brainstorming! The worst that will happen is that you won't quite fulfill any brainstormed goal if you write it down and go for it. If you restrict yourself from writing down a goal you want but are afraid to go after, the best that will happen is you will fail.

Keep in mind that you are not carving your goals in stone. As your life changes and your desires change, you'll be able to adjust your goals as necessary. Goals are a fluid process, always based on who you are and the dreams you desire today. So don't be afraid to stretch, thinking you'll never be able to change your goals in the future. Have a blast in this process, becoming the Michelangelo of your own destiny!

3. Choose deadlines for your Personal Goals.

On the same "Brainstorm/Deadlines" worksheet, place a number by each of your goals representing within how many years (or months) you would like to fulfill that goal. Place a 1 for within one year, a 5 for within five years, a 10 for within 10 years, etc. If you're not exactly sure what to put down, estimate based on what you know today. You can always adjust later as you're pursuing your goal.

You may have listed some goals that will never truly have an end or deadline. I call these continual improvement goals. These are goals such as having an ever-improving relationship with your family or Creator and learning more and more about an area of interest. Your focus is to keep improving and growing with these goals and never take these areas of your life for granted. Great! I have several of these, and list all of them with a one-year deadline.

Remember, the purpose of deadlines are to tell you how much energy to put toward your goals and when. No negative pressure, just the positive pressure to create the actions you desire.

4. Choose your top three short-term Personal Goals.

Now choose the three top short-term Personal Goals that you will apply the Push-Pull Principle to create the all-important purpose discussed earlier. Look at your deadlines and circle, check, or highlight the three goals you would like to fulfill first. If you didn't list at least three Personal Goals, don't worry. Just use what you did list.

These three goals are going to be the ones that require the most energy for action the earliest. If you have three one-year goals and all of the rest are later, highlight your three one-year goals. If you have more than three one-year goals, choose which three are the most important to you to accomplish over the next year. If you have a one-year goal, several three-year goals and the rest are later, highlight the one-year goal and choose the two most important three-year goals. I think you get the picture. Remember, this is a tool to help you. When in doubt as to what to do, make up your own rules. You're the ultimate boss.

Why choose only three goals and not more? In behavioral-based goals, focus is just as important as purpose, and focus comes from reviewing your goals at least five days each week. If you applied the Push-Pull Principle to all of your goals, your goals would be cumbersome and take a long time to review. This would easily lead to excuses not to review your goals as frequently and would cause you to scan your Push-Pull for each goal rather than "feel" the costs and the rewards.

I want you to work off of the KISS Principle again, Keeping It Short and Simple. With three Push-Pulls for each goal category, you'll still have nine to review almost daily. This will take you about five to 10 minutes each time—easily manageable through Bit by Bit. In time, as you get used to reviewing your goals, you can add an extra Push-Pull here or there as long as you review frequently and with proper *emotion* for your costs and rewards for each. Keep it simple! Simplicity will be a key to your success.

Don't worry about your long-term goals not having a Push-Pull. You'll be creating Push-Pull's for them in time as you fulfill your short-term goals. Be patient and trust the process.

5. Apply Push-Pull Principle to three chosen Personal Goals.

Using the three Personal Goals worksheets with the subtitle "Purpose is power!" list each of your three chosen short-term goals on a separate worksheet. Write each goal into the blank, "I am totally committed to _____." This commitment to paper is the beginning of your journey to your chosen goals' fulfillment.

Now complete the Push and Pull for your chosen short-term Personal Goals on your three worksheets. For the Push, list all of the applicable emotional, financial, physical, social, and spiritual costs if you do not achieve your goal. Do the same for the Pull, except now you're focusing on the rewards for the same five areas when you do achieve your goal.

Be emotional. The more personally painful you list your costs and the more personally enjoyable you list your rewards, the stronger this tool will be and the greater your chances of fulfilling your goal.

6. Clean up your listed Personal Goals.

Now simply go back to the Personal Goals you've brainstormed and rewrite them in a neat, chronological order. This is where I list the specific year by which I want to accomplish each goal. You can use the worksheet you brainstormed on or write on a clean one. Organize this so it suits your tastes. Again, your rules.

The rest of the workshop follows the exact same routine, except now you're focusing on your Financial and Material Goals.

Repeat steps one through six for both your Financial Goals and Material Goals.

Using Your Workshop Results

Now let's put everything you've learned and created all together.

Review your Personal, Financial, and Material Goal's Push-Pull worksheets daily, meaning at least five days every week. This creates the focus to build the necessary blinders to your daily distractions. Take your time and review your costs and rewards with emotion to generate the purpose you require for action. The all-important focus and purpose for success!

Review the chronological listing of all of your short and long-term goals at least once a week. This allows you to be on a frequent and consistent lookout for opportunities for action to fulfill long-range goals.

Every three months or so, reevaluate all of your goals. This allows you to create new Push-Pulls to replace goals you may have accomplished over the last few months. It also allows you to change, eliminate, or add new goals based on your current situation and desires. This may only require minor peeking and tweaking, or it may call for you to go through an entire new workshop, using your old goal set as a guide. Situations change; our lives change; our tastes change; so make sure you keep your goals up to date. A quarterly review should be sufficient.

Commit to taking some form of action on your goals every day if possible. You don't have to act on every goal daily, but you want to move forward on your goal set as a whole based on your chosen deadlines. Your action can be substantial or very minor. Just putting good thought into your goals is extremely beneficial. This mentality and commitment puts the power of continual success to work for your success. Just improving by 1/2 percent a day five days a week can make your goals come true much quicker than you think! Remember the power of the Continual Success Improvement Formula combined with Bit by Bit. Use these tremendously powerful tools to help you with your goals.

The Power of "Top of the Mind" Visual Review

A great tool you can add to your goal arsenal if you choose is the power of "top of the mind" visual review. For the goals you have where you can cut out pictures of or obtain artifacts that remind you of them, create a goal collage or scrapbook or prominently display the artifacts as a visual reminder of your desires. Material Goals work great here, but Personal and Financial Goals can fit, too.

A Material Goal example is a Bose Wave Radio brochure I displayed in my office when I first started my company. I wanted the radio as part of my seminar multimedia, and through daily visualizing of the pictures in that brochure, I fulfilled my goal within a few months.

Personal Goal examples are the Ensign shoulder boards I kept at the top of my bed headboard at the Naval Academy to inspire me to become a naval officer and the Navy "Wings of Gold" I coveted that I displayed at my desk as I was going through flight school. Both helped me see the future I so desired and helped lead me to action.

Keep this tool readily available for you to look at and visualize through each day. Be creative and make this powerful tool fun!

How does this tool work? Like a lightning rod for your purpose, color images or artifacts that remind you of a particular goal concentrate the costs and rewards for that goal into one area. Every time you see the tool, you subconsciously review your purpose for that goal's fulfillment. This generates incredible subconscious blinders to the distractions of the day. The more frequently you view your tool, the stronger your blinders become.

60-Second Power Summary

▸ Setting goals works!

▸ Behavioral-based goals create the blueprints of the direction you want your life to follow and build the blinders necessary to greatly reduce the daily distractions that will try to detour you from your chosen path.

▸ Focus and purpose are the secrets of behavioral-based goals.

  ▹ Focus: frequent review.

  ▹ Purpose: Push-Pull Principle.

▸ Guidelines to Your Goals

  ▹ Written down.

  ▹ Clearly defined.

    › Specific.

    › Measurable.

    › Realistic but not limiting.

    › Time-specific.

▸ The Workshop

  1. Relax.
  2. Brainstorm your Personal Goals.
  3. Choose deadlines for your Personal Goals.
  4. Choose top three short-term Personal Goals.
  5. Apply Push-Pull Principle to three chosen Personal Goals.
  6. Clean up your listed Personal Goals.
  7. Repeat steps one through six for both your Financial and Material Goals.

▸ Review Push-Pull worksheets at least five days a week.

▸ Review chronological listing of all short and long-term goals at least once a week.

▸ Reevaluate goals every three months.

▸ Use "top of the mind" visual review for goals you have where you can cut out pictures of or obtain artifacts that remind you of them.

Put Your Knowledge Into Action

You should have a good idea as to what the action plan is for this module. Go through the goal-setting workshop and begin building the habit of reviewing and acting on your desired goals. Take a week to complete your worksheets, and then focus your next three weeks on building the habits of reviewing your goals with your Clarity.

Also, don't lose sight of the Time Control tools you've already learned and put into habit. Continue the work you started with the Continual Success Improvement Formula and Bit by Bit as needed.

TIME CONTROL

Personal Goals Worksheet 1
(Brainstorm / Deadlines)

Personal Goals Worksheet 2

(Purpose is power!)

I am totally committed to

_____

_____

_____

_____

_____

_____

Push:

The *costs* if I do not achieve this goal. (emotional, financial, physical, social, spiritual)

_____

_____

_____

_____

_____

_____

_____

_____

Pull:

The *rewards* when I achieve this goal. (emotional, financial, physical, social, spiritual)

_____

_____

_____

_____

_____

_____

_____

Personal Goals Worksheet 3

(Purpose is power!)

I am totally committed to

_____

_____

_____

_____

_____

_____

Push:

The *costs* if I do not achieve this goal. (emotional, financial, physical, social, spiritual)

_____

_____

_____

_____

_____

_____

_____

Pull:

The *rewards* when I achieve this goal. (emotional, financial, physical, social, spiritual)

_____

_____

_____

_____

_____

_____

_____

Personal Goals Worksheet 4

(Purpose is power!)

I am totally committed to

_____

_____

_____

_____

_____

_____

Push:

The *costs* if I do not achieve this goal. (emotional, financial, physical, social, spiritual)

_____

_____

_____

_____

_____

_____

_____

_____

Pull:

The *rewards* when I achieve this goal. (emotional, financial, physical, social, spiritual)

_____

_____

_____

_____

_____

_____

_____

Financial Goals Worksheet 1
(Brainstorm / Deadlines)

_____

_____

_____

_____

_____

_____

_____

_____

_____

_____

_____

_____

_____

_____

_____

_____

_____

_____

_____

_____

_____

_____

_____

_____

_____

_____

_____

_____

Financial Goals Worksheet 2

(Purpose is power!)

I am totally committed to

_____

_____

_____

_____

_____

_____

Push:

The *costs* if I do not achieve this goal. (emotional, financial, physical, social, spiritual)

_____

_____

_____

_____

_____

_____

_____

_____

Pull:

The *rewards* when I achieve this goal. (emotional, financial, physical, social, spiritual)

_____

_____

_____

_____

_____

_____

_____

_____

Financial Goals Worksheet 3

(Purpose is power!)

I am totally committed to

_____

_____

_____

_____

_____

_____

Push:

The *costs* if I do not achieve this goal. (emotional, financial, physical, social, spiritual)

_____

_____

_____

_____

_____

_____

_____

_____

Pull:

The *rewards* when I achieve this goal. (emotional, financial, physical, social, spiritual)

_____

_____

_____

_____

_____

_____

_____

_____

Financial Goals Worksheet 4

(Purpose is power!)

I am totally committed to

_____

_____

_____

_____

_____

_____

Push:

The *costs* if I do not achieve this goal. (emotional, financial, physical, social, spiritual)

_____

_____

_____

_____

_____

_____

_____

_____

Pull:

The *rewards* when I achieve this goal. (emotional, financial, physical, social, spiritual)

_____

_____

_____

_____

_____

_____

_____

_____

Material Goals Worksheet 1
   (Brainstorm / Deadlines)

_____

_____

_____

_____

_____

_____

_____

_____

_____

_____

_____

_____

_____

_____

_____

_____

_____

_____

_____

_____

_____

_____

_____

_____

_____

_____

_____

_____

_____

_____

_____

Material Goals Worksheet 2

(Purpose is power!)

I am totally committed to

_____

_____

_____

_____

_____

_____

Push:

The *costs* if I do not achieve this goal. (emotional, financial, physical, social, spiritual)

_____

_____

_____

_____

_____

_____

_____

Pull:

The *rewards* when I achieve this goal. (emotional, financial, physical, social, spiritual)

_____

_____

_____

_____

_____

_____

_____

Material Goals Worksheet 3
(Purpose is power!)
I am totally committed to

_____

_____

_____

_____

_____

_____

Push:

The *costs* if I do not achieve this goal. (emotional, financial, physical, social, spiritual)

_____

_____

_____

_____

_____

_____

_____

Pull:

The *rewards* when I achieve this goal. (emotional, financial, physical, social, spiritual)

_____

_____

_____

_____

_____

_____

_____

Material Goals Worksheet 4

(Purpose is power!)

I am totally committed to

_____

_____

_____

_____

_____

_____

Push:

The *costs* if I do not achieve this goal. (emotional, financial, physical, social, spiritual)

_____

_____

_____

_____

_____

_____

_____

Pull:

The *rewards* when I achieve this goal. (emotional, financial, physical, social, spiritual)

_____

_____

_____

_____

_____

_____

_____

MODULE

REDUCING DISTRACTIONS

It's Okay to Waste Time!

We all waste time! I've been studying time intensely for the last 19 years, and I have *never* come across someone who did not waste some time every day.

From my experiences, each of us wastes an average of two to four hours each day. It's part of our behavioral programming to be playful, frolic, and waste time. It's who we are as human beings.

So how do you become successful in controlling your time, knowing this? It's easy! The secret to permanently gaining at least one more hour a day in this category of controlling your time is through balance. The focus of this module is for you to learn that you will never fully eliminate time wasters and distractions from your life. That's perfectly okay, though. You should focus on reducing, not eliminating, your time wasters.

If you've ever tried to completely eliminate your time wasters, my guess is that you may have succeeded for a couple of days, but sooner, rather than later, you reverted back to where you started, or close to it. This probably frustrated you to no end and may have even caused you to momentarily give up your search to gain more control of your time. Trying to succeed in this pattern is like going on a crash diet or starting an overly intense exercise routine. Over time, you end up right back where you started—falling victim to the yo-yo syndrome.

Balance is the key! Why fight yourself when you can work with your natural tendencies much easier and with less stress? Through balance, allowing your natural human tendency to play and goof off still exist while just halving the time you waste now, you'll be able to gain immense control of your time—permanently. It's like tweaking your healthy eating habits while still allowing yourself to enjoy the less healthy food you love in moderation. You won't feel like you're fighting yourself and will have a much better chance of instilling permanent positive lifestyle changes.

You Have More Time Than You Think

Understanding that you want more time and that you are behaviorally inclined to waste some daily, you should understand just how much time you have every single day of your life to use as you wish.

You have 24 hours in a day. To look at your time wasters in this unit of time is somewhat deceptive, though. Why? Most of the time you waste comes in much smaller units. These units are usually one and five-minute increments that add up slowly but surely throughout the day.

Looking at five and one-minute increments then gives you 288 five-minute and 1,440 one-minute increments each day. If we factor in a decent night's rest of about seven and a half hours of sleep, you have, on average, 200 five-minute increments and 1,000 one-minute increments of awake time every day. That's a lot of time! How so? Just remember the lesson of Bit by Bit—how five little minutes a day applied consistently can absolutely change your destiny.

Another way of looking at your daily time is through a great visual I use in my training. I place 1,440 pennies into a jar to symbolize the number of minutes you have daily to apply toward your awake and sleep periods. I take out one penny and pass it around the room to have everyone feel how light a single penny is. I then take the jar, weighing in at eight pounds, and slam it on a table in the front of the room. Boom! The thunderous sound the jar makes when it slams onto the table catches everyone's attention. When I pass the jar around the room, everyone is shocked at how heavy it is compared to the single penny. That's how much time you have every day! More than you think, when you compare one penny to an eight pound jar representing the entire day.

The Killer 13

From my research and experience, I've found that there are 13 main areas of our lives where we tend to get distracted and waste time. I call these areas the Killer 13 because of their ability to silently kill valuable time in your life. Halving their effects is your goal! Do this and you'll see instant leverage in your control of time.

Simply identify which of these Killer 13 time wasters affect your time on a consistent, daily basis and concentrate on reducing, merely halving, their effects with the simple, behavioral tools provided for you. One of the worksheets in this module will walk you through this process for both work and home.

All of the Killer 13 have the same potential, time-stealing effects in your life. They are listed in no particular order of importance because they affect each of us to different degrees.

1. Telephone/E-mail

The telephone and its modern counterpart, e-mail, have their greatest time-stealing effects at work. Although they are incredible time-saving devices, it's the abuse of them that creates their time-wasting tendencies. This abuse is almost always rooted on a social level.

Whether in the office or on a mobile phone, how much time do you tend to spend on the phone every day at work? Of that time, how much of it is spent on a social rather than business level?

I'm not going to judge you. I'm not asking you to become a stiff robot and not talk to your loved ones or friends from work, and I'm definitely not asking you to stop building business relationships from your phone. I just want you to face how much time you average daily talking to your loved ones or friends on the phone from work. I want you to realize how much time you spend socializing with clients and prospects in the name of building business relationships and networking. What would happen to those relationships if you halved how much time you spent in those conversations on the phone? If you maintained the same frequency of contact but just reduced how long you spent in each one?

My experience is that it would have little to no negative effect at all! Frequency is the key to relationships. Showing you care by picking up the phone and calling someone has little difference in effect whether you talk 15 minutes or just five. Think about it.

E-mail is right in line with the telephone. How much time have you spent responding to e-mails with lengthy details that could have carried the same effect with a short note?

I have worked with clients who spent one to several hours a day responding to e-mails or looking for others to forward them on to. Unfortunately, many of these e-mails were from friends and family and had nothing to do with business. They easily got caught up and distracted from work. By halving their responses, they gained hours back each day and still were able to keep in touch with those they cared about.

The same applies at home. If you feel you don't have enough time at home to do what you need or want to do, look at how long you spend on the phone or responding to e-mails from your home PC. If you cut back in half what you spend right now, how much extra time would that give you daily?

2. Surfing the Web

The Web is a great tool for business, education, communication, and entertainment. But how much time do you waste on the Web?

Have you ever been working on business on the Web and found your-self surfing from link to link and suddenly realized you were completely wasting your time? Or have you ever found yourself taking a few minutes before bedtime to surf the Web for relaxation and then found yourself several hours later massively cutting into your sleep time? The Web trap to waste time is huge if you're not careful! But it's not that hard to control. You simply need to compartmentalize what you do on the Web and stay aware of the trap.

At work, stay focused on what you are working on when on the Web. Create a mental alarm to go off when you find yourself getting distracted. When you begin to check the sports scores or surf the news of the day or research your next vacation, seriously ask yourself if you are on break or on your lunchtime. If you're not, then realize you are walking the path of one of the Killer 13! Get back on track as soon as possible.

At home, if you find that your Web browsing is cutting into your sleep, harming your relationships, or keeping you from your Clarity in any way, avoid one of the Killer 13 by just turning off your computer and walking away.

3. Interruptions

According to Rita Davenport, a success and time management speaker and author, the average executive has only seven to 20 minutes a day of uninterrupted time.

Some of the clients I work with are a little more fortunate, averaging interruptions every 30 minutes, and some actually get interrupted even more often, closer to every five minutes. The bottom line is that we all face inter-ruptions throughout the day.

Do you know what the difference is between distractions and interrup-tions? Interruptions are caused by others, and distractions can be either from others or ourselves. We have our goals created, and the blinders they create will help us through many of the interruptions we'll face daily. But wouldn't it be nice to just get rid of as many interruptions as possible? Sure it would!

The best thing you can do is to anticipate the interruptions in your life and plan accordingly to reduce them. I would be willing to bet there is a pattern to the interruptions you face at both work and home. Be observant and notice when and where the interruptions come from, then work around them to maximize the time you need.

Interruptions at Work

At work, most of us face interruptions during primetime of the business day. This varies from industry to industry, but most fit into the window of 9 a.m. to 5 p.m. If you feel overwhelmed by interruptions during the day and want more time to work on projects, consider a test. Try arriving at work 30 to 60 minutes earlier than you do now over the next week or so. In this short addition of time, you should be able to get done the same amount of work you would normally accomplish in two to four hours during primetime hours. But don't take away from your sleep to arrive earlier or your efforts will be counterproductive, and if possible, go home a little earlier to compensate for your extra time.

Another tool you can use when you're working on an important project is to refuse visitors or calls during a certain period of time during the workday. Basically lock yourself away for an hour or so to create the uninterrupted atmosphere you need to be creative and productive. Have someone else take your calls and screen out any internal or external visitors. If you work by yourself, let your voice mail or answering machine take your calls and put a "do not disturb" sign on your door.

You'll be amazed at how much you can accomplish when you drastically take out your interruptions for even just a small one hour window. You'll also amaze yourself at how you can make up any lost calls that same day and how your visitors will adapt to your schedule.

I also don't suggest you try to put this undisturbed time at the end of the day like so many people try to do. Many of my clients come to me saying they can only get paperwork or project work done between 5 p.m. and 7 p.m. in the evening. The idea to find undisturbed time is commendable, but putting it at the end of the workday is counterproductive.

Studies show that after you work eight hours, your productivity begins to drop. Between eight and 10 hours of work, your productivity drops by about 25 percent. After 10 hours, it drops by 50 percent and after 12 hours, even further. Mix any form of sleep deprivation in with this, and the results are even worse.

You'll be able to get so much more accomplished in your uninterrupted time if you are fresh and at your mental peak. Take advantage of this, and focus on the early part of the business day rather than later.

4. *Socializing at Work*

Socializing is something that almost every one of us does to some degree while at work. A work environment where you did absolutely no socializing, where you never bonded with any of your coworkers, and where you only cared about their contribution to the company, would not be a pleasant place to work.

Because, on average, we spend over one-third of our lives at work, most of us are naturally going to bond and become friends with at least some of our coworkers. When I flew P-3 Orions in the Navy, it was a critical part of our aircrew's success, 12 people working together to carry out one plane's mission. Socializing was not only accepted, it was encouraged to create the important trust needed to perform in dangerous situations.

But there is a line to socializing at work. If not respected and contained, socializing can easily fall into the Killer 13 zone. It can easily wreak havoc on your productivity. Just be aware of how much you're doing and the effect it's having on both your own and others' jobs.

Knowing that your human behavior leads you to socialize at work, look for ways to do it that minimize the impact, not only on your job, but on your coworkers as well. Be respectful of their time and need to get things done. Look to socialize on breaks, at lunch, and during company functions or after hours. Find ways to socialize while you work that can actually increase your productivity and creativity.

Remember that frequency is more important than length of each contact in growing a relationship. If you were to halve how much time you spend socializing each day, how much more time would that give you?

The exact same principle applies to socializing with clients and prospects. Building these relationships is important, but are you spending more time than you really need to at each lunch or meeting to build the relationship and show that person that your company values them?

Easy rules to remember if you want to avoid the Killer 13 trap of socializing at work: know its okay to do it, be aware of its impact on your and others' time and productivity, and focus on halving how long you spend doing it.

5. Procrastination

For most of us, procrastination is one of the most dangerous time stealers of the Killer 13. I like to call it the silent killer, because it does its dirty work much more subtly and quietly.

Procrastination is solidly based in our behavioral roots of avoidance. When we procrastinate, we choose inaction over action to avoid something. That something is fear. Fear of criticism and failure, fear of success, fear of boredom.

When you learned the Push-Pull Principle earlier, I explained how one of the greatest motivators in our lives is the avoidance of pain. Well, fear can be very painful, and we will avoid things we are afraid of to escape that possible pain. A good way of looking at the accumulative effects of procrastination on your control of time is to view it as the evil twin of Bit by Bit. As Bit by Bit adds up subtly and consistently to eventually grow your success to unbelievable levels, procrastination does the same thing, but in a negative way. Procrastination accumulates its negative effects slowly and consistently each time you avoid taking action. Eventually, if you don't change your behaviors, the lost opportunities and recourse on your life become exponential and weigh heavy on your self-confidence, self-esteem and your drive to succeed!

So how do you get a handle on procrastination?

Module 11 is dedicated solely to this topic, but in the meantime, here are two simple tools to curb the effects of procrastination in your life. Remember that you don't have to eliminate procrastination completely to enjoy success. Just work on reducing its effects and you'll add an immense amount of control to your time.

The first tool is simple awareness. Just focus more on being aware of when and where you tend to procrastinate—where you fear action to some degree. Ask yourself why you are avoiding action. Confronting your answer, confronting your fear, may be enough to make a major difference.

The second tool is what I call Fast Forward. For the areas of your life where you know you are procrastinating, perform this simple visualization. First, visualize the effects on your life on emotional, financial, physical, social, and spiritual levels (sound familiar?) if you continue to procrastinate in this area over the next year. The next five years. The next 10 years. The next 20. Second, visualize the effects on your life if you were to take consistent action, however small, in this area of your life. Again, address the same emotional, financial, physical, social, and spiritual levels for one year, five years, 10 years, and 20 years.

Especially if you are emotional in your visualizations, you should see enough of a drastic difference in your future between procrastination and taking action that you generate enough motivation to move forward with action.

6. Personal Disorganization

For many of us, being disorganized at both work and home steals hours and hours from us each week. Being unable to find things when you need them, losing important documents, losing track of when things are due, all stem from personal disorganization.

Usually, the attempted cure for this is to focus on being completely organized and to try to force yourself into somebody else's mold of being organized. It's a no-win cure! First, you go against your human nature in trying to program yourself like a fully organized machine. Second, because we all have such different personalities, rarely does one person fit the mold of another in how they are best suited in their organization skills. Trying to force yourself into someone else's mold of organization, rather than adapting it to your own personality rarely produces results that last very long.

I have seen organization self-help books that are hundreds and hundreds of pages long. But from my 19 years of experience in finding how we best perform in time, I have found that a few strategic guidelines are all that's really needed to give you more organization in your life.

Strategic Guidelines for Organization

The first and most important is to focus on *simplicity*. Make your organization simple. The simpler the better. What can you do to simplify how you do your work, how you store documents, how you keep track of your projects, or any other area of your life where you want to be more organized?

Listen to your answers and test your own advice. Ask yourself the same question every couple of weeks to make sure you're focused on simple, constant improvement. This would be a great candidate for the Continual Success Improvement Formula.

The second strategic area to focus on is maximizing your working environment. Ask what you can do to make where you're working more comfortable and more conducive to your ability to work productively. Again, take action based on your answers. Be sure you act based on your tastes and personality. What is comfortable and conducive to productivity to you may be completely different from my tastes. Just be sure that you do not infringe on others who may share your working area. Compromise may be necessary so that the change benefits everyone.

The third strategy is to realize that its okay to organize differently based on the particular project. Don't try to fit everything into the same mold. Keep things simple and consistently ask yourself what is the best way to organize this particular task based on my personality. Test your answers.

The fourth organizational strategy is to make sure you have the proper tools for your tasks or work. The big three you want to make sure you have covered are support, equipment, and education. You'd be amazed at how many people jump right into or are thrown into a project without making sure they have the proper tools covered.

Without covering your big three, how can you possibly be organized enough to get any semblance of productivity? Support is simply the need for help from others. In order for you to best do your job, do you need the assistance of others? What about equipment or resources? Are their physical items that would make your productivity soar in a project? The last tool is education. Do you need courses or training to better enhance yourself for this particular project? Again, match the tools to your personality and tastes.

Once you've identified what you need to cover your three tools, do your best to get them! I realize that your budget or personnel restrictions might not allow you to get everything you want, but do your best. Finding substitutes or creative partial solutions will leapfrog your organization compared to not addressing the task's tools in the first place.

The fifth strategy to better organize yourself is to use some form of a planner to keep track of appointments and tasks. A good planning tool will ease your control of time and tasks. Use one that works for you—not someone else's. You must be absolutely comfortable with your tool or it becomes a time waster itself!

If you don't currently have a day planner of some sort already, I suggest you start simple and work your way up to something more complex if you ever do outgrow it. Your goal is to find a tool that will help you simplify your time and tasks, not one that will create frustration and wasted time.

Having said all this, don't overly organize! Organizing is designed to help give you more time. Beware—it can be abused, and turn into one of the Killer 13.

Spending more time organizing and less time doing is a waste of your time. That's what I mean by focusing on simplicity! Apply the KISS principle to your organizing and you should be good to go. Keeping It Short and Simple is the key to your success, so you can spend more time in effective action toward your Clarity.

7. Cleaning Your Desk — the Paradox

Why would cleaning your desk be a waste of time and part of the Killer 13?

It's a paradox! Having an organized desk that allows you to focus on effective action is a great way to control your time. But a lot of times we go too far—especially near lunchtime or the end of the day just before we go home. Many times when we have only five or 10 minutes left, we would rather straighten up our desk than put that time in toward action to an important project or task. We feel that five minutes or so is not enough time to make a difference. So to gain a sense of accomplishment, and we as human beings love accomplishment, we choose to straighten our desk so we can pat ourselves on the back on the way out the door.

This results from not focusing on the power of Bit by Bit in our lives. If you were to apply those five minutes every day toward something important, just improving it a little or completing a small part of it, it could add up to geometric growth over time. If you are in sales, what could one extra sales call a day mean over the course of a month or a year?

8. Inability to Say No

The inability to say no can cause you to take on projects that you really don't want to do, but currently feel obligated to take on. This can only lead to the wasting of your precious time.

I'm not talking about saying no to projects that fall into your realm of responsibility at work. And I'm not telling you to become a no machine at home and not volunteer. I'm asking you to seriously evaluate what projects you are agreeing to take on from someone else and the impact they will have on your Clarity.

Evaluate the situation at both work and home. How many times have you agreed to take on a project at work knowing full well that it would negatively impact your primary responsibility or take away time with your family? Why did you say yes?

The same goes for home where this killer of time tends to have a worse effect. How many times have you been talked into doing a community, school or church project, and less than a few minutes after saying yes you're frustrated and unhappy how the project is going to impact your personal and family time? Again, why did you say yes?

Most of the time we cannot say no when we want to because of our social upbringing. We've been raised to think that saying no would be rude to the person asking for our help. We have guilty feelings when we turn someone down, no matter how full our schedule is. You must break free from this behavior and guilt if you want to gain massive control of your time!

Think about how much better you could perform your main responsibility at work if you didn't say yes as often. How much more time could you spend with your family and fulfilling your Clarity if you didn't have as many personal projects on your plate?

Again, I want to stress that the objective of this thinking is not to turn you into a non-volunteer who is solely self-absorbed. Helping others at work is fantastic, and so is community involvement and volunteering. What you need to do is prevent yourself from being overwhelmed and understand that it's okay to say no when you have other priorities. It's your life! And it's your absolute right to say no in your personal time and at work as long as it is not part of your job expectations.

So how do you say no? It's a little harder than it looks due to years of social programming. It will take a few learned strategies and some practice on your part.

The strategies are easy and straightforward. When asked for help, first evaluate whether you want to take the responsibility and commitment of the project on your shoulders. If you do, great! Accept or volunteer. If you don't want to take on the project, first thank the person for thinking about you. Let them know you are honored they thought of you for help.

Second, being sincere, pleasant, and direct, rapidly tell them no. It usually goes something like, "Thank you for thinking about me, but the answer is no this time." You want to tell them as soon as you have decided not to accept the project to give them a fair chance to find someone else in a timely manner. It's simple respect.

Don't tell them you're sorry, either; because you should have absolutely nothing to be sorry about. Your social programming may try to trip you up here. It takes some practice to break the habit of saying "sorry" when you turn someone down. Saying sorry is a way of dealing with the guilt of rejecting someone.

You also don't have to tell the person you are saying no to your reasons for declining. Don't create or give them excuses! Your social programming may make you feel like you have to justify why you are not taking on the project. Again, it's a way of dealing with the guilt. Avoid giving excuses. If the only reason you don't want to take on the project is because you want to rest in a chair and watch cars pass by your house—that's your right.

By creating or giving an excuse, you open the person you are rejecting up to judge your excuse compared to the importance of the project in their eyes. They may consciously or subconsciously try to make you feel guilty if they are desperate. Don't give them ammo! Stay strong and just give them a polite, respectful, and brief no. If they ask you why you are turning them down, simply tell them that you have other personal or business priorities that require your time. Remember, anything that moves you toward your Clarity is a priority.

9. Lack of Delegation

Lack of delegation is a major player among the Killer 13.

Having less of an effect at home, improper delegation focuses its negative effect more on those who lead and manage others in business. Whether you're a business owner, executive, manager, or supervisor, failing to delegate correctly can waste unbelievable hours of your time and create untold stress.

Poor delegation skills have three major negative effects, depending on your delegating style. The first is when you fail to delegate at all or you do so very infrequently. Your personal workload eventually becomes unmanageable with all of the projects you've personally taken on, and your work performance and personal life begin to suffer. This is how many workaholics are born.

The second negative effect from poor delegation is improper project completion or missed deadlines. This happens when someone does delegate, but they fail to create a good communication and follow-up system for tracking the progress of the project or task. They delegate a project but forget to ever check up on it properly. By the time they do check on the progress, usually from a reminder from their boss or the business client, the deadline has already passed and/or the work was not completed as expected.

The third poor delegation negative effect is severely decreased employee morale. The person who creates this effect delegates projects but micro manages their progress every step of the way. Micro managing is when a manager tells his or her employees exactly what, how, and when to do something for a project. Every step of the way they control the actions of their employees on a project. The employees assigned these projects feel like robots, having little or no free will to creatively work on the task at hand. This ultimately results in frustration, anger, and resentment toward the person delegating the projects.

Creating Effective Delegation Skills

The strategies for creating effective delegation skills are really simple. Just put them into practice and try to improve upon them through time and you'll begin to see increased control of your time and an increased team environment at work.

The first strategy is to avoid the "I can do it better myself" fallacy. If you have a lot of experience in the areas you delegate in, the odds are high that you could do each project better than those you assign them to. But realize that you can't duplicate yourself and you are better off working on managing your area of responsibility rather than working in it. This means you will need others to help you out.

The second delegation strategy is to allow your employees to make mistakes. If you are a perfectionist, not only are you practicing procrastination, but you are also stifling your employees' morale and ability to grow. Educate them; train them; help them close the gap between your abilities and theirs. Expect the best from your employees based on their abilities and experience, but allow mistakes. Mistakes are nothing but a growing process.

If you instill proper communication and follow-up, which is the third strategy, you'll drastically reduce the number and severity of these mistakes and still help your employees grow. Simply create a system of how and when your employees will keep you posted on the progress of their projects and tasks. This will keep you informed and create a safety net for you to offer advice or direction if needed.

The final strategy is to avoid micro managing at all cost. Let your employees come up with their own solutions and use their creativity in their assigned projects. It gives them a sense of ownership and pride in what they're doing, increasing their morale, and ultimately their productivity and worth. This doesn't mean you can't offer direction and advice. Just be careful not to stifle your employees.

10. Indecision

Indecision, being frozen from taking action, leads to lost opportunities and the waste of massive amounts of time.

Indecision is caused by the fear of making mistakes. Usually from a lack of self-confidence, when we are caught in the trap of indecision, we are afraid that if we take action we might make mistakes or even fail. As we've seen before, this fear triggers our motivational avoidance mechanism to avoid pain and to avoid action.

Sometimes we try to disguise this fear in our planning. Instead of acting after we have looked at the information at hand, we try to analyze the situation even deeper, looking at constantly deeper and deeper angles in the name of protecting ourselves when we finally decide to take action. We become subject to "paralysis by analysis."

By the time we do act, we have lost a great deal of time that could have been invested in action and even correction if we did make some mistakes. So much more has been accomplished in action and flexibility than in over-planning.

As usual, the general strategies for defeating indecision are easy to pick up. Your model is to be quick to make intelligent decisions, flexible in your approach and slow to change your decisions, avoiding the waiver principle when you encounter obstacles.

You want to have a philosophy of spending more time in the solution to a project or challenge and less time in defining the issues. You want to think things through and make an intelligent decision, but you don't want to take a lot of time to do so. Remember, it's action that will lead you to success.

Your tools or tactics to aid you in your strategies are to set deadlines for a decision and to act when you have about 60 percent of the required information to act. By setting deadlines for a decision, you force yourself to analyze a project in a timely manner, focusing on the major issues, challenges, and solutions at hand. This will help keep you from getting lost in unnecessary minutia.

Train yourself to take action when you have 60 percent of the required information. Why 60 percent? Well first, obviously you don't have a meter somewhere that spikes at 60 percent to tell you exactly when to act. I'm talking about a good gut check. By 60 percent, I mean look to act when you feel you have enough information that the odds are in your favor to act successfully. Setting a deadline for a decision will make this tactic easier. Another reason I chose 60 percent as a standard for action is that it is a number very similar to the one used by Secretary of State General Colin Powell, former Chairman of the Joint Chiefs of Staff for the U.S. Armed Forces and Commander of Allied Forces in Desert Storm. If it worked as successfully as it did for him, it can work for you, too!

11. Unimportant Paperwork and Reading

How many hours a day do you spend doing paperwork and reading? I'm sure a lot of it is needed and relevant, even if it's part of your mental rest and unwind time. But how much of that time is spent on paperwork and reading that does not move you forward toward your Clarity? How much of it is a waste of time? If you could recuperate just half of that time each day, what would it mean to your control of time?

When you read throughout the day, what topics do you focus on? The newspaper, business education, business reports, personal education, personal entertainment, junk mail? Think about what you read; then decide if any of that reading is done for the wrong reasons. What I mean by this is that some people read the newspaper for 30 minutes to over an hour every day, then complain that they never have enough personal time. Ask yourself why you read the newspaper. Make sure it fulfills some role in your Clarity, even if it's relaxation, and has not become a time-wasting habit with no true recognized purpose. Do this same process with all of the other reading you do.

Notice that junk mail is included on the list. Do you ever find yourself reading junk mail or junk e-mail, even for just a few minutes? If you do, that time could be used for Bit by Bit toward an important part of your Clarity. You could take that five minutes a day and explode your business's marketing ability, learn to speak a foreign language, or enrich your relationships. Your choice—unimportant reading or your Clarity.

When your hear the word "paperwork," what do you think of? Most of my clients have negative images come to mind because of the time that paperwork tends to dominate in their workday. As we discuss this particular Killer 13, keep in mind that when I say paperwork, I'm referring to all forms of data storage. This includes paper, computer files, scannings, and e-mail.

According to efficiency and time management expert Michael Leboeuf, most companies could cut costs by 20 percent if they streamlined paperwork. For a lot of companies, that's the equivalent of making an extra 20 percent in gross revenues. Most companies would call a 20 percent increase in sales a banner year!

Rita Davenport also adds that 80 to 90 percent of all stored paper will never be referred to again. Part of the problem stems from the fact that the more you store, the harder it becomes to find anything of value in all of the stored paperwork and files. It quickly evolves into an organizational nightmare!

During a recent Earth Day, I heard a fact that blew my mind away. Almost one million copies a minute are produced each business day! Besides the obvious environmental impact on our planet, those copies cost about $27,000 a minute to produce. Beyond the cost of storing the paper and the time costs spent in handling it, how much of that $39 million a day is wasted? If Rita Davenport is correct, about $33 million worth of copies are wasted each business day and will never be referred to again!

There are two important paradigms to keep in mind about paper in order to keep it in proper perspective. The first is that paper is to business what fat is to a diet. It's necessary to be healthy, but we tend to go way overboard in our consumption or use of it. The second paradigm is that paper is money. Every copy you make, every computer report you print costs money. Some is directly spent on the printing costs as discussed above with the Earth Day fact, but paper also costs money to store and to retrieve when needed.

So how do you defeat this Killer 13? If you just half-heartedly follow this strategy and a few of the 13 tactics, you can't help but gain more control of your time. The strategy is simple. Start a war on paper! That's it. Look at reducing paperwork and how much you store as a challenge to gain not only more time but to increase your company's profits as well.

The following tactics are listed in no particular order of importance:

1. **Reduce the fear that you have to protect yourself by putting everything in writing.**

Some things are important to keep a record of, but as usual, some people tend to go overboard. If you have a working environment were fear dominates over trust, you have some major issues to deal with before serious success for all can be achieved.

2.   Get in the habit of throwing things away!

Your first instinct should be to throw a piece of paper away over storing it. Ask yourself, "What is the worst that can happen if I throw this away?" If you don't like your answer because it is crippling to yourself or the company, by all means, file the document appropriately. But if your answer is acceptable, such as having to ask for another copy from someone else if you ever need it, then throw it out.

3.   When in doubt, throw it out.

Throw paper away when you're sure you don't need it, but also throw it away unless it could harm you if lost.

When I was in the Navy, not only was I part of an aircrew with the responsibility of our aviation missions, but I was also assigned an officer position to run part of our squadron. Every other aviator did the same thing, whether an officer or an enlisted member of the aircrew. It was how we kept a squadron of about 12 aircrafts and 300 people running.

The standard operating procedure for junior officers was to move us from position to position in the squadron every few months to expose us to a wide variety of experiences and develop our leadership skills. Our responsibilities usually increased with each new position we assumed throughout our three to four years with a particular squadron.

Whenever I was assigned a new position, the first thing I would do beyond getting to know my people, was to completely revamp the files from the previous officers before me. I went into purge mode to simplify my paperwork and would invariably throw out about 50 to 75 percent of all the paperwork and files that had accumulated for years. As I got to know my job better, I would always look to streamline it even more.

Using this attitude of throwing things away, even when I was in doubt, never, ever burned me and still hasn't to this day. My corporation's files are only about one foot thick, and I am constantly trying to streamline my computer files to keep them simple and manageable.

4.   Create a paper safety net.

From experience I learned not to fear throwing things away. The freedom of having simplified, streamlined files drastically increases my control of time. This fourth tactic may help alleviate some of the nervousness and fear of throwing away paper. Create a special drawer in a file cabinet for the exclusive purpose of holding papers you would like to throw away but are still afraid to. It's a safety net of sorts.

After several months of seeing if you really need the paper you have in there, and I would bet you need very little if any at all, toss the drawer full of paper away and start again. As you become better at predicting what paper you can throw away and less afraid to do so, you'll become less dependent on this tactic.

5. Put only the bare necessities in writing.

When creating any memo or letter, stick to exactly what you need to get your point across and nothing more. This will not only save you time and paper, but will also save time for the person eventually receiving it.

6. Answer memos on the originating memo.

This is a great tactic to save paper, time, and confusion. By answering back on the original memo, the person getting your reply instantly knows what you are talking about because they recognize their own memo.

7. Copy only what you need at the copy machine.

How many times have you made a few extra copies of material for a meeting just to make sure you covered anyone extra who might be there? How many times have you walked away from a meeting with extra copies that you ended up throwing away or recycling? Try to break the mentality of making extra copies!

Find out how many people will be in attendance and make that many copies. If anyone extra shows up, just create the copies they need following the meeting. It's that easy.

8. Use the KISS Principle when creating computer reports.

Again, focus on keeping these reports short and simple. In this information age of business, it's so easy to print out information in a myriad of different formats and presentation styles. It's easy to fall into the trap of information overload and create reports that are almost overwhelming.

This tactic asks you to focus on keeping your reports brief and to the point. I would focus on the introduction and summary. When asked for more detail, I would be prepared to easily and quickly print out the specific detail being requested following the meeting and put it in a format that the person asking for it prefers. This saves time, money, and the frustration of trying to guess what everyone wants and how they want to see it. Give them what they want, when they want, and how they want it and you can't go wrong with your computer reports.

9. Reduce your filing.

Do what you can to simplify and streamline your files. Not only reduce how many you have, but also reduce how much you place in each.

10. Go through your files several times a year.

Every quarter to six months is great. You want to basically apply the Continual Success Improvement Formula to keeping your files streamlined and effective. Create a system that is simple and has as little fat as possible so you can easily find pertinent and valuable information when you need it.

11. Handle paper only once if possible.

You want to get into an "act now" mode on each piece of paper that finds its way into your hands. Read it, delegate it, pass it on to the appropriate person, take action on it, throw it away, file it, or put it somewhere to be acted upon at a specific time. Do not create piles and piles of paperwork that you eventually plan to get to. Rarely will you ever catch up if you fall into this trap.

Act on it now! If it's a document that will take you extensive time or research to complete, take some action now, even if it's just planning on when you *will* act on it. Don't let it pass by your fingers without some positive action.

12. Dot your paper corners.

One way to prevent from falling into the trap of picking up a piece of paper, doing very little to nothing with it, then placing it back in your in-box only to repeat this procrastination again later, is to dot the corner of that document every time you handle it. When the paper starts looking like it has the measles from all of your dots, it should be a sign that you're procrastinating and need to take immediate action now to get it out of your hands permanently.

13. Use the telephone or e-mail instead of writing a formal memo.

Any time you can take a few minutes to answer someone by phone or shoot a quick e-mail to do the same, you save not only paper, but also the time involved in creating a formal memo. Most of the time, the people you're responding to will be flattered that you answered back so quickly.

Be formal when the situation dictates; but if you don't have to be formal, settle on saving time and money through quick calls or e-mails.

12. *Poorly Planned Meetings*

How many times have you been in a meeting and thought it was a waste of time? All of us have at some point or another!

I'm amazed at how few meetings are as organized as they should be and take as little time as they should to accomplish the same end result. Meetings are essential to business, but more often than not, they waste valuable time because of how they are conducted.

The first thing you want to do to help avoid this Killer 13 is to ask yourself if the meeting you have planned is absolutely essential to all parties invited. Make sure you are not requiring people to be at the meeting who have nothing to do with the topics being covered or that have only a small portion of the schedule for them. Ask if there is another way to deal with these people to get the information out or the decision input needed.

Many times speaking to them for a few minutes offline, away from the meeting will get you the same result and save them hours to put toward other company projects.

If you are not in charge of the meeting and your attendance is required, you can save time by studying the agenda or meeting topics ahead of time, even for just a few minutes, so you can be better prepared to participate. Be prepared to answer any questions in your area of expertise for the meeting topics at hand and be prepared to help participate in a decision if required.

A few simple strategies exist to help make meetings you're in charge of more productive and require less time. The first is your meeting time. Take this at two levels, how long your meeting will be and when you will schedule it. Try to keep your meeting length to no more than an hour and a half. Anything longer and your meeting's effectiveness and productivity begin to deteriorate.

If possible, schedule your meeting around your participants' peak periods of attention and effectiveness. For most of us, this is late mornings Tuesday through Friday. Beware of afternoon energy drops due to lunch and our natural biorhythms, and do everything you can to avoid meetings Monday mornings and Friday afternoons.

The second strategy is to make an agenda for your meetings. Very few business meetings follow this timesaving plan. Try it—it absolutely works! An agenda is a simple document you create prior to your meeting and distribute to all meeting participants one to two days before the meeting. In it, you place the focus of the meeting and what your intent is—information passing, decision making, or a combination of the two. You state where the meeting will be held, when it will start, when it will end, and who is to participate. You then list a schedule for the meeting with topics, how long each will be discussed, and who is responsible for presenting that topic. That's it! It's simple to make, and once you make one, you have a model for future agendas, taking only about 15 minutes to create each time, but saving hours at the actual meeting.

The third strategy to improve your meetings is to start on time, end on time, and stick to the agenda during the meeting. If everyone is not at the meeting at the scheduled start time, start anyway! People adapt to your expectations. If you constantly start meetings late because you are waiting on attendees, then others will not make it a priority to be on time for future meetings. You'll be amazed at how quickly people start arriving on time once they know it's expected.

Ending on time and sticking to the agenda are just as important. If you or someone else doesn't complete their topic during their scheduled limit according to the agenda, quickly make arrangements to complete discussion of the topic at a future date or at the end of the meeting if there is time left over. Don't let your agenda schedule be ignored. That's the only way to cover all of the topics in your meeting with equal importance. Ending the meeting on time is an important sign of respect for the time of all attendees. Make it a priority!

I guarantee you the first few times you start using an agenda it will be hard to stick to the schedule. Do your best. The more you stick to the agenda's schedule, the more attendees will conform to covering just the important points of their topics so they can finish on time. Set the standard and others will follow in gaining tremendous control of your time through meetings.

13. Television and Video Games

Television and video games have an absolute huge potential to be large time wasters and a major Killer 13 in your personal life. They are perhaps the greatest distractions you face at home while trying to gain more control of your time.

The average American spends about four hours every single day staring at a non-interactive, flickering box called a television. Our children mirror this statistic very closely, being partially raised by an electronic babysitter or substitute parent and often learning their values from video games, many of them violent.

Let me put this into perspective for you. For most of us, television eats up half the time we're not working or sleeping. Add that up through our lifetime, and most of us can expect to waste almost 12 years of our lives with this time killer!

You do not have to throw away your television and burn your video games, although there are some experts who would suggest we all do that. I don't think television or video games are inherently evil. I recognize both as entertainment distractions that need individual parental supervision for our children. I enjoy both in responsible moderation and feel they have a place in my life. How do they impact your life?

Take a moment to recognize how much time you spend with this Killer 13. Estimate how much time you spend in front of the television and playing video games, if this applies to you at all. If you want, keep a viewing log over the next week to get a more accurate, probably eye-opening account of your habit.

Now to add more time to your personal life. If you were to halve how much time you spend viewing television and playing video games, how much time would that add to your average day? If you fit into the typical American profile, this could mean about two more hours a day just at home! What could you do with this extra time? How much closer could it help you get to your Clarity? This could literally give you back years of your life.

The Laws of Time

Having learned the 13 primary ways people tend to waste time and some strategies and tactics to help reduce their effects in life, here are three powerful behavioral laws of time and how to avoid their time-stealing traps. These laws, when you enact them in your life, act as magnets to the Killer 13. They each create situations that make you much more vulnerable to distractions and time wasters.

The first law is called Parkinson's Law. You may not recognize its formal name, but I can almost guarantee you've run into it before. Parkinson's Law states that work expands to fill the time you allow it. A good example of this law is when you only have a small bit of work to do and you have all day to complete it. Because you have so little to do and have so much time, you don't want to get started on it right away, so you instantly jump into one of the Killer 13. You socialize for a little while, maybe talk on the phone socially, surf the Web, grab some unimportant but entertaining reading, maybe watch some television if at home, and definitely procrastinate. You might start your real work a little before lunch, then take an extended lunch break. You come back from lunch and follow the same pattern as the morning. Next thing you know, you have to rush to complete your work before going home.

Has this or any variation of it ever happened to you? If it has, you've suffered the time-stealing effects of Parkinson's Law. What can you do about it in the future?

The best strategy for defeating Parkinson's Law is to have incentives for completing your work. If you control your day, the incentive to go home early is very powerful. If you have to stay at work for the day, seek an extended lunch if you can finish your work in the morning. Or find some other project that moves you toward your Clarity that you can get excited about and start once you complete you work. If you're at home, allow yourself to have an enjoyable afternoon in a favorite sport or recreational activity if you can finish your work in the morning. The possibilities are endless. Stay aware of the dangerous effects of this law and be creative in your incentives.

The second law is the Law of Diminishing Returns. This law affects those who tend to put in long hours at work, especially workaholics. It basically states that the longer you work in any one day, the less effective and efficient you become. As you progress through the work hours of a day, you become more and more susceptible to the time wasters and distractions of the Killer 13.

As I already taught you with the Killer 13 Interruptions, studies show that after you work eight hours, your productivity begins to drop. Between eight and 10 hours of work, your productivity drops by about 25 percent. After 10 hours, it drops by 50 percent and after 12 hours even further.

The reason your productivity drops is as you slowly wear down mentally and physically throughout the workday, your blinders to distractions steadily erode as well, making time wasters harder to avoid.

If you exercise consistently, eat a healthy diet, and have good sleep habits, you can reduce the effect of this law to some degree. But all of us, no matter who we are, will suffer a consistent loss of productivity throughout the day. I never recommend working longer than eight to 10 hours a day on a consistent basis.

The third law of time that can aggressively attract the Killer 13 is the Law of Sleep Deprivation. As its name implies, this law affects those of us who suffer from sleep deprivation, no matter how small. This law states that the more sleep deprivation you suffer from, the more time you will be prone to waste—the bigger your sleep debt, the worse the time-stealing effects of this law. Combine this law with a long workday and you'll find yourself hard pressed to be productive at all.

As we discussed in Module 4, you begin to accumulate a sleep debt and suffer from the effects of sleep deprivation the moment you don't get your optimum sleep amount. If you accumulate a large sleep debt through an extended period of poor sleep habits, you could be a walking magnet for the Killer 13, finding it consistently and progressively harder to be productive than to waste time.

The tool for beating this law of time is simple and easy. Get enough sleep!

If you've accumulated a large sleep debt over the years, work hard at eliminating that debt and establishing positive sleep habits. It may take months to do this, but the payoff is not only increased awareness and energy, but also in much improved blinders to distractions are absolutely worth it.

Be Perceptive

All of the material you've learned so far in this module can be condensed into one simple, easy to remember question that will give you the true secret weapon to reducing distractions and time wasters in your life.

"What is the best use of my time right now?"

Make it a habit to consistently and frequently ask yourself this question throughout the day and listen to your answer. Many times we don't realize when we're wasting time. We're on auto-mode, blindly caught up in the trap of our human behaviors. Anything you do to catch yourself and break your pattern of behavior can make a tremendous difference in getting back on track to producing toward your Clarity and goals. This simple question can create the simple awareness you need to recognize your pattern of wasting time. Many times awareness is all you need.

I want you to learn to recognize when you're wasting your time. Make this question your secret weapon in doing so! Admit it to yourself when you catch yourself wasting time, recognize it's okay to do so and part of your human programming, and then get back on track to effective action toward your Clarity and goals right away.

60-Second Power Summary

▸   It's okay to waste time.

▸   Focus on halving your time wasters.

▸   The Killer 13

1. Telephone/E-mail.
2. Surfing the Web.
3. Interruptions.
4. Socializing.
5. Procrastination.
6. Personal Disorganization.
7. Cleaning Your Desk.
8. Inability to Say No.
9. Lack of Delegation.
10. Indecision.
11. Unimportant Paperwork and Reading.
12. Poorly Planned Meetings.
13. Television and Video Games.

▸   The Laws of Time (Killer 13 magnets)

▹   Parkinson's Law.

▹   Law of Diminishing Returns.

▹   Law of Sleep Deprivation.

▸   "What is the best use of my time right now?"

Put Your Knowledge Into Action

Your action plan for this module is easy and will not require that much time. There are two worksheets to complete.

The first worksheet is titled "Time Wasters Worksheet." It has six simple, yet eye-opening steps that show how you're wasting your time both at work and home and what it's costing you in time. When filling out this worksheet, try to be very honest with yourself. Keep in mind as you look at your numbers that we have a tendency to understate our weaknesses and faults. The numbers you arrive at in this worksheet are the ones you're willing to admit to yourself. The truth is probably somewhat different.

The first part of the worksheet focuses on work. Step one asks you to list specific ways you are consistently wasting your time at work. Refer back to the Killer 13 and list the time wasters that have a tendency to grab you daily.

Step two asks you to write by each time waster you listed in step one the average amount of time you estimate you lose for that time waster each day. Be honest!

Step three asks you to total the times you listed in step two then to divide them in half.

The first total in step three is the total amount of time you estimate you waste at work every day. The second total in step three is how much time you can gain daily if you simply were to halve how much time you waste. Go through the questions I've listed to get a feel for the specific impact reducing your time wasters at work can have in your life.

Steps four through six are very similar to the first three steps, except this time you're focusing on time wasters at home. Again, be honest with yourself.

The second worksheet in your action plan, titled "Time Wasters Motivation," should look familiar. It's a Push-Pull Principle worksheet designed to create awareness and motivation in reducing your time wasters. The drill for completing this worksheet is the same as for the past few modules' action plans. Brainstorm all of the costs in your life on emotional, financial, physical, social, and spiritual levels if you continue to waste the same amount of time as you do right now. Remember to be emotional. In the Pull section, do the same thing for the rewards in your life if you just halve the time you waste now.

Review this sheet as necessary to help you create the critical awareness and motivation needed for success in this important area of your life. For the next few weeks review once every day or so; then you can steadily reduce your reviewing as you build your positive behaviors. If you find yourself slipping, simply increase how often you review. Keep in mind to review with emotion to gain the most benefits.

Use the two worksheets you've completed plus the strategies and tactics for the Killer 13 you learned this module to help create the extra time you desire. Remember, your focus is to reduce the time wasters and distractions in your work and home lives. If you can just halve their time-stealing effects, you can't help but gain at least—the very least—one more hour a day! Concentrate on this for the next three to four weeks to build power and positive change; then move on to the next module.

Time Wasters Worksheet

How are you wasting your time and what is it costing you?

1. List specific ways you are consistently wasting your time at *work*:

_____

_____

_____

_____

2. Next to each item above write the average amount of time you lose each day for that particular time waster.

3. Total the times above: Divide this total by 2:

    This is how much time you could gain at *work* on an average day.

    ▹   What could you accomplish with this extra time?

    _____

    ▹   How much closer could you get to your Clarity?

    _____

    ▹   How much more productive and effective could you be?

    _____

4. List specific ways you are consistently wasting your time at *home*:

_____

_____

_____

_____

5. Next to each item above, write the average amount of time you lose each day for that particular time waster.

6. Total the times above: Divide this total by 2:

    This is how much time you could gain at *home* on an average day.

    ▹   What could you accomplish with this extra time?

    _____

    ▹   How much closer could you get to your Clarity?

    _____

    ▹   How much more quality time with your family could you have?

    _____

Time Wasters Motivation Worksheet

I am totally committed to *reducing time wasters at work and home to create the time I desire to reach my destiny!*

Push:

The *costs* if I do not achieve this goal. (emotional, financial, physical, social, spiritual)

_____

_____

_____

_____

_____

_____

_____

_____

_____

_____

_____

Pull:

The *rewards* when I achieve this goal. (emotional, financial, physical, social, spiritual)

_____

_____

_____

_____

_____

_____

_____

_____

_____

_____

_____

MODULE

MOTIVATION
CONTROL

Enthusiasm!

Motivation! Enthusiasm! Energy!

Motivation is the energy for positive action. And focused action is one of the best tools for creating more control of your time. From the Greek origin meaning "in God" and "inspired," enthusiasm is the energy to get things done—to move from inaction to action. It is a real force and plays a real and measurable part of your success in time. As Ralph Waldo Emerson said, "Nothing great was ever achieved without enthusiasm."

Your level of motivation affects *everything* you do! How motivated you are determines how much effective work you accomplish. It determines how productive you are in a sales call. It determines how much you enjoy your business or job. It determines how much joy you get from your relationships. It determines the benefit you receive from your exercise. It determines the level of enjoyment you receive from your sports or other personal hobbies and interests. Bottom line—it determines your time. It determines the quality and quantity of time you have every day.

As an example, let's say there are two employees who are equally qualified and physically skilled for a particular job, with one exception. One would rather be doing something else and carries a minimal attitude toward the outcome of the job. The other is motivated and excited to be working on this particular task and cares how the job impacts the company. Who would accomplish more?

There's no doubt about the answer. Although both have equal skills and qualification, the worker that is more motivated will accomplish more and have a greater residual impact on the morale of others around them. Who would you rather have working for you and who would you rather be?

All because of one difference—motivation! We can't directly measure it, but motivation is a very real energy. And it has an incredible impact on your business and personal life. One study on motivation and its impact on sales revealed that motivated salespeople sell, on average, 15 percent more than their counterparts who aren't as motivated. Fifteen percent more! Most businesses would love a 15 percent increase in sales over the course of a year. One factor—motivation—can make that happen.

Your Motivation Measurement

Before you can learn the tools of short- and long-term motivation, you must know where you stand in your level of motivation. Similar to your Clarity, knowing where you are in your motivation level and where you want to be makes a tremendous difference in your outcome of producing motivational energy.

Without knowing these points in your level of motivation, you stand a very good chance of taking your enthusiasm and motivational energy for granted and failing to leverage them to your advantage. Knowing where you are is achieved by a simple process of taking a motivation measurement. Its basic premise and advantage is to force awareness. It forces you to take stock in yourself at any one moment to see just how much motivational energy you have for positive action. Awareness. It forces you to confront if you are at your best for a particular task or event in your life or just dragging your feet.

There are several ways to measure your motivation, and they are all subjective in nature—meaning you do not have a needle inside you that points to some magical reading of your motivational energy at any one time. All work off of relative or comparative estimates for you—your best guess. The measurement tool I recommend is a percentage scale from 0 to 100 as seen below.

0—10—20—30—40—50—60—70—80—90—100

Zero percent motivation means you're as motivated as a rock—nothing, nil, no energy whatsoever for positive action. One hundred percent motivation means you are absolutely at your best mentally to apply positive action toward something—you're enthusiastic, you're mentally clear, and you're tightly focused. At a 100 percent measurement, you may still experience fear toward some action, but it is quelled by your absolute confidence in your abilities.

Being near a 100 percent motivation level doesn't mean you have to be jumping out of your pants with enthusiasm. It means you're mentally at your best to do your best. You can be wildly excited and enthusiastic, but you can also be peacefully motivated to spend precious time with those you love. When I'm reading to my boys or sitting with them watching a special show or spending time with my wife, I'm very close to a 100 percent level of motivation. I am completely in tune with the moment, focused, not letting myself take the time for granted.

Most of the time, when you take your motivation measurement, you'll be somewhere between 25 and 75 percent on the scale. If you are a 50, you're fairly neutral to the event, meaning you enjoy it, but could easily be distracted by something else. If you are less than a 50, you have some motivational energy toward what you're doing, but you would rather be doing something else. The closer you are to 0 percent, the more you would rather be doing something else. The same goes for the other side of the scale. The closer you are to 100 percent, the more you are motivated toward the event and the less likely you are to being distracted.

Take a motivation measurement of yourself right now while studying this module. At this very moment, where are you between being as motivated as a rock, a 0, and being at your absolute mental peak toward absorbing new, beneficial information that can make a difference in your control of time, a 100? External and internal factors will make a difference in your measurement. How tired you are, what time of day you're doing this, any distractions around you—all make a difference in your measurement.

So, what's your measurement? Again, the number you pick is subjective, based on you. But it will tell a story. In my seminars, I've seen numbers all across the scale, but most fit somewhere between a 60 and a 90 for this example. If you had a measurement less than 50, I would guess you've had a long day, are tired, have distractions around you, or a combination of the three. If your measurement fell between 50 and 100, this probably means you're motivated toward studying this module, but do have some room for improvement in your level of motivational energy.

The difference between your motivation measurement at any one time and the 100 percent mark is how much more motivated you could be—how much more positive energy you could generate—toward the event. This difference is where extra control of your time can be found!

Taking a simple motivation measurement before or during an event forces awareness. And awareness is one of the simple keys to change. Change in where you want to be in your level of motivation—your energy for positive action!

Once you know where you are in your level of motivation, you then need to know where you want to be. Based on the event you are about to do or are in the middle of doing, decide how much motivational energy you would like to have. How mentally clear and focused do you want to be? How much enthusiasm do you want or need to accomplish or take part in this event? Do you need or want to be at your absolute mental best, in other words a measurement of 100 percent, or would an 80 or 90 percent do just fine?

It's your decision. You get to make the rules to your internal motivational energy level. Others may try to help motivate you or external factors may try to bring you down, but you ultimately decide at what level you want to be performing. Your rules! Do understand this—your choice of where you want to be will impact your time. The closer to 100 percent you are, the more focused and in control of your behaviors you'll be. The closer you perform at your mental peak, the stronger your blinders to time wasters and distractions become. In other words, the more control you have of your time.

For any event, you should be able to quickly decide where you are and then make a decision as to where you'd like to be on the motivational scale. The difference between the two is the key; it is where all of the tools you'll soon learn in both short and long-term motivation will come into play. The short-term motivation tools will help you quickly close that gap when you apply them, and the long-term motivation tools will keep that gap minimized through time.

Let's look at a few quick examples of using motivation measurement to make sure you've got the concept in proper perspective.

On your way to work, take a quick motivation measurement to how motivated you are for your job or business. Decide where you want to be and note the difference. Decide if you want to apply any of the tools from this module to close the gap.

Before a sales call or important presentation, take a quick motivation measurement. Decide where you want to be in order to perform at your best. Again, make a decision as to applying any of the motivation-increasing tools to close the gap and increase your chances of success.

On your way home from a long day at work, take a motivation measurement for spending time with your family. Once again, decide where you want to be and take action to make it happen with the simple tools that will soon be at your disposal.

I think you get the idea. You can apply this awareness to checking your motivation level at any time, toward any event. Sports, relationships, sales, marketing, performing your job, phone calls, live events…anything!

Remember, you ultimately control your enthusiasm. You get to decide and you make the rules for your motivation. Don't depend on others and on external factors to motivate you. You get to decide where you want to perform for all of the events in your life. Take advantage of this control and apply it toward accelerating your control of time. Get in the habit of measuring your motivation and taking action from your results.

How to Change Your Motivation Level

Once you know where your motivation level is and where you want it to be, the rest is easy. All you have to do is apply tools—simple tools to increase your short and long-term levels of motivation. For short-term motivation we're going to focus on tools that involve your body. For long-term motivation we'll teach you tools centered on your mind.

Your Body: Key to Short-Term Motivation

You can change your level of motivation instantly with your body. Taking action physically, performing certain functions with different part of your body, can very quickly close the gap between where your motivation measurement is and where you want it to be.

Again, realize your have total control in this process. If you want to be more enthusiastic, if you want to have more energy for positive action, you must accept responsibility that the power sits within you—nobody else. Take charge of your motivation, take charge of your actions, and take charge of your time!

All of the six body tools for short-term motivation are directly affected by your energy level. Your diet, exercise level, and sleep all factor into how much of a motivation increase you get from applying these tools and how long it will last.

Your Diet

I'm sure I'm not the first to tell you that what you eat impacts your energy level. I want to make sure you understand that it directly impacts your ability to generate energy for positive action—your enthusiasm.

Your diet does this on two levels. The first is your overall diet. If you consistently eat a poor diet in both content and quantity, the body motivation tools will increase your motivation level but to a reduced amount and last a shorter period of time. I'm sure this is rather obvious.

But I also want to make sure you're on top of the second level of how diet impacts your motivational ability, the short-term meal. If you have decent eating habits, then you realize that one heavy or fatty meal can impact your ability to generate motivational energy for several hours after you've eaten. Skipping a meal can have a similar effect.

If you've got an important presentation or meeting in the afternoon, be aware that your natural biorhythms will be working slightly against you in the mid to late afternoon with a dip in your energy level. Add a heavy lunch or skip a meal and the negative effects to your energy level are compounded. Keep this in mind when you get too busy to grab a bite to eat or when you pull up to the drive-thru and are tempted to "super size" your lunch for only 39 cents more.

Your Exercise

If you're a couch potato and never do any form of consistent exercise or physical exertion, then your ability to close the gap in your motivation levels between where you are and where you want to be will be reduced. When you do generate increased motivational energy from the upcoming body tools, the lasting effect will be diminished. The good news is you don't have to be an Olympic athlete to maximize the effect of these body tools. Any moderate exercise, even a simple walking program, will greatly impact how much and how long these tools help you.

Your Sleep

You should know by now how much sleep can impact your time. Of the three energy level factors, sleep can have the greatest impact on your benefit from the body tools. Any sleep debt at all will reduce these powerful body tools' ability to increase your motivation level and keep it there. The more sleep deprived you are, meaning the larger the sleep debt you carry, the greater the negative impact on your ability to generate energy for positive action for any sustained amount of time.

Your Body Motivation Tools

There are six short-term body tools that you can use to instantly increase your level of motivation in any situation. Use them in combination and their positive effects compound to give you more leverage to perform at your best.

1. Deliberate Movements

Powerful, fast, deliberate movements can instantly increase your heart rate and clear your mind for more energy for positive action. Clapping your hands, snapping your fingers, stomping your feet, jumping up and down, and taking deep breaths all fall into this category of instant improvement to your motivation.

These gestures and actions force your body to go into increased movement, circulating your blood at a faster rate, unpooling it from your legs if you've been sitting for a long period of time, and increasing the amount of air filling your lungs. With an increased heart rate and more oxygen flowing from your lungs to your bloodstream, it's much easier to focus and perform at a higher mental rate.

Right now do another quick motivation measurement for studying this module. What percentage do you have?

Now, do what I call a Power Breath. Take a deep breath in, hold it for a few seconds, and let it out nice, slow, and strong. Don't overdo this. You should not feel lightheaded or dizzy. Your fitness level will determine how long you should hold your breath. Start with just a few seconds at first. If you ever feel dizzy, shorten how long you hold your breath and slow down when you exhale. It should be relaxing and invigorating, not strenuous. Your object is to increase your oxygen flow to your blood stream. The more oxygen in your blood, the more your cells can perform at their best, giving you increased energy and mental clarity. In other words, increased motivation.

To best maximize your breath, let your stomach expand when you breathe in and tighten when you breathe out. This involves your diaphragm properly and is the way our body was meant to breathe. Sucking in your stomach and lifting your chest up when you inhale actually limits the capacity of your lungs.

Go ahead and perform three Power Breaths right now.

How do you feel? Do you have more motivation? Take a quick motivation measurement and see. Did you increase your measurement from where you were just a few moments ago? If you did, how long did this exercise take and what benefits can you give yourself with this quick, easy exercise in the future?

How long the positive effects of a Power Breath last depends on your big three factors for your energy level—your diet, your exercise, and your sleep. On average, you can expect a few Power Breaths to increase your motivation for about 15 to 30 minutes. Keeping this in mind, how hard would it be to do a few Power Breaths a few times an hour? Try it over the next week and see if it makes a difference in your daily motivation.

Try a few Power Breaths right before special events and see what they do to your performance. Before you speak, before you give a presentation, before a phone or in-person sales call, before an important meeting or phone call, before walking in your door to greet your family from work, or before important parts of a sporting event. Try it! Note if it gives you more focus, more positive energy, and calms any nerves you may have. It takes only a few seconds to do, but has amazing results.

This is a great time to bring up a point about a diminished, yet still very established tradition in the workplace—the smoke break. Have you or have you ever heard others say they need a smoke break to get a boost in their energy? I want you to think about this for a minute. Most workers are in enclosed buildings. How do we tend to breathe when we are in these work environments? Short, shallow breaths—right? When a smoker takes a smoke break, where do most have to go? Outside! And when they take a drag on their cigarettes, how do they tend to breathe? Long, deep breaths! Not realizing it, smokers are doing Power Breaths during their smoke breaks.

I grant you that the nicotine in cigarettes, like caffeine, artificially boosts energy to a degree. But while smoking outside, in fresh air, smokers are filling their lungs with more oxygen than they did when cooped up inside. Even when mixed with deadly smoke and tar, they are getting more oxygen to their blood stream for increased energy. It's not the cigarette that's making a positive difference; it's the Power Breaths!

The lesson here is to imagine how much more energy smokers could have if they took the same breaks and took the same breaths minus the deadly cigarettes. If you don't smoke, learn something valuable from this. If you work in a cooped up building, take a few Power Breath breaks throughout the day. Go outside, away from the smokers, and do a few Power

Breaths with some fresh, outside air. These breaks should take you only a few minutes each, but see the positive impact they have in your mental clarity and motivational energy.

Here is another exercise to try.

Stand up, put your arms straight out to your sides, and then clap your hands in s-l-o-w motion. Do this a few times and decide if this deliberate movement has increased your motivation level.

I bet clapping at this slow speed had no effect, or maybe even a negative one, on your motivation level. It's a deliberate movement, so why didn't it work? It was too slow!

The key to this tool increasing your motivation is in speed and power. Your deliberate movements must have power. Yes, when you do Power Breaths go slow so you don't get too dizzy. But make them strong. Everything else—clapping, snapping your fingers, stomping, jumping—should be done with speed and power to generate the extra energy you desire.

Clap again. But this time, clap with speed and power. Try it a few times! Don't worry about what others around you might think as you try this exercise. They might just learn something.

Did it make a difference? I bet it did. I bet your blood flow increased and your hands are tingling a little. Where are you now in your motivation measurement?

Sports teams, especially football players, and the military use these same deliberate movements to pump themselves up before and during special events. If it works for them, why can't it work for you?

2. Your Voice

How you use your voice directly impacts your motivation level. Changing it by making it stronger, louder, faster, or more passionate can instantly increase your motivation and give you more energy for positive action.

Let's start out with an exercise I call a Power Scream. Depending on where you're studying this module, you may want to try the silent version of this. Hold any air from passing into your windpipes, but contract your stomach and mouth muscles as you silently go through a scream.

Scream for about three seconds. Don't strain your voice, but get all of your tension and stress out in one powerful, sustained scream.

Even if you had to do the silent version to prevent scaring any coworkers, I bet you feel a physical difference in your body. Probably increased blood flow and a release of tension. If you found yourself smiling or laughing a little afterward, even from a bit of embarrassment, all the better. Smiling and laughing increase your motivational potential even more!

The Power Scream is a great motivation-building tool. Use it to pick yourself up or to release built up stress that holds back your energy for positive action. Again, I'm sure you've heard athletes scream at times during competition. Many tennis players do a short Power Scream with every stroke to focus themselves and boost the power of their hits. Many forms of martial arts use versions of the Power Scream to generate power and focus and have effectively done so for thousands of years. I've seen basketball players do the same thing after a dunk or big shot to pump up themselves, their teammates, and the crowd. The military does the same thing—especially the Marines.

Don't dismiss the Power Scream as being silly and not applicable to your life unless you truly don't care about improving your control of time. I know you care about your time! So give the Power Scream a test over the next week or so and prove to yourself that it really helps or has little to no impact at all. Then you can make your decision from a position of strength, not speculation.

Besides a Power Scream, there are other ways you can use your voice to increase your motivation. Have you ever heard someone give a presentation who spoke in a slow, monotone voice? How about someone who spoke so soft and timid that you had to strain to hear them even though you were only a few feet away? I'm sure you have. How did either of these speaking styles affect your ability to focus on their topic and be swayed by their arguments? Probably negatively. Why? Their voice style was actually draining your motivational energy because you had to pay close attention and be enthusiastic about their presentation.

Has either of these speaking styles ever affected you directly? Understand that speaking dispassionately, not only drains the motivation from your audience, but it also drains your motivational energy as well. Communication studies show that 80 percent of the message you convey is from physical actions and only 20 percent is from the actual words you say. How you use your voice to speak your message plays a *huge* part in 80 percent of the message you deliver.

Be more passionate when you speak and you'll generate a huge amount of motivational energy for both yourself and your audience. How can you do this? Just being aware can help you tremendously to speak stronger, louder, faster. Don't be unnatural, though. Just experiment with conveying passion through your voice to find what works best for you.

Here are some great examples to how your voice can affect your motivation level.

When I was teaching history to freshmen in college, I had my students give a short speech about the topic we were studying every week. At first many were nervous about speaking in front of a group. But as the semester wore on and they were aloud to be as creative as they wanted to be, their nerves were replaced by passion and motivation. These freshmen learned to give presentations leaps and bounds ahead of the graduating seniors. Their use of body motivational tools was a big key to their success!

Adolf Hitler was one of the greatest terrors to ever walk this planet, but he was also one of history's greatest speakers. He had the ability to convey unbelievable passion to hundreds of thousands of listeners through his voice alone. American reporters in Germany just prior to World War II consistently reported that even though they could not understand the German language Hitler was speaking, his passionate speaking style wrapped them up into the motivational energy swelling in the crowd.

3. Your Posture

How you sit, how you stand, and how you carry yourself when you walk all instantly affect your motivation level.

Think back to high school when you had to sit through an hour of your most boring class. How did you sit in your chair or desk? Try it now and see how it feels on your body.

I bet you were slouching. Did it motivate you to sit like that? How did it just feel when you tried it again? I bet boring and de-motivating! It may have even helped you feel like it was time for a nap.

The same goes for now in your career. When you are in a long, boring meeting, one in which five minutes of the entire one to two hour session is dedicated to things you care about, how do you tend to sit? What is your posture like? Loose and probably slouching again—just like in high school (maybe not that dramatic!). Again, do you think sitting like that improves or takes away from your ability to generate motivational energy for positive action in that meeting?

Take another quick motivation measurement. Try sitting like you do in those boring meetings and note how it makes you feel. What does it do to your motivation measurement? Drops it, right? How much depends on you.

Use your posture to your advantage! I want you to sit like you are in an interview with Bill Gates, Microsoft's multi-billion dollar founder. Bill is looking for someone to head a new project, and you're a frontrunner for consideration. If he picks you, you will receive a billion-dollar budget at your complete disposal, a 10 million dollar a year salary, and a five million-dollar, tax-free signing bonus.

How would you sit for this interview? Do it now! Are you sitting upright, confidently, and attentive? Probably something close to this. What does sitting like this do to your motivation measurement?

Try this exercise that vividly shows you the impact posture has on your motivation level. For the next minute, alternate sitting like you are in that boring meeting and then quickly shift to how you would sit for the Bill Gate's interview. Stay in each position for a few seconds, then quickly shift to the other. Do this several times.

Beyond the possible aerobic benefit of this exercise, can you feel the distinct difference in your muscle position and tone between both positions?

Keep this lesson mind the next time you're in a meeting. Choose your posture and choose your level of motivation.

4. Your Facial Expressions

Believe it or not, how you use the muscles in your face can instantly play a major part in your motivation level at any one time. The best way to see how this works is through another demonstration exercise. I first saw Anthony Robbins use a similar form of this exercise several years ago in demonstrating what he called "state management." I found the exercise to be a great demonstrator for the facial expression impact in your motivation as well. If there are others around you, you might improve their motivation as they watch you perform this. If you are one who tends to get embarrassed easily, you might want to try this somewhere where you have a little privacy.

Put the biggest smile on your face that you can possibly muster. Keeping the smile on your face, try to feel frustrated. Don't lose that smile! Try to feel mad. You can smile better than that—come on, give it a good try!

How hard was it to feel frustrated and mad with a smile on your face? From all of the seminars and training sessions with thousands of people trying this, the answers are almost always the same. It's very hard to almost impossible! It's hard to feel mad and frustrated when your facial expression is positive. Time and time again, it has been proven that your physical facial expressions guide your emotions and ultimately your motivation level.

So what do you take away from this? I'm not suggesting you walk around all day with an exaggerated Howdy Doody grin on your face. But do try to be more aware that positive facial expressions can instantly leverage your emotions and your motivational energy.

Be aware of the opposite, as well. Negative, grumpy facial expressions can drain your motivational energy in a heartbeat. Have you ever seen someone with a permanent scowl on his or her face? Do you ever remember that person being motivated for anything? I doubt it.

Laughter is one of the best medicines in the world for a couple of reasons that are perfect to point out now. Laughing causes you to have positive facial expressions, increasing your motivational ability. It also causes you to use your voice in a more passionate way whether giggling, having a full blown belly laugh bringing tears to your eyes, or anything in between. Laughing has been proven to improve your health. If it can do that, imagine what it can do for your ability to generate energy for positive action.

5. Music

Music is an outstanding tool to instantly improve your motivation. How so? Music has the ability to tie the four body tools you have just learned—deliberate movements, your voice, your posture, and your facial expressions—together for instant geometric improvement in your motivation measurement.

When you listen to the right song for the right situation, it improves your motivation by causing you to immediately and effortlessly use some or all of your body tools. For deliberate movements, you might dance or move your body to the beat of the music. For your voice, you might sing. Your posture is likely to become positive and confident. And your facial expressions might become expressive and vibrant. Add all these movements together and your motivational energy can elevate to incredible levels.

Here are a few examples to illustrate this powerful tool.

Weight lifting. Have you ever lifted weights? If you have, can you lift more and do more repetitions if you have music with a strong beat that you like playing loudly around you? You bet you can! The music focuses you and increases your motivation to try harder and do more.

Aerobics. If you've ever done aerobics, can you imagine doing the same routine for the same amount of time with the same intensity with no music? Aerobics without music goes from motivational exercise to a torturous activity.

Movies. How different would movies be with no musical score to set the theme and energy of the production? Take the same actors, the same action, the exact same dialogue, but subtract the background music, and you have a completely different experience.

These examples make it clear that music makes a difference in motivational energy. This energy can also be applied at both work and in the home.

First, understand that there are different levels of motivation where music can help you. You may be looking for motivation to relax and unwind, inspire and motivate, gain extra focus and productivity, or get completely pumped up. Music is available, music I can almost bet you own right now, that can help you achieve these different kinds of positive motivational energy. You just need to take an inventory of your music collection and categorize selections to work for you in the appropriate situations.

It doesn't matter what style of music you like. Classical, jazz, pop, rhythm and blues, country, to just name a few styles, all have different musical pieces that fit the different levels of motivation. Pick selections of music that touch you personally for each of the levels and use them when you want to move toward that motivation style. Have musical selections readily available to relax you when you want to unwind, to inspire you when you want to reach higher levels of success, to spiritually lift you when you are challenged, and to kick you in the rear and light your fire when you want to go further in something than you ever have before.

Keep these selections readily available for use when you're at home, in your car, and at work. Before your next sales call, presentation, or important meeting, take a few minutes in your car or with a portable cassette or CD player to listen to the selection that will best fit the motivation you want for the event. I guarantee that it will increase the motivational energy you have available for positive action.

I've worked with senior sales representatives that swear by this simple motivational tool. The few minutes they spend listening to a certain piece of personal motivational music crystallizes their focus and boosts their confidence immensely. It helps them visualize a positive sales outcome and do what it takes to ethically bring it about.

6. Your Sense of Smell

The smells around you have an amazing, but often overlooked, ability to instantly change your level of motivation.

It's easy to illustrate this on the negative end. Imagine the worst smell you can think of surrounding you right now. What would that do to your motivation level to stay in your seat and continue to study this module? It would plummet it in a heartbeat, with your only focus being to get away from the source of the smell.

Well, your sense of smell can also work to your advantage, shrinking the motivational gap between where you are and where you would like to be. An Australian dentist named Patty Lund decided to address the instant fear many patients associated with the typical dental office medical smell. He purchased an espresso machine and hired a part time baker to cook bakery goods in his dental office every morning. The rich cafe smell that immediately enveloped Patty's patients when they entered his practice did wonders on calming their fears and increasing their motivation level for receiving dental treatment. One positive factor did this—smell.

In Japan many offices are practicing the art of aromatherapy in the workplace. Following studies that determined how smells affect workers' motivation, offices are using office fresheners that change smells throughout the day. In the morning the fresheners emit citrus, mint, and cinnamon smells proven to boost productivity and motivation. As the workday draws to an end, the fresheners switch to calming flower smells such as lavender, proven to relax and unwind the workers before they go home.

The scent of a bar of soap first thing in the morning shower, coffee brewing for breakfast, potpourri in your home or office, incenses to relax you, fresh flowers, perfume or cologne—all can increase your motivation to perform or relax, depending on the smell, its intensity, and your situation. Experiment and test different smells to see if they help increase your motivation. Once you find some that work, put them to work for your benefit.

Keep in mind that we each can react very differently to the same smell. What inspires and motivates others may actually decrease the motivation of someone else. Some of us are attracted to someone wearing a particular perfume or cologne. Others could be completely turned off by the same. Be aware of this when using the motivational tool of smell around others.

Your Mind: Key to Long-Term Motivation

As much as your body impacts your motivation level on an immediate basis, your mind impacts your motivation level to an equal degree over the long haul.

I want to start this section off with a simple exercise. I want you to read the sentence below and count the number of letter f's you can see. Only spend about 15 to 20 seconds max on this.

The wedding gift of the bride's father for his famous son-in-law was to leave him half of the bill for the festivities.

How many did you count?

The answer is nine. Did you get the write answer or did you fall a few short? If you didn't quite get nine, go back and see what words you passed over. If you missed any, I bet you left out the f's in "of" and "for." Am I right? Of the thousands and thousands I have tested with this exercise, most fall into the range of seven or eight in their count. Why? Simple—your focus. As you read, you learn to skim over very common words to speed your reading process up. Even when you try to break from reading in your usual skim mode, your mind's focus can be difficult to break. In other words, your human behavior took over. Sound familiar?

Your brain, your mind, is simply the most powerful computer in the world. As technology outgrows itself at an exponential rate, the gap is closing somewhat, but to date, no computer has been able to match the non-linear processing capability of the human brain. By processing power, I am referring to your brain's ability to interpret all of the information your body collects. Your guide to this processing capability is through your mind's focus.

Every single second we have billions of sensory inputs into our brain. Sounds, sights, smells, tastes, and touch feed a never-ending stream of data to be sorted for interpretation. How your brain sorts all of this almost overwhelming information determines your reality.

Even as great as our brain's processing capability is, we cannot analyze all of the information we are fed at once. It's too much and would fry our mind if our brains did. We are "selective" with the data we collect, choosing only a minute portion of our environment on which to focus. We then mix the data we select with our interpretations and past experiences. What you are selecting, what you are focusing on, mixed with how you interpret it, is the world you know—your reality.

Focus is the key to your long-term motivation! You have control over what your mind selects and chooses to focus on and ultimately your long-term motivation, the consistent energy for positive action you possess through time.

Here are some examples to illustrate the power of focus and how it bears on your long-term motivation.

In the beginning of this module I alluded to an example of two equally skilled workers with a vastly different focus on their jobs. One enjoyed the job; the other didn't. The worker with a positive focus easily accomplishes more and has their time go by at a faster rate through the day. The worker who does not enjoy the job will focus on how long the day is and how much more time they had to go before they could go home. That focus would directly impact the quantity and quality of the work they produced.

Roller coasters are a great example of focus and its effects. Do you enjoy riding roller coasters? Most of us usually fit into one of two categories—you love them or you absolutely hate them.

Let's go on a mental roller coaster ride for a minute. If you love roller coasters, you'll have a focus on fun, and this will be an exhilarating experience for you filled with laughter and positive adrenaline. When finished with the ride, you may still want to go back again and will have produced chemicals in your body that actually improve your immune system.

Our roller coaster haters will have a completely opposite experience based on a focus of fear. After the ride is over, they may be so physically and emotionally drained that they literally need help getting out of the car. Not to mention the need for a cleanup crew. The roller coaster haters will have produced chemicals in their body as well. But these chemicals literally break down their immune system, aging them and leaving them more susceptible to sickness.

One factor was the difference in these two very different roller coaster outcomes. Focus. The single power behind your long-term motivation!

Your Mind Motivation Tools

There are only three simple tools to keep in mind when you are trying to maximize your long-term motivation for your success in time.

1. Your Attitude

I know I'm not the first person to tell you that your attitude is important to your success. But remember way back to our introductory module when I explained that knowledge is not power, only its application is? This is the case with your attitude! It's not what you know that's important. I know you know attitude is important. It's what you do with what you know that counts. That is the job of this tool. To get you to really pay attention to the long-term motivational power of your attitude. I want to show you some incredible examples—unique, very illustrative ones that you may not have heard before that show attitude's true potential in your life.

Your attitude is simply how your mind interprets your brain's focus. Whether you interpret a roller coaster or airplane ride as terror-filled or pure enjoyable bliss is a function of attitude. Whether you view your job as fun, fulfilling, and productive or boring and a waste of your talents is a function of attitude. Whether you view challenges and obstacles as daunting and hopeless or exciting and filled with wondrous opportunities is a function of attitude. And whether you love marketing and sales or are fear of constant rejection is a function of attitude.

Your focus is purely your choice. The moment children learn to ride a bike, their focus shifts from fearful of falling to the exhilaration of speed and control. That transition time is a little different for each of us. Some of us switch instantly; others take more time. But the full control of our focus lies within. We are the masters of our focus, our attitude, and ultimately, our motivation for positive action.

The challenge falls in your ingrained behaviors—how strong your current focus is. To shift it may take time, but the awareness of your current attitude and knowing where you want it to really be is a very powerful start.

Believe in yourself no matter what others believe. Most people, especially your loved ones, often hold you back from taking risks and growing, pursuing your goals and dreams, because of their focus. Their focus is often not on your dreams and happiness but on their fears for you and for themselves for not having the attitude, the courage, to take the risks you are. Our loved ones often mean well, but stay aware that their fearful attitude can hold you back.

Never, ever forget that your attitude can create absolute miracles in your life. So many great stories are testimonies to this, but I now want to share with you some of the best that I have come across in my studies and experiences.

I'll start off with two sports stories. Even if you aren't into sports, their lessons apply to all of our lives.

The first story is about an amateur track and field athlete named Roger Bannister. For thousands of years through time's recorded history, no person had ever been able to run a mile in less than four minutes. During the first half of the 20th century, scientists and doctors seemed to be in agreement that it was humanly impossible to break the sacred four-minute barrier. Our human bone and muscle structure could not generate enough sustained power and speed to overcome the friction of our human frame, they thought.

Until 1954, Roger Bannister, as an amateur participant in an English track and field competition, broke the sacred barrier in the mile run with a time of 3 minutes and 59.6 seconds. He had no special training; he had no special diet; he had no special equipment. What he had was attitude!

But the amazing thing about this story is not even Roger Bannister's accomplishment. By breaking the barrier and showing the world it could be done, he instantly shifted the attitude of mile runners around the world. Knowing that an amateur athlete had done it, professional and amateur athletes alike changed their focus and gained the motivation they needed to succeed in what they once thought impossible.

Before Roger Bannister, no one had broken the four-minute barrier. The year he did it, he was the first and only. The next year, 37 athletes broke the barrier. And the year after that, 300 athletes broke it!

The second sports story I want to share with you centers on modern day golf icon Tiger Woods. Tiger was touted as one of the best golfers to ever play the amateur circuit. In his first year on the pro tour the expectations, media coverage, and endorsement opportunities for this young man surpassed any golfer who had come before him. That same year, 1997, Tiger participated in his first major event, the coveted Masters in Augusta, Georgia.

Prior to starting the event, Tiger was interviewed by sports media and asked if he thought he could win the Masters. His reply was that he was confident in his abilities and felt he could win every tournament he entered. His attitude for winning was rock solid.

Tiger's play in the Masters matched his attitude. He didn't just win the event, he shattered it! He was not only the youngest player to ever win the Masters, but he also set a course record that had stood for over 100 years. In that weekend at Augusta, he set the largest margin of victory in any PGA major at 12 strokes—a record that had stood for 130 years. It's the equivalent of winning a basketball game by over 100 points. Not bad for the new kid on the block. His attitude played a major role.

But Tiger's attitude would shift after that tournament. After such a convincing victory at the Masters, the media went crazy. The hype went so far in the media as to discuss changing all of the golf courses to handicap Tiger and give the other golfers a chance. Tiger was still only 21, and the barrage of even higher expectations began to weigh on him in the year's later tournaments. He began to press in his game, and his attitude shifted. As the stress built higher and higher, Tiger commented in interviews that he couldn't win all of the tournaments because he was only human. He began to doubt himself, and his attitude for winning followed.

Tiger still played well enough to compete, but not to win. He finished the year as the top-ranked golfer in the world, but had dropped well below the level he was capable of playing. He carried this attitude and play through the next 1998 golf season, slipping his ranking and shrinking his number of tournament victories.

In 1999, Tiger began to mature and gain his confidence back, learning how to handle the pressure and expectations. His attitude shifted positively back again and his dominant play followed. Since then, Tiger has gone on to become one of the most dominant golfers in history, setting the scoring record at every single PGA major event in just a few years and even stringing an unheard of four major tournament victories in a row. Once again, his attitude has been the difference.

Translate Tiger's story to your life. No matter what your skill level is, it's attitude that makes the difference. Attitude gives you the motivation, and motivation gives you the energy for positive action in all of your life.

The next few stories show the clear power of attitude in the most important game of all—our will to live.

Arturo Garcia was a commercial construction worker in California. One day in 1999 near the end of his shift, he fell through some weakened platforms covering a hole in the ground. As he fell through, the massive volume of loose dirt surrounding the hole was jarred and began to bury him alive. Arturo quickly remembered the simple but life-saving training he had received and covered his face with his hardhat. This created the only small pocket of air for him to breathe.

Arturo's coworkers heard him when he fell and quickly called emergency crews. For the next eight hours the rescue crews faced an amazing dilemma. The dirt around Arturo was so loose and shifted so much that every time the frantic rescuers would use a large suction hose to remove the dirt around Arturo, more dirt would quickly fill in. Each time he was completely buried again. Worse yet, he was slipping further down the hole and was about to fall through a gap that would be his instant death.

Over the eight-hour ordeal, Arturo was buried alive eight times! Each time his attitude to survive for the sake of his wife and young children kept him from panicking. After his eighth burial, as he was slipping into the perilous gap, Arturo managed to free a pocketknife from pants pocket and cut his belt off. This allowed him to wiggle out of his pants, and rescuers could finally pull him free.

What was the difference? What allowed this man to face death eight times over eight hours, buried alive each time? His attitude! His will to survive made the difference. If Arturo's attitude could do this for him, imagine what an attitude shift could do for you in your day-to-day life. The next time you have a bad day, compare it to his "bad day" and remember his attitude for motivation.

As a Training Officer for my P-3C Orion squadron in the Navy, I had the opportunity to study the crash reports from the very few P-3C ditchings that had taken place in the 30-year long history of the plane. Designed to hunt submarines for long periods of time, the Orion is the largest tactical plane in the Navy's arsenal. It is 100 feet from wingtip to wingtip and carries up to 23 people, much too big to land on an aircraft carrier. Our aircrews consisted of 11 to 12 people, and our missions often took us thousands of miles from land for over 10 hours at a time.

Ditching is when a plane has to land on the surface of the water because of an emergency. Because of its size and construction, the Orion is one of the best planes in the Navy at ditching with a high probability of survival. Fortunately, only a handful has ever had to prove this. Most of these have been close to land, and in one case after the ditching, the crew was able to swim safely to land with the plane's tail sticking out of the water in less than 20 feet of water.

But one ditching incident paints a very clear picture of attitude and its power on your motivation. A P-3, thousands of miles from land over the Pacific Ocean, incurred engine problems that the crew instantly knew would keep them from making it back. They flew back toward base for hours as their fuel level fell lower and lower. The crew managed to call for help, and another plane flew by their side as everyone waited for the inevitable crash landing into the cold ocean waters below.

When the pilots finally put the Orion into the water, all crewmembers survived the impact and made it to the life rafts. The emergency plane that flew by their side could offer little more help than to direct a ship to their eventual location. The rest was a matter of survival and attitude in the harsh ocean elements as they waited for over a day for a ship to rescue them.

Through all of their survival training and all of their teamwork, the will to live was a very personal but crucial element in their survival. In the end, all of the married crewmembers survived, and all of the single crewmembers couldn't hold on to life and died before help arrived. In the interviews that followed, each survivor pointed to their intense desire to see their wives and children again as the key element to their survival. Their attitude! Their attitude gave them the motivation to stay alive in the harshest of elements. What can your attitude do for you?

The final story on attitude I want to share with you is one I will never forget. It's about a survivor of a World War II Nazi concentration camp named Victor Frankl and how his shift in attitude saved his life.

Prior to the Holocaust, Victor was a successful psychiatrist in Vienna. When the horror hit, Victor, like millions of other Jews, was quickly thrust into Hitler's hell. He soon lost his wife and children in the concentration camps and looked for a way to hold on to his own survival in the midst of his swelling grief. Using his background as a psychiatrist, he began to observe the motivational patterns of those Jews who seemed to have a higher will to survive. He discovered it was their attitude in how they focused on the horror around them every day that made the difference.

One day in camp a Nazi soldier noticed that Victor was still wearing his wedding ring, his only physical link and memory to the family he had violently taken away from him. The soldier decided to taunt him and took the ring from his finger. In his book *Man's Search for Meaning*, Victor points out that in that very instant he discovered, "The last of the human freedoms is to change one's attitude in any given set of circumstances."

He changed his attitude in an instant! Victor decided the only victory he could have would be his attitude, so he did nothing when the soldier took his ring. The soldier wanted him to react, wanted him to show pain and sorrow, but he gave no quarter. He simply stood and won that small victory when the soldier walked away angry and disappointed at losing his mentally tortuous game.

Victor created a purpose to enduring all of the Nazi torture and pain with his newfound attitude for survival. Through the rest of his days in camp until freed by the Allies, while others gave up hope and perished, he dreamed of telling others about the horrors he experienced and saw and how he had survived. Over and over, retold thousands of times, Victor visualized the details of giving his post Holocaust speeches and never letting the world forget about what had happened in those camps.

His will to survive became his torch to carry him through. His attitude allowed him to endure and eventually persevere. Remember Victor's story and how you can change your attitude whenever you want—no matter what your circumstances

2. Your Questions to Yourself

The second simple tool that can help you maximize your long-term motivation for your success in time is the set of questions you ask yourself on a frequent basis.

You are constantly asking and answering questions to yourself. These questions and how you answer them are the instruments of your focus. They help you select what you focus on in your environment. Your questions determine your focus, and your focus then determines your motivation.

Your mind will answer every question you ask of it. The answer you receive and act upon depends upon your experiences and your attitude.

When you consciously or subconsciously choose weakening questions as your primary set of questions, you will focus on the negative and daunting obstacles of your life. The following questions, and others similar to them, fit into this category:

▶   Why am I a failure?

▶   Why does this always happen to me?

▶   Why do others always get the lucky breaks?

▶   Why can't I succeed?

▶   Why can't I stop   ?

What happens when you ask yourself these questions? Your mind sifts through your experiences, your fears, and your attitude to give you an answer. Most of the time the answer you get when you frame a question like those above is negative and motivationally draining. Your mind tends to justify why you're a failure, why you can't succeed, why others are "luckier," and why you will never be able to stop a destructive habit. What do you think this does to your focus and your motivation to create positive action? It kills it! Weakening questions will create a "poor me" attitude and stifle your ability to ever control your time.

Notice that all of the weakening questions began with "why." "Why" can begin worthwhile questions, but it almost always begins negative and motivation draining ones. Be constantly aware of this and monitor the questions you ask yourself and the answers you give.

I want you to begin choosing empowering questions over weakening ones. It may not happen overnight, but I want you to begin the process of replacing any frequent negative questions you ask with ones that shift your focus to the positive and possible. Following are examples of empowering questions, ones that give you control:

▸ How can I succeed in   ?

▸ What can I do to improve?

▸ How can I get by this challenge?

▸ What can I do to stop   ?

Notice the difference. Shifting to "how can I" or "what can I do" forces your mind to come up with solutions instead of excuses. It opens the door for opportunities to move you forward instead of reasons to hold you back.

3. Daily Motivation Questions

Because questions are so powerful at directing your focus and your focus is so important to your long-term motivation, I want to help you create a question set to start your day out right.

What questions do you normally ask yourself within the first few moments of getting up? Are they similar to the ones below?

▸ Why do I have to get up so early?

▸ Why can't I sleep in?

▸ Why do I have to fight traffic to get to work again?

▸ Why didn't I go to bed earlier?

▸ Why me?

There's that dangerous "why" creeping in to your head. If the questions you go through are at all similar to the ones above, how do you think your answers set you up to be motivated for the day ahead? Negatively and pessimistically. Right?

Answer a few questions right now. Take your time for each and use emotion and feeling.

▸ What are you grateful for in your life?

▸ What are you committed to being or achieving?

▸ How are you wealthy right now?

▸ How are you healthy right now?

▸ What are you or what could you be excited about today?

If you went through honestly and with emotion and feeling, how did your answers to these questions make you feel? If you were to ask and answer all or some of these or similar personally empowering questions every morning, what difference could it do for your daily focus and motivation?

As part of this module's action plan, create a Daily Motivation Questions set to answer every morning for the next two weeks to see if it makes a difference. There is a worksheet included to help you. If you find the questions make a difference after two weeks, make it a daily habit for the rest of your life.

Choose a few questions like the empowering ones you just went through in the exercise above. Keep it simple and have no more than five questions to start with. If you find this question set very beneficial and you want to add more in the future, feel free. Just keep it manageable so that you don't find yourself creating excuses not to go through it.

Of the questions I listed for you, I highly recommend three of them for you try. Their simple but very powerful impact has paid huge dividends in my daily motivation to control my time and my life.

"What am I grateful for?" keeps me aware of just how blessed my life is no matter what the circumstances are at the time. It keeps me from taking the important things for granted.

"What am I committed to?" keeps me focused on my Clarity and purpose. As an example, I answer this question every morning with I am committed to being the best Christian, the best husband, the best father, the best family member and friend, the best speaker and teacher and motivator and author and business coach and business man and marketer I can be. I use it to remember the gifts I have been blessed with and to make sure I use them to positively impact others that day.

"What am I excited about?" helps me find the excitement and motivation surrounding every event in my day ahead. It keeps me appreciative of the gifts of the day and helps me face them with the proper respect they deserve. This question helps me find the joy of every single day and not take where I am in my life's journey for granted.

Once you've chosen your questions, realize you can change them at any time to match your current tastes in life. Now make sure you answer them at least five mornings every week. Everyday would be great, but don't beat yourself up for being human. Consistency is the key.

Use simple tools if you need reminders to go through the questions. Use this module's worksheet or put your questions on index cards. Keeping them readily visible in the morning works great in forcing the habit of going through them.

I always start my questions as my feet hit the floor from my bed and continue to answer them as I take my shower and get ready for the day. If you want, you can answer them on your way to work. Just put a reminder in your car to get you started. The idea is to use what works for you, but be sure to go through the questions before you hit the first event of your day.

60-Second Power Summary

▸ Motivation is the energy for positive action.

▸ Frequently use motivation measurement to determine where you are and where you want to be in your level of motivation.

▸ Physically using your body is the key to your short-term motivation.

▸ Your Body Motivation Tools are directly affected by your energy level
  ▹ Diet.
  ▹ Exercise.
  ▹ Sleep.

▸ Body Motivation Tools:
  1. Deliberate Movements.
  2. Your Voice.
  3. Your Posture.
  4. Your Facial Expressions.
  5. Music.
  6. Your Sense of Smell.

▸ Your mind's focus is the key to your long-term motivation.

▸ Mind Motivation Tools:
  1. Your Attitude.
  2. Your Questions to Yourself.
  3. Daily Motivation Questions.

Put Your Knowledge Into Action

Your action plan for this module is simple but extremely beneficial and empowering. I want you to create the habit of taking motivation measurements and using your body motivational tools to close the gap between where you are and where you want to be. Look for ways to do this everyday, both in your personal and business lives, over the next three to four weeks.

Monitor your attitude and questions to yourself daily. Remember the lessons of the stories on attitude and their impact on your focus and motivation and find ways to implement them into your life. Begin choosing empowering questions over weakening ones.

Create your Daily Motivation Questions and commit to going through them every morning with feeling and emotion for a two-week trial. Continue for the rest of your life if they help bring positive focus to your days.

Daily Motivation Questions Worksheet

Question 1:

_____

_____

_____

_____

Answer with feeling and emotion!

Question 2:

_____

_____

_____

Answer with feeling and emotion!

Question 3:

_____

_____

_____

Answer with feeling and emotion!

Question 4:

_____

_____

_____

Answer with feeling and emotion!

Question 5:

_____

_____

_____

Answer with feeling and emotion!

MODULE

INCREASING YOUR ENERGY LEVEL: THE LESS THAN 6 % SOLUTION

Knowing what to do, how do it, and being motivated to do it mean nothing if you don't have the energy to do it.

This module is about your energy and how it directly and proportionately affects your ability to control your time. It's a large part of what separates Success-Centered Time Management from time management. Of the three categories you learned to gain more control of your time, increasing your energy falls into the Increasing Your Human Performance category. Along with the power of sleep and motivation control, increasing your energy will help you use the gift of your body to raise control of your time to a completely different level.

Your Doctor: An Important Start

The first, quick order of business we have to cover in this module involves your protection and safety.

Usually, disclaimers for media that involve health issues are encoded in legal-speak and flash by before you have a chance to understand them. It seems strange that someone is offering you advice to help you, but then jumps behind the legal protection of saying their material is advisory in nature only and that you should consult your doctor before trying any of the advice.

Here's my take on this.

This module contains the collection of the best diet, exercise, and rest lifestyle adjustments that I've studied, personally tested, and continue to use through my 19 years of experience as a Naval Academy midshipman, naval aviator and officer, and success coach. The advice I will give you is simple, proven, and it works.

But there is a catch. I don't personally know you. I don't know your current physical condition or your medical history. I don't have the years of medical training and experience necessary to tell you without a shadow of a doubt that what I am asking you to consider doing to help you gain more energy is safe for your particular situation.

As an example, for over 95 percent of us, doing light aerobics is healthful and builds our energy. If you blindly take my advice and you fall into that small 5 percent with joint problems or a heart condition, light aerobics could do much more harm than good. The same goes for dietary adjustments if you happen to be allergic to any of the foods I suggest you eat.

My concern is that you do not get hurt. There is someone who can help and protect you. Someone who knows your condition and medical history and has the training and experience necessary to either give you the green flag to go ahead with the advice in this module or make adjustments to safely fit your particular situation. That person is your doctor.

Whether from this module or any other source with tips for improving your health, for your safety, please consult your doctor before following through on any advice that might put you at risk for illness or injury.

Just 6%!

How big is 6 percent?

For most of us it's not that impressive nor does it mean very much. If your favorite store had just a 6 percent sale, would you drop everything you're doing and go right away? Probably not. It would take a 10 or 20 percent discount before you would probably start to get excited.

As you learned in the Reducing Distractions module, we all waste time every day. It's part of our human nature. On average, each of us wastes between two and three hours a day. That's 12 to 18 percent minimum of your awake time every single day.

What I want you to realize is that just a 6 percent commitment of your daily awake time, one-half to one-third of what you waste, is all you need to completely supercharge your energy level and maintain it for peak time control performance.

What exactly is 6 percent of your day? It's on daily average, just one hour out of your 16 hours of awake time if you're getting optimal sleep. A total of seven hours out of your week.

I can imagine that right now you are thinking that I'm going to ask you to work out one hour a day, seven days a week. There's *no way* I'm going to do that, you're saying to yourself. Don't worry! Half of that time, three and a half hours out of the weekly seven, you'll commit to mental rest at a rate of about 30 minutes a day. I'll soon show you how mental rest and recharging, something most of us take for granted in the importance of our control of time, actually asks you to take half of your 6-percent commitment to slow down and take it easy.

In the remaining 3 percent, or a total of three and a half hours of your week, you'll perform a combination of moderate anaerobic and aerobic workouts that fit your lifestyle and tastes. No workout is over 40 minutes long in any one session, and a good majority of that time is spent in the gradual warm-up and cool-down phases.

Six percent of your time in a program that isn't hard and matches your current level of fitness is not much to ask. Especially when you consider the benefits you'll receive in your increased capacity to do more for longer periods of time throughout the rest of your day. If you keep in mind that this 6 percent investment will positively affect the remaining 94 percent of your awake time and make your sleep time more productive, what excuse do you really have not to try it? If you realize that this small commitment of your time will positively affect every single part of your life and that the time can be easily found for it if you simply try, you have no excuses.

The Forgotten Keys to Energy

Increasing your energy to improve your overall control of time is about simple choices Lifestyle choices that add up their beneficial effects to your health and increased energy. The choices aren't hard, don't take a lot of your time, and definitely don't demand strenuous exercise. But they do demand two things—frequency and consistency.

As discussed in earlier modules, we live in a time where our culture is dominated by a "miracle pill" mentality. Most people want results, want positive changes in their life, but they want them *now*! They want to take a pill to solve their problems. They want a pill that allows them to eat anything and everything they want, that burns away unwanted fat and pounds, that sculpts their body so they don't have to exercise, and that massively increases their energy.

Many companies are preying on this mentality by offering bogus products that actually claim to do all of the above desires with no side effects. What's sad is that millions of us, like lemmings to a cliff, are drawn to the hype over and over again, throwing away billions of dollars and rarely achieving a fraction of the results we desire.

Be forever cautious of the instant fix!

The keys to a healthy life and more energy, resulting in more time to you every day, are easy, however. They don't take long, and they don't care about what current shape you're in. They do demand simple diligence.

If you frequently and consistently add healthy foods to your diet, still enjoying your favorite dishes and snacks, you will gain more energy. If you frequently and consistently perform simple exercises that match your lifestyle and current health situation, you will gain more energy. And if you frequently and consistently give your body and your mind the rest and rebuilding time they need, you will gain more energy. It's that easy, but it does take a little work on your part every day. No "miracle pill" to swallow for instant gratification, just a miracle that is easily within your grasp.

The Continual Success Improvement Formula and Bit by Bit are perfect Time Control partners for frequency and consistency. By trying to improve your diet, your exercise, and your rest by just a little bit on an almost daily basis, you will improve your health, your energy, and your control of time more and more. An extra glass of water, an extra piece of fruit, a little more grain and fiber, a little less white sugar and processed flour, one less bite of a big dinner, a little less dessert. A few minutes of stretching, a few stomach exercises, a few push-ups, walking a little bit more, working out one more minute, taking the stairs instead of the elevator, a few minutes of light weight training, playing your favorite sport one more time every couple of weeks. Going to bed 15 minutes earlier, taking a 20 minute nap, relaxing for 30 minutes before going to bed, taking breaks while working, sitting outside and watching the world go by for five or 10 minutes. All are small; all add up!

3-Pronged Attack

To gain the maximum amount of energy you can in the least amount of time and effort requires a balanced, three-pronged attack focusing on what you eat, how you move your body, and how you rest.

Improvement in any one area will give you additional energy. But improve and maximize all three, asking only a 6 percent commitment of your awake time from yourself and you will exponentially grow your energy level. What do you think this will do to your control of time?

Eating for More Energy

What you put into your body has a definite effect on your energy level. What you eat and drink right now will determine your energy level over the next several hours. And what you frequently and consistently eat and drink will affect your overall energy level through time. I'm sure this isn't news to you.

What you should know is that making small changes here and there, adding a little something healthful here, taking away a little something there, while still enjoying your favorite foods and beverages, is all it takes to add more energy to your life.

I'm not going to share a special diet with you. Lord knows that there are more out now than ever before—creating a spiral of confusing options to choose from. Go to any local bookstore, and I can almost guarantee that you'll see stacks and stacks of the latest diet books right up front. High carbohydrate and low fat diets on one stand and low carbohydrate and high protein on another—all backed by medical experts and celebrities. What I'm going to do is share the few dietary adjustments that have had the biggest impact on my life and my overall energy level.

1. Add more fruits and vegetables.

I know you've heard this before, but it does make a big difference to your energy level. The U.S. National Cancer Institute recommends we shoot for five to nine servings of fruits and vegetables a day. A combination is best, allowing you to get a variety of healthy vitamins, minerals, fiber, and roughage.

Ask yourself how many servings you average a day right now. If you're below the mark, try adding one or two more a day. You don't have to go for it all at once. Make small adjustments, just one more apple or orange or carrot or tomato or salad to your entire day. Add a little more later on, and before you know it, through the power of continual success, you'll reach the recommended range.

This is a good place to give you my opinion on what some high protein/ low carbohydrate diets say about fruits and vegetables. Through all of my studies, in all of the nutritional courses I went through at the Naval Academy, and in all of my experience, I have never heard a recognized nutritional authority say that eating fruits and vegetables in any quantities can be harmful to your diet. Several of these diets, have experts claiming that fruits and many vegetables are bad for you because they contain sugar. I would be cautious of someone telling me not to eat fruits or vegetables such as carrots and to watch how much lettuce I eat each day. If you are considering going on one of these diets, please talk to your doctor first before you cut out fruit and vegetables from your daily intake.

2. Replace simple sugars with more complex carbohydrates.

The high protein/low carbohydrate diets do make a very good point about processed sugar in our society. Most of us eat way too much!

You do not have to eliminate sugar from your diet. I enjoy my wife's homemade peanut butter cookies more than anyone does. What I'm suggesting you do to improve your overall energy is to replace some of the processed sugars in your diet with more complex carbohydrates.

What exactly does this mean? It means cutting down on some of the white breads, candy bars, sugar cereals, sodas, chips, and desserts a little and adding a few more grains, such as wheat and oats. You don't have to go overboard. Just a few small changes here and there will add up to a healthier lifestyle and increased energy.

Doesn't fruit have sugar and isn't it bad for me, some are asking? Yes, fruit has sugar. And this is the argument that some of the high protein/low carbohydrate diets are trying to use in telling you why not to eat fruits and some vegetables. But what they fail to point out is that the sugar in fruit is chemically different than processed sugar. The natural sugar in fruits and some vegetables is much more easily processed by your body to maintain a good chemical balance and promote long-term energy.

3. Reduce your fat intake.

Fat is important to your diet, but most of us go way overboard in our consumption. As a matter of fact, obesity is now considered a national epidemic according to many health studies. Sugars are a big part of the problem, but it's not to be outdone by how much fat we eat.

Diets are not always the answer. I think that, in the long run, most diets do more harm than good. When you focus on short-term gains to your system, you usually pay for it over time. Lifestyle adjustments are the key! Making small adjustments to what you eat that add up over time will give you the results you are shooting for in a diet and give you the best odds for enjoying your benefits through time. The problem is that this approach will not make you drop 30 pounds in 30 days. Diets that claim they can do this become very attractive—setting you up for the rebound effect to gain even more weight in the future. Beware of miracle pills!

In focusing on your fat intake and how it relates to your energy level, I want you to think bit by bit. If you cut out a bite here, avoid a candy bar there, and refuse to clean your plate when you're not hungry anymore, you'll begin to add more energy to your life. Enjoy the foods you like, but do so just a little less, and your positive efforts will stack up over time. Use time to your advantage with this mentality.

One last suggestion on your fat intake is to spread it out over the day, giving your body an increased chance to burn a lot of it. Make sure you get some fat in your breakfast and lunch, so that you are not craving as much fat at dinnertime. If you eat the majority of your fat at dinner or in the evening, your decreased metabolism at night and while you sleep will convert more of what you eat to fat stores in your body.

4. Drink more water.

Water is one of the main building blocks in your body. I find it amazing that many of us get most of our water through processed, sugar drinks such as coffee and soda. Our bodies then have to work hard to not only get the water, but they must also process the sugars and chemicals in the drinks.

This takes away from your potential energy!

If you are not getting enough water, which most experts claim to be about 64 ounces a day, or eight small glasses, then drinking a few extra glasses of water every day is one of the easiest and sure-fire ways to gain more energy. Many studies are also showing that increasing your water intake even more, to between 64 and 128 ounces a day can even give you even greater benefits. So when you feel your energy slipping, drink some water. Then notice what happens to your energy level over the next few minutes.

You don't have to drink bottles of water at a time. I've seen people go overboard and almost gag and drown themselves in the amount of water they try to drink at once. Moderation is all you need. A half of a glass (a simple 4 to 6 ounces) of water added to each of your hours can create a tremendous boost to your overall energy level.

5. Drink less caffeine and alcohol.

Caffeine and alcohol are diuretics, which mean they cause you to go to the bathroom more often in order to relieve your bladder. They force precious water out of your body.

If you drink a lot of coffee and soda throughout the day, then top off the evening with a few alcoholic drinks, you're killing your energy level. Cutting out just a few of these drinks will begin to give you back the hydration your body needs. Drink a little more water as well, and you'll begin to feel instant results in your energy.

6. Monitor your vitamin and dietary supplement intake.

This is an area you should really talk to your doctor about. There are so many vitamins and "healthy" supplements on the market now that it can literally make your head spin when you go to the store to purchase any. Vitamins for everybody, vitamins just for men, vitamins just for women, vitamins for your immune system, vitamins for your bones, vitamins for active people, vitamins for stressed people, to name just a few. Supplements for cold prevention, supplements for more energy, supplements for increased memory and brain function, supplements for stress control, supplements for your prostate, supplements for your eyes, supplements for your sex drive, supplements for joint pain relief—it's numbing!

I have studied quite a bit in this area for myself and for my family, and I have personally tried a variety of vitamins and supplements over the years. I feel some have made a difference; others seemed little more than a placebo.

The U.S. National Cancer Institute says that the majority of vitamin and mineral benefits should come from the foods you eat. They recommend you take a cautious stance to the clever and very persuasive marketing and advertising hype surrounding most vitamins and supplements. Consulting your doctor is the best key in making your decision.

Most of the reputable studies I've seen suggest taking a generic multivitamin and maybe an extra dose of natural vitamin E (no more than 400 IU's a day). Vitamin E is a blood thinner. So if you have a medical condition that could be negatively affected or are taking medication, you know whom to talk to first. For all other vitamins and supplements, you want be cautious of the side effects and possible overdose problems.

Exercising for More Energy

Recent studies show that less than 40 percent of Americans exercise on a regular basis. From my experience, I think that fewer people than that move their body to any consistent degree.

Most of us associate the word exercise to pain, drudgery, and boredom. Unfortunately, for most people in our culture today, there's no contest in choosing between avoiding exercise and exercising. Avoiding exercising wins, hands down.

The philosophy I want you to develop about exercise is probably an approach you haven't followed before. I don't want you to worry about being perfect, and I want you to realize that doing any movement, any exercise is so tremendously better than doing none. Moderate. Frequent. Consistent. These are your pillars to my philosophy to gaining more energy through exercise and to enjoy the process pain free.

Most of us who haven't exercised for awhile and then get motivated to do so for some reason, consistently make the same mistakes that doom our long-term benefit. We inevitably fall into the too much, too soon syndrome. This is when we exercise beyond what our bodies are adapted to, too quickly. It doesn't feel so bad the first day we exercise too hard or too long or both. Sure we're tired, but we're also invigorated and motivated. But wait until that second day! The next morning we wake to pain and stiffness, lactic acid making the simplest of movements excruciating. We decide to wait a few days before working out again, and our motivation soon fades. Before long, we create excuses and we're right back where we started.

Exercise shouldn't be painful. Exercise shouldn't be hard. Exercise doesn't have to take long to give you an energy boost you will notice and be able to apply toward your increased control of time. Don't forget— moderate, frequent, and consistent.

Exercise should be moderate. This means exercise to your level of health. Especially when you're starting your program, don't push yourself too hard. If this means you can only walk for 10 or 15 minutes comfortably before having to stop, that's fine. Don't overdo it. That's key. By sticking to moderate exercise, you'll keep yourself from getting sore and burned out. I want you to look forward to exercise, not dread it.

Time is on your side. You'll grow your energy level by adding, bit by bit, to your exercise as your body adapts to a new level of fitness. If you walk only 10 minutes the first time you start your program and add only one minute a week to your walk, you'll easily be able to walk over an hour at a time within just one year.

You can apply this same concept to any exercise program. In aerobics, for example, even if you can't get past the warm-up the first time, adding a simple minute every other week will easily get you to over 30 minutes in one year. In weight lifting, even if you can only lift three-pound barbells, adding a few ounces a month will get you noticeably stronger through time.

Moderation. Working out to a comfortable level and slowly, but surely adding a little to it through time will get you to any level of fitness and energy you desire. Let time work for you!

Exercise should be frequent and consistent. You're energy will be much higher and your health benefits greater if you workout, even for just a few minutes each time, five to six days a week. Your body adapts to shorter, more frequent exercise periods over longer, more intense but less frequent workouts.

I faced an interesting challenge several years ago. I came down with pneumonia and completely lost all of my strength and lung endurance over the course of a month. After I rid myself of the pneumonia I could only take my young boys trick-or-treating on Halloween to about five houses before I got too tired and had to go home and rest for the remainder of the night. I had barely walked more than 100 yards! I had a long road to recovery to get back to my level of fitness prior to my sickness.

I got excited, though. I was in as bad of shape as any of my students and coaching clients had ever been in, and I wanted to be a perfect example to my philosophy of moderation, frequency, and consistency.

When I started my program, I could only walk about five minutes comfortably. I walked three to four times a week with very light weight lifting in between. I tried to add a minute to my walks each time. Within a few weeks, I was walking slowly for five minutes then speed walking for five minutes then slowing down over the next five. In the second month, I was walking a total of 20 minutes and began to lightly jog for one minute. Every time after that, I tried to add one minute to my run portion. The workouts were never hard or strenuous, each moderately paced at my level of fitness at the time.

After month two of the program, I was walking five minutes, speed walking five minutes, lightly jogging for 15 minutes, speed walking for five minutes, then walking moderately for five more minutes. I continued my slowly increasing pace, until after the third month I was jogging for 30 minutes in the middle. After month four, I had my run portion up to 40 minutes and then began to add sprints to the middle of my runs. Within four months of barely being able to walk without shortness of breath and dizziness, I had easily and moderately grown my endurance up to a one-hour program. I knew I could go further, but was satisfied to workout no longer than one hour at a time. If I did it from my level of fitness after my pneumonia, I know you can too.

Create an exercise program that works for you based on your level of fitness and your tastes. Walk, play golf, do some pushups and stomach exercises, do Tae Bo, ride a bike, swim, whatever turns you on. Do something for a while, and then change it to keep it fun and fresh. Make exercising a permanent part of your life, something you look forward to and enjoy.

Exercising doesn't have to take long to give you an energy benefit, and it should be balanced. Even after you work your endurance and fitness level up, you don't need to work out any more than a total of three and a half hours a week. No session needs to be more than 30 to 40 minutes, and this includes proper warm-up and cool-down periods. And the exercise you get throughout the week should be balanced to include aerobic benefit, anaerobic benefit, and stretching.

Aerobic Exercise

Aerobic exercise means to exercise with oxygen. Increasing your lungs' and heart's ability to transfer oxygen to your cells is a critical key to increasing your energy level. The greater your ability to transfer oxygen to your cells, the more energy you'll have.

During aerobic exercise, you move your body to increase your heart rate, thus forcing more oxygen into your cells. A good rule of thumb is that if you are exercising so that you cannot carry on a conversation with someone because you're breathing too hard, then you have crossed from aerobic exercise to anaerobic exercise. You need to slow down if you want to gain aerobic benefit.

Aerobic exercise includes speed walking, jogging, biking, swimming, aerobics, stair climbers and other aerobic machines, and any other movement that gets your heart rate up for a sustained amount of time.

We've all heard the American Lung and Heart Association recommend that we should aerobically exercise for at least 20 minutes three times each week to maintain a healthy heart. Usually what happens when we hear this and haven't exercised in a while is that we push ourselves too hard too soon to reach this goal. We think we have to start there to get a benefit. Wrong!

Make aerobically moving for 20 minutes three times a week a goal, something you want to shoot for—not something you have to start at. Like I told you before, moderation should be your focus. Through time, you can reach that goal and without pain or stress to your body.

One of the most important aspects of aerobic exercise is reaching and maintaining your target heart rate. There are a few ways to track your heart rate during a workout, but I would like to recommend that you make a purchase that will make an incredible difference to your workouts and ability to grow your energy level. You may have heard that you can monitor your heart rate while exercising by using your fingers to check your pulse at your wrists. This does give you a very basic ballpark figure, but when you're moving about, it's hard to get an accurate figure and it's inconvenient to constantly take this measurement.

If you're serious about easily improving your health, I recommend you purchase a heart monitor. These are comprised of a strap that goes around your torso and that sends a radio signal to a digital watch-like device that gives you an instant readout of your heart rate. They range in price from about $75 (US) to several hundred dollars, depending on how many bells and whistles it comes with. You should be able to find one at any sporting goods store.

The reason I love a heart onitor and recommend one to you is that ur heart rate while working out. This al- properly and gives you unbelievable still get great aerobic benefit. It also ard, letting you instantly know when ements.

differs in heart rates from warm-up er what I do, so long as I meet these onsist of me playing a selection of my , jumping, Tae-Bo-ing, and chasing my I meet my heart zones, and the heart hen I can do just about any movement

e with you before we move on to the le importance of a proper warm-up and rk out assign too little importance in er 10 years before I finally understood. ng or before sporting competition and n't put nearly enough time or structure s as I should have. Not even my military training showed me the proper way.

It wasn't until I was researching for my recovery from pneumonia that I found an incredible way to warm-up and cool-down that was easy and incredibly effective. In a health tape series, Tony Robbins, famed peak performance consultant, demonstrated the warm-up and cool-down philosophy of ultra-marathon runners. Ultra-marathon runners compete in races that exceed 50 miles in distance at a time. On average, ultra-marathoners recover more quickly from their competitions and have fewer injuries compared to marathoners that compete in races only half the distance.

Robbins found that the ultra-marathoners' secret lies in their simple approach to warm-ups and cool-downs. They warm-up and cool-down for longer periods than most, and they do so with a stair step mentality. They don't stretch too long or too hard prior to their warm-up, which allows their gradual warm-up to loosen and stretch their muscles.

The warm-up I took away from Robbins' research was to walk (or whatever movement you're going to do for your workout—bike, swim, etc.) for five minutes at a very slow pace in order to gradually move the muscles you intend to use for exercise. I equate this pace to one you would use to walk to your mailbox to check the mail. Then, for the next five minutes, pick up the pace just a little, almost like a speed walk if you are intending on jogging for your workout. This moves more blood to your muscles in a gradual pace and increases your heart rate another notch. Then, for the last five minutes of your warm-up, pick up your pace to just below where you intend to workout.

The cool-down is very similar to the warm-up, except you're working your way down the stairs, instead of up, in your pacing. Go from your aerobic target zone to a notch below for five minutes. Then go down to a speed walk pace for five minutes. Then go down to a very gradual walk pace for the last five minutes. Again, this brings your heart rate down nice and slow and gives your muscles a chance to cool down gradually.

This stair step mentality slowly warms up your intended muscles and gradually works your heart rate up to an aerobic level, then does the opposite for the cool-down. This simple 15-minute process before and after your workouts does wonders for your joints and keeps you from shocking your heart with too big of jumps in your heart rate.

Everyone I've shared this simple warm-up and cool-down plan with has seen major reductions in their injury and soreness rates and has found reaching and maintaining their aerobic zone much easier.

Here are the heart rate numbers, as promised. Keep in mind that these are zones you want to shoot for as you progress in your workouts. If your fitness level only allows you to do the warm-up or cool-down before calling it quits for the day, that's fine. That's exactly what I had to do when I was building back up after pneumonia. Keep your workouts moderate and build on them slowly.

There are several heart rate zones to choose from. The most common and recommended formula is to subtract your age from 220, then multiply this number by 0.6 and 0.8. This gives you an aerobic range to target your workout in. The following chart shows this formula applied to some age ranges:

Age	Low Range (0.6)	High Range (0.8)
20	120	160
25	117	156
30	114	152
35	111	148
40	108	144
45	105	140
50	102	136
55	99	132

Keep in mind that these numbers are targets. You do *not* have to start your workouts here. They're ranges you want to work toward through moderate growth based on your current level of fitness.

Start your workouts at a moderate length and pace. Understand that in the beginning, especially if you are out of shape, it will be very easy to get your heart rate up. Simple walking may get you into your aerobic zone. Take it easy and work up to your zones gradually; then do the same for your cool-down. As your fitness level increases, you will have to do more movement to get your heart rate up.

Of the recommended three and a half hours per week of exercise to gain more energy, two hours of it should go toward aerobic exercise programs. Shoot for three days a week with workouts totaling about 40 minutes each. This 40 minutes includes a 15-minute warm-up and a 15-minute cool-down, giving you about 20 total minutes in your age group's aerobic zone. If you enjoy your workouts and want to do more or go further, that's great!

If you already exercise quite a bit and want to find a way to supercharge your workouts to build your endurance and speed, try this great maximizing tool. The latest research shows that adding short bursts or sprints to the middle of your aerobic workouts can boost your endurance and speed ability immensely. When you do the same movement at the same pace over and over, you will eventually hit a plateau of growth. By adding a few 20 or 30-second sprints, you force your heart beyond your aerobic zone for a very short period and then have it recover back into the aerobic zone. This raises your plateau of ability through time. Adding just one more sprint a week or month to your workout will give you unbelievable potential.

One last thing on aerobic activity. If you decide that a heart rate monitor is not for you and that you could care less about heart rate zones, then just try to add movement to your day through sports or any activity for at least three days each week. If you frequently and consistently move more than you do now, you will gain more energy. You don't have to be perfect, and any movement, any exercise is much better than none.

Anaerobic Exercise

Anaerobic exercise means exercising without oxygen. It means strengthening your muscles. It breaks down your muscles and gives them the ability, with proper rest, to recover to an even stronger level than before. Anaerobic exercise includes weight lifting, weight resistance machines, sprinting, and resistance exercises such as pushups, sit-ups, abdominal crunches, pull-ups, dips, and squats.

Why, if you're not an athlete in training or a bodybuilder, would I recommend you spend an hour and a half a week performing anaerobic exercise? Aerobic exercise is a great energy builder, but it can be hard on your joints and muscles. By building up your muscles, especially those that are involved in your aerobic workouts, you'll reduce your chances of injury and make your aerobic workouts easier and more enjoyable. You'll also reduce how tired you get from the day's requirements on your strength, building your energy reserves for better use of your time. Supporting your own weight, carrying your kids, and performing household or job-related chores will become easier and less stressful.

Although not as much as aerobic activity, anaerobic exercise increases your metabolism and your body's ability to burn fat and produce energy. Combined with beneficial aerobic activity, resistance training will increase your metabolism to an even higher level.

The keys to successful exercise fit perfectly for anaerobic exercise. Moderation, frequency, and consistency. Starting at a level that is easy and comfortable for you, exercising anaerobically two to three times a week, and building on it gradually will build and maintain your strength through time.

So what should you do for your workout? It's up to you. Like your aerobic exercise, choose exercises that match your personality and physical requirements. You can go to a gym or fitness center and use their weights and resistance machines. You can create your own program of home resistance exercises such as pushups, dips, squats, and abdominal exercises. You can create your own home gym. Or you can purchase a couple of barbells and free weights. Your choice.

Even if you can't do one pushup, you could do a couple of pushups with your knees touching the ground. Add a few pushups to this a week, and before you know it, you will be able to do a full pushup. Then you could add one more pushup a week, getting stronger and stronger. The same concept applies for your abdominal exercise and all of your resistance exercises. Don't worry about how many you can do. Pick some that work your arms and chest, your abs, and your legs. Do them easily and safely and let time work for you.

Lifting weights or using weight resistance machines follow the same concept. Moderation!

A great time saving tool you can apply to your weight training is knowing that two sets of any weight resistance exercise will give you about 80 percent of the benefits of three sets according to a Duke University study. You can use this when you don't feel you have the time to workout.

For my simple, energy building program, do an aerobic exercise three times a week for a total of one and a half hours a week. Each session can be as little as 20 to 30 minutes to include light stretching before and afterward. You can also do light resistance exercises such a pushups and abdominal exercises more often to count toward your total time. Two to three minutes a day, five days a week, can accumulate to 10 to 15 minutes of your weekly hour and a half. Keep in mind this is a goal, don't feel you have to start here to gain benefit. Start slow, grow at your own pace, and make it something you look forward to.

Don't be too strict with yourself on your time. Just do your best, keeping in mind that frequent, consistent exercise, no matter how long, will produce positive results.

Stretching Exercise

Stretching is often the overlooked exercise that completes the balance of aerobic and anaerobic exercise.

What does consistent stretching do for you? It reduces the amount of painful lactic acid your muscles produce while exercising, reduces your chances of injury to your muscles and joints, and keeps you limber for required activities throughout your day.

Try to stretch at least five days each week. I do a few minutes of light stretching as part of a morning routine and make stretching a part of every aerobic and anaerobic workout.

There are a few things to keep in mind about stretching to make sure you don't injure yourself.

1. **Start out slowly and don't overdo it**. Don't push yourself when stretching. Go just far enough until you feel resistance and hold.

2. **Don't bounce**. Stretching should be fluid. If you bounce while stretching, you greatly increase your chances of injury to your muscles and joints.

3. **Do most of your stretching when your muscles are already warmed up**. You actually increase your chances of injuring yourself while stretching when your muscles are cold, such as when you wake up or right before exercising. I stretch in the mornings, but I do so very lightly, more like a cat stretching after a nap to work out the kinks. I use my 15-minute warm-ups for my aerobic workouts to slowly stretch the muscles I will be using. I use my five-minute warm-ups for my weight lifting to increase the blood flow to my muscles and lightly stretch them. Following my workouts, when my muscles are already warmed up, I do the majority of long-term stretching to my hamstrings and other major muscles groups.

Resting Your Body

Giving your body proper rest between your workouts is critical to your gaining of energy. You do not achieve growth in strength or endurance while you perform the actual workout. In your workouts, you break your body down to some degree. It's the time between workouts when your body repairs from your exercising and rewards you with greater endurance, more strength, and increased energy.

Your body responds to the demands you put on it by adapting. It will grow your strength if you break your muscles down through resistance training. It will grow your endurance if you walk or run or bike or swim or do aerobics to compensate better next time. Our bodies are truly incredible adaptive miracles.

But the only way your body can adapt from your workout is to give it the time it needs to recover and build for the future. This is why physical rest is so important.

There are two things I want you to focus on to give your body the rest it needs to reward you with more energy.

The first is resting between exercise activity. Your heart can handle aerobic activity every day if you don't push yourself too hard. But the question is, can your muscles and joints handle the strain of whatever you are doing for aerobic benefit? To prevent strain on your joints, perform aerobic activity three times a week, giving yourself a day off in between from your endurance activity. If you want to do aerobic exercise more often, vary your aerobic workout to prevent strain.

Anaerobic exercise is a different animal. With the exception of light resistance exercise such as pushups or abdominal exercises, you need to give yourself at least one day off between workouts of a muscle group. Professional weightlifters are able to lift almost daily because they work on different muscles groups every other day. So conduct your three weekly anaerobic, resistance workouts every other day.

What's great is that you can do your aerobic exercise on one day and then your anaerobic workout the next with no harm to your body and vice versa. So spread your aerobic workouts and your anaerobic workouts between each other and you'll give your body the time it needs to recuperate and grow in energy and strength.

The second area to focus on to give your body the physical rest it requires is to get a consistent, good night's sleep. You have read the whole module on the importance of sleep to your time. As a quick review, though, giving your body the adequate deep and dream cycles it needs each night will allow your body and brain to repair and recharge physically. Failing to give your body the sleep it needs to repair from your workouts and your full day of use will cause your immune system to break down quickly, making you weaker instead of stronger through time.

Resting Your Mind

As important as resting your body is to allowing you to physically gain more energy, resting your mind on a frequent, consistent basis will help keep your stress level down and your mental focus and clarity high. Stress chops away at your available energy. Everything you do to keep it down will help you maintain a higher level of energy for positive use toward your time.

This area is so important to your ability to consistently maintain a high energy level that you should put half of the 6-percent commitment you made for your energy toward it. That's three and a half hours a week. That's 30 minutes a day! You not only deserve it, you need it to maintain a balanced level of energy. I want you to look at this time as an investment in your overall control of your time.

What do you do to rest your mind? All kinds of things are possible for you to choose from. Relaxing reading, quiet sitting, listening to music, prayer, meditation, taking a bath, and a multitude of other possibilities that relax you and require little or no thought. Try to avoid the television during this time. What time of day you choose to accomplish this is of no importance.

You want to quiet your mind and relax during this time. If you live a very active and hectic lifestyle, this may seem hard at first. Your mind may be active and hard to quiet and you may feel jittery trying to sit in one place for a 30-minute period. The harder it is for you to relax and unwind, the more you need this time. If you want, start with shorter periods of time; and like your exercise goals, work at a moderate pace until you can reach them comfortably.

Because this seems so easy to do, please do not underestimate its cumulative importance to your energy. Make quiet time for yourself every day a priority. Give your mind the break it needs.

60-Second Power Summary

▶ Knowing what to do, how to do it, and being motivated to do it mean nothing if you don't have the energy to do it.

▶ Consult your doctor.

▶ 6 percent commitment of awake time (seven hours a week)

▶ Frequency and consistency are keys to gaining and maintaining energy.

▶ Eating for More Energy

1. Add more fruits and vegetables.
2. Replace simple sugars with more complex carbohydrates.
3. Reduce your fat intake.
4. Drink more water.
5. Drink less caffeine and alcohol.
6. Monitor your vitamin and dietary supplement intake.

▶ Exercising for More Energy

   ▹ Moderate. Frequent. Consistent.

   ▹ Aerobic Exercise.

      › Heart monitor.

      › Proper warm-up and cool-down (stair step approach).

- › Three 40-minute workouts a week.
- › Supercharge workout with short sprints.
- ⊳ Anaerobic Exercise
  - › Strength training.
  - › Two sets of any weight resistance exercise will give you about 80 percent of the benefits of three sets.
  - › One set will give you about 40 percent of the benefits.
  - › Three times a week (about 30 minutes each).
- ⊳ Stretching Exercise (daily)
  1. Start slowly and don't overdo.
  2. Don't bounce.
  3. Do most of your stretching when your muscles are already warmed up.
- ▶ Resting for More Energy
  - ⊳ Resting Your Body.
    - › Between exercise activity.
    - › Sleep.
  - ⊳ Resting Your Mind.
    - › 30 minutes a day.

Put Your Knowledge Into Action

So what will be included in this module's action plan? Pretty simple, really. Add the elements you have learned in this module to gain more energy for your life. Concentrate on making them habit over the next three to four weeks before moving on to the next module. Commit to adding more energy to your days and adding a new level of control to your time. To help, there is a simple Push-Pull worksheet for you to go through to create the motivation for you to succeed.

Gaining Energy Motivation Worksheet

I am totally committed to creating a healthier lifestyle and increasing the energy in my life!

Push:

The *costs* if I do not achieve this goal. (emotional, financial, physical, social, spiritual)

_____

_____

_____

_____

_____

_____

_____

_____

_____

_____

Pull:

The *rewards* when I achieve this goal. (emotional, financial, physical, social, spiritual)

_____

_____

_____

_____

_____

_____

_____

_____

_____

_____

MODULE

REMOVING STRESS FROM YOUR LIFE

The Dynamics of Stress

For starters, I want you to fully understand that stress is a behavior. It's not something that is outside of you. It's simply an internal reaction to events in your environment.

When you experience this behavior, you feel a swelling of pressure build up inside you. Depending on the event and how you interpret it, this stress may be positive or negative. Positive stress usually comes from an event with some urgency, but is tempered by a sense of control on your part. You know something has to be done or you have to face something, but you are confident in your abilities to handle it. The pressure from positive stress manifests itself in heightened senses and a physical energy boost. For short periods of time, this stress can help you get things done quickly and accomplish great feats.

I know you've amazed yourself in the past with how quickly you have accomplished something when you had a deadline and you were determined to succeed. Positive stress probably was the boost that helped you. While flying a thousand miles north of Iceland, just a few hundred feet above the icy North Atlantic waters, my crew and I successfully tracked Russian submarines on multiple occasions due to this positive behavior. And I'm sure you've heard stories of parents performing superhuman feats to save their children, refusing to let harm come to their loved ones. Again, positive stress gave them the physical boost and immense will to succeed.

Although positive stress is beneficial over the short-term, prolonged time spent in this behavior can begin to break you down mentally and physically. Without proactive measures to reduce stress from other areas, positive stress can shift to negative stress, resulting in burnout. Athletes no longer enjoying the thrill of the game; military, police, and rescue personnel losing their edge and confidence; and business professionals no longer finding their businesses or jobs fun and exciting, are all good examples of burnout.

So what about negative stress? This behavior comes from your interpretation of an event where you are losing some control and it triggers frustration, anger, depression, fear, overwhelm, or a combination of these. Depending on the event, this loss of control and resulting emotions can be slight to extreme. And their effects add up through time and multiple events if not controlled. As a result of prolonged negative stress, you can experience loss of confidence, extreme mood swings, loss of sleep, and physical breakdown from decreased immunity to lethargy, ulcers, and possibly cancer.

I'm sure you've experienced negative stress when things didn't go your way at work or home. I know you've tasted it when taking a test you didn't feel prepared for. How about when faced with a deadline you didn't feel you could meet or when facing financial challenges? When your children wouldn't cooperate? When your spouse or significant other didn't behave or act as you had hoped or expected? When you had to give a speech and weren't confident in yourself? When you tried something new and didn't know what would happen? Of course! All of these normal events have triggered negative stress in us at one time or another because we experienced a lack of control and focused on the negative possibilities.

Which brings me to what triggers our stressful behavior in the first place.

Remember back to the Motivation Control module where. You learnd about the immense power of your mind. Your mind receives billions of sensory inputs every second. Because you can't possibly process all of this information at once, you subconsciously filter it through your mind's focus. This focus is a creation of your culture, in other words the environment in which you were raised, and your past experiences. From these, you have forged an unconscious question set to direct your focus when faced with certain stressors. Your specific questions for an event, or stressor, and your answers to them determine if you will experience negative stress, positive stress, or nothing at all.

Stressors are simply events in your life or things in your environment that have the potential to be filtered through your focus and processed by your mind and body as stressful. Everything is a potential stressor on some level. Time, money, work, business, family, relationships, health, sports, your home, your car, your drive to and from work, Christmas, the new millennium, your computer, the air you breathe—everything! Each of us has a different filter for these stressors. Some of us let a stressor pass right by and not even give it a second look; others of us will focus and dread over it creating immense negative stress.

Let's look at some interesting examples of how our focus on stressors influences potential stressful behavior in our lives.

A great example I see over and over again in the business world is a result of perfectionism. When you're a perfectionist, the stressors you face on a daily basis center on your ability to make a project "perfect" in your eyes. Usually your question set is a failure mindset where very little if anything ever meets the over-zealous high standards you've set for yourself and others. As a result, you never quite feel in control because things routinely tend not to go right for you. This focus on constant perceived lack of control builds up negative pressure and stress causing the emotions of frustration and overwhelm.

Another good example is going to the dentist's office. Depending on your past experiences, your focus on this stressor may be anywhere from pleasurable to light discomfort to terror. Most of us associate some form of discomfort and pain to this event, creating the potential for high levels of negative stress from the very first second of stepping into a dental office. In the Motivation Control module, you learned the body tool of smell. Smell can be a strong trigger for your focus question set for the dental stressor. Since most dental offices have the same medical smell, you stand a high chance of focusing on this smell when you first walk into a dental office. If you associate fear and pain with dentists, this smell alone could trigger negative stress and heighten your sense of pain.

The next three short examples involve our day-to-day lives.

Relationships are always great places to find stressors and to see a wide variety of focus question sets. When you are dating, your focus on asking someone out on a date makes a very big difference in your stress. If you have low self-confidence and self-esteem, you will focus on the probability of rejection and how it will make you feel. This can only result in negative pressure harboring fear and physical discomfort. If you are confident in yourself and find it a thrill to ask people out no matter what the result, you will focus on the possibilities of success and the rush of acceptance. This would result in positive stress, heightening your senses and giving you a natural high. The stressor of asking someone out is the same, but the resulting stress results are at opposite ends of a spectrum depending on your focus.

Money is a very interesting stressor. It seems to be the answer to all of our problems and the reason for a lot, if not most, of our problems. A true Catch-22! Almost all of us have created negative stress from our focus on money at one point or another in our lives. In our American free economy culture, the heavy focus on money permeates throughout our society every single day. Children are pressured at a young age to study hard in school so they can go to college, get a good job afterward, and make a nice financial living. Couples routinely fight over financial matters, creating the greatest reason for most divorces. Parents worry about being able to help their kids through college. And those nearing retirement generate negative stress when focusing on their financial security for the remainder of their lives.

The last day-to-day stressor that has a high potential for stress for many of us is our family. How you focus on your parents' expectations of you, how you focus on your children's behaviors, how you focus on your spouse's or significant other's actions or inactions or perceived faults, and how you focus on any sick family members makes a major difference in your stress level. Keep in mind that your stress in all of these situations is not determined by the stressors themselves, but by your focus and internal and external reaction to them.

How Stress Impacts Your Time

For starters, let me remind you that positive stress can actually improve your performance in time for short durations. With positive stress you have urgency but also a sense of control, or at least a strong determination to succeed. The key to keep in mind for positive stress is the short-term increase in time-based performance. If you have a stressful job you enjoy or live a lifestyle with a multitude of positive-based stressors and you do not frequently reduce your stress and blow off steam, your positive stress can easily shift to negative stress as you begin to deteriorate your sense of control.

So what happens to your control of time when you begin with or shift your behavior to negative stress?

Your questions to yourself lead to your focus, and your focus leads to your motivation level. When you have a poor question set for a particular stressor, your negative focus leads to severely reduced or negative motivation. We've already seen in the Motivation Control module just how much your level of motivation affects your time. The more often you slip into this negative stress pattern, the greater the negative impact on your time.

When stressed, your negative motivation and focus drain your physical, mental, and emotional energy levels. Your attention is split, always focusing at least in part on the stressor causing your stress. Due to increased anxiety over your stressor, it becomes harder and harder to get the critical sleep you need. Your immune system breaks down and physical ailments such as ulcers and possibly cancers form. You experience mood swings and a loss of emotional control, quickly shifting between anger, depression, and overwhelm.

Depending on how much stress you create and how often you find yourself living through this behavior, the effects above can range from minor to very severe. The negative effects create and feed off each other, forming a time-stealing spiral in your life that can get out of control if you don't consciously work at shifting your negative focus and building defenses against it.

The cumulative end result to your time from these negative effects is reduced productivity, reduced creativity, lost opportunities, degraded relationships with those you love, and an increased susceptibility to compromise your values.

Shifting Your Attitude

The amazing thing to keep in mind is that you have complete control over your focus. You have full control over what questions you ask when faced with a stressor and more importantly, how you answer them. And you ultimately have the ability to control your stressful behavior if you choose. It's completely up to you!

You have your work cut out for you though. You're going to have to face years of programming that created your present focus question set for your stressors. The keys to your success are patience and continual success. If you expect to study and apply the tools in this module toward gaining control of your stress and see instant, perfect results, you'll be disappointed. This is not a "miracle pill." It's a solution that will make a difference, but it requires you to have patience as you slowly but surely replace negative programming with positive.

Remember the power of improving any part of your life by half of a percent a day, five days a week? Apply this philosophy of conquering your stress just a little at a time on a daily basis and you'll see hundreds and thousands of percent improvement in this critical area of controlling your time over the next few years.

Patience. Continual success. Cherish these and you will see success. Once you catch yourself slipping into your stress producing focus one time and are able to shift your attitude to prevent or greatly reduce stress you would normally experience, you will realize for yourself just how much control you truly possess. From that point on, increasing your control will be a simple matter of maintaining awareness toward your stressors and adjusting your focus on them.

The rest of this section shares some tips to help you develop a more positive and stress-reducing attitude concerning the day-to-day stressors you face.

First, keep in mind that change and obstacles are constants in life. No matter who you are, no matter what your age or background or education or financial status, the one thing you can always bet on is that life is never predictable or fully controllable. If your focus is centered on trying to bring complete normalcy to your life and prevent change, the natural and unavoidable challenges of life will become a wave of negative stress-building stressors. However, if you realize that change and obstacles are normal and constant and you shift your focus to all of the wonderful opportunities each carries with them, you'll greatly reduce your stress and open doors to success you've previously blinded yourself to.

Secondly, begin focusing on these natural stressors as challenges instead of problems. This simple mental shift has amazing power. When you see a stressor as a problem, you tend to feel a sense of loss of control and focus on the negative impact. Negative stress is a natural byproduct. However when you view a stressor as a challenge, you inherently feel a sense of control and your focus shifts to the solution instead of the possible negative impact. Stepping back from a stressor with this positive attitude gives you the ability to eliminate it or adapt and innovate around it. It will give you a much better chance of uncovering any opportunities that exist or, if none do, to at least grow in your reaction to a particular stressor even if it's just strengthening your patience.

The third thing you should start doing is consciously learning from your mistakes. Mistakes are a normal part of growing in your success, and failure at an attempt or test of something should be nothing more than a learning experience. The best way to learn from your mistakes without stress is to develop a testing and continual success attitude.

We all had this attitude when we were young kids learning how to walk and speak. We didn't care if we made mistakes or what others thought about us. We just tried and tried until we eventually amazed our parents and ourselves with our progress.

Somewhere along the line in our life we shifted this attitude. We began to care about mistakes because we now cared what others thought about us. Remember high school? By this time in our lives most of us were very conscious of our mistakes and tested our limits less and less. If we had to learn to speak or walk from this point on, most of us would give up saying it's too hard or we're not good enough.

Regain your attitude that testing and making mistakes and learning from them is not only fine, but also a critical step to controlling your time. Those whom we consider to be successful fully understand and use this attitude to their ultimate advantage. Think about it. Who makes more mistakes, successful people or those who wish they were successful? Successful people, by far! Why? They understand and apply the fact that the more they try and learn, the more successful they will be. As long as they learn from their mistakes and try another approach based on what they've learned so far, they are assured of even greater achievements. Most of those who wish they were successful are too afraid of making mistakes. So they take fewer chances in life, resulting in less growth and numerous lost opportunities.

Through past and modern history, the world's greatest achievers prove this fact, having made many more mistakes than successes. Thomas Edison, perhaps the greatest inventor of all time, had an estimated 9,999 failed attempts to invent the light bulb. With each new failure, he applied what he learned from the mistake and was driven by the fact that he was one step closer to his goal. Finally, he reached success at his estimated 10,000th try.

Ten thousand tries! Was Thomas Edison a failure? Not by any stretch of the imagination. He fully embraced the power of testing, continual success and not being afraid to make mistakes.

NBA superstar Michael Jordan was previously listed as ESPN's top athlete of the 20th century. He is arguably the greatest basketball player of all time. In 1997, he did a commercial for Nike shoes where he stated all of the "mistakes" he made in his NBA career through the 1996 season. Having already won a national college championship, two Olympic gold medals, and four NBA championship rings, Michael listed how he had missed over 6,000 shots, lost over 300 games, and missed 26 potential game-winning, last-second shots. Because he fails, he claimed, he succeeds. Why? Again, because he understood the power of learning and growing from his mistakes. Michael used this attitude to claim the next two NBA championships in 1997 and 1998 for a total of six. Not bad for someone who didn't make the cut for his high school basketball team.

Thomas Edison and Michael Jordan may seem out of your league as good examples to the power of mistakes, but Steven Schussler shouldn't. He is an entrepreneur in the restaurant industry that put this same attitude toward his success. Steven had a lifelong passion for raising tropical birds and bore a vision to create a family entertainment restaurant that combined animation, live animals, retail, and incredible food. But first he had to get funding. To attract investors, he turned every inch of his home into a tropical rainforest. He created the night sky on his ceilings, giant cascading waterfalls, rock formations, mist rising from his floors, giant fish tanks, over-sized vegetation, simulated thunderstorms, jungle soundtracks, and wild animal statues. For five long and financially lean years he lived with 45 tropical birds, two 150-pound tortoises, an iguana, and a baboon as he paraded 200 potential investors through his home. Eventually, one investor was impressed with Steven's creativity and enthusiasm and hired him as a consultant to some entertainment projects. On his 27th visit to Steven's home, the investor finally decided to give Steven's concept a try. The Rainforest Cafe was born.

Steven's Rainforest Cafe was an instant success and became a publicly-held company after just one year of operation. This was a first in the retail-restaurant industry. Five years and 37 restaurants later, including 10 internationally, the Rainforest Cafe is still going strong with crowds waiting up to three hours for a chance to experience Steven Schussler's vision. How many investors and how long would you have been willing to go to make this dream come true? Steven learned from each investor that paraded through his transformed home for five years, until he finally met success with the 200th.

Mistakes. Don't be afraid to make them and learn from them! I want you to remember back to the last time you gave up on something. Something that at one time was important to you, but you became just too frustrated with it and gave up. Starting your own business. Getting a degree. Trying a new position or a new job. Trying to grow a relationship. Trying to improve yourself. Whatever. Now ask yourself, did you try at least 10,000 new ways to make it work, as Thomas Edison did with the light bulb? Did you miss at least 6,000 shots in whatever area of your life you were trying to improve like Michael Jordan? And did you give everything you had for at least five years and go through at least 200 no's before you hung up your hat in defeat? Most of us would answer no, not even coming close to the number of "mistakes" that were needed to become successful. For most of us, the greatest mistake we can make is being too afraid to make mistakes. Don't be afraid of mistakes! Test, learn, and apply—the power of continual success.

Finally, the last thing I want you to develop as you try to create a more positive and stress-reducing attitude is to learn to forgive yourself. This is a natural but very important progression from understanding that mistakes are a normal part of growing toward success. Forgiving yourself is the foundation of being able to make mistakes with confidence. Don't worry about what others think. Just experiment, make inevitable mistakes, and then learn and grow from them. Most people who would judge you rather than support you or those who suggest you not do something in the name of "just protecting and looking out for you" are usually people who are afraid of making mistakes themselves. This doesn't mean you shouldn't listen to advice or take counsel; it simply means to not be afraid of trying uncharted territory in your life.

Your greatest obstacle to this attitude shift of self-forgiveness is perfectionism. If you're a perfectionist you have a need for something to be perfect before you take action. This can only serve to create a delaying pattern for attempted tests and prevent you from seeing wonderful opportunities to accelerate your success. Get in the habit of making something good before taking action, but realize it will be in action, mistakes, and adjustment where the greatest progress and achievements will lie.

The Sword and Shield Technique

You now have some attitude-building tools that will help you immensely with developing a positive focus on the stressors you face in life. The following is a set of stress-combating tools that will wield great power directly against the negative focus systems you've developed over the years.

These tools form a single stress-busting technique I call the Sword and Shield. The Sword is an offensive weapon against the stress in your life. It is a simple series of questions I want you to ask yourself, and more importantly answer, when you feel stress building toward a particular stressor in your life. It will serve to shift your focus from problems to challenges and quickly move you into the solution stage of eliminating, reducing, avoiding, or gaining control over a stressor.

The Shield is a defensive weapon against stress. It is a series of things you can do on a routine basis in you life to greatly reduce or even eliminate the need of using your Sword against stressors. It will serve to reduce the overall stress you feel toward stressors. I'm talking about lifestyle changes with this weapon.

The Sword

The Sword is your offensive weapon against the stressful focus you've developed toward particular stressors. Its purpose is twofold—to create awareness toward your negative focus system and to shift that focus toward a solution where you would normally build negative stress.

Your questions lead to your focus and your focus leads to your motivation. If the subconscious question system you have toward a particular stressor is negative and defeating, then your focus will be negative, leading you into stressful behavior. However, if you can catch yourself building toward stress when confronted with a particular stressor and consciously replace your negative question set with a predetermined positive one, your focus can improve immensely and lead you to greatly reduced or even eliminated negative stressful behavior. The formula is simple.

First is awareness. We are automatic beings to a very large extent. Through all the years and experiences of our life we have created automatic reactions or focus to certain stressors. I want you to begin monitoring your reaction to these stressors—all of the stressors you face every day from the very common to the unique. You know when you begin to feel stressed. There is a very definite physical and mental process that takes place. It's a little different for each of us, but common reactions are butterflies in our stomach, a tightening of our muscles, a very real temperature rise, sweating, anxiety, anger, hopelessness, and overwhelm to name a few. What happens to you physically and mentally when you are stressed? Take a moment to think about it.

Now lock this image and feeling into a mental radar that rings a bell in your head or sounds a blaring alarm or whispers in your head a warning every time you begin to slip into this behavior. Call this your stress early warning system, the first part of using the Sword! The awareness you create by mentally catching yourself slipping into stress when faced with a stressor will go a long way toward improving your control.

Awareness is powerful. In and of itself, it can help you take great strides toward reducing stress. Why? As soon as you catch yourself slipping into stress, you put yourself at a fork in the road of your behavior. You now have a choice. Rather than going on automatic mode walking the path of your unconscious negative question set and eventual focus, you can now consciously choose your questions, your focus, and the road either to stress or solution.

Awareness, consciously developing the ability to catch yourself slipping into stressful behavior, gives you options for action. It's your radar in your war against stress. Now how do you conquer your negative focus and choose the path toward solution when your awareness picks up stress on your radar screen? That's the job of the second half of the Sword—to cut your stressful focus to pieces!

When you catch yourself slipping into stress, go through a simple series of questions to shift your focus toward a particular stressor. This active part of the Sword will lead you toward a positive solution and a path with greatly reduced or even eliminated stress altogether.

Now for the Sword's questions. Don't worry about memorizing them. One of the worksheets for this module contains a simple listing of the questions that you can copy, cut out and place in your wallet, pocket, or purse. Wear it out and make other copies as needed.

Even once you memorize these questions, still carry a hard copy with you and pull it out for review when your awareness radar finds stress brewing on the horizon. From experience, trust me when I tell you that your behaviors can outwit your memory. Keeping a physical copy of the Sword allows you to pull out this weapon like a real sword and wield it toward your success.

When you feel yourself slipping into stress and standing at the crossroads ask and answer to yourself:

1. What is the stressor causing my stress?
2. How am I focusing on it to make me feel stressed?
3. What is the worst thing that can happen?
4. How am I or can I be grateful for this stressor?
5. How can I can I eliminate, reduce, avoid, or gain control over this stressor?
6. How can I make my solution fun?

That's it! Six simple questions that can immensely improve your control over the stress-building stressors in your life. Let's go over them one at a time.

1. What is the stressor causing my stress?

Once you understand that you are beginning to slip into stress, it's important to know what, exactly, is triggering it. Identifying the stressor will help you figure out exactly how to deal with it.

2. How am I focusing on it to make me feel stressed?

You know what the stressor is; now look inward at yourself to see how you are focusing on it to create stress. An example might be my kids getting ready to go somewhere with me. If I feel stress building in this, I might identify that my kids not cooperating as much as they could to get ready on time is my stressor. Looking at my focus to discover why, I could see that being late is causing me to be frustrated and feel a lack of control in the matter. If I don't act to shift my focus, I will slip into the stressful behavior of being angry and frustrated at my kids.

3. What is the worst thing that can happen?

By answering this you'll find that most stressors won't lead to anything horrible. As a matter of fact you will find that many are really insignificant with little or no real negative impact. It's just that our negative focus has a strong tendency to blow things out of proportion. This question will knock things down to their unexaggerated, real size. By seeing the worst that this stressor can cause, you will be better armed to find a solution for it.

Following the example of my kids causing me to be late as a stressor, I would find by answering this question that being late with my kids is not that big of a deal.

4. How am I or can I be grateful for this stressor?

What a strange question to ask of something that is causing you to slip into stressful behavior. Take this question seriously and its effects on your focus can be absolutely transforming. What about the stressor you're facing could you be grateful for? If it's your family, are you grateful for having them in your life? If it's something to do with your job, are you grateful for the career or employment you have? If it's your business, are you grateful for owning it and all of the freedoms that come with being your own boss? Shifting your perspective from something negative caused by the stressor to something positive about it really begins to put you in control of the situation. It diffuses your automatic negative response and makes it incredibly easier to find a solution. Shifting from problems to challenges—remember?

5. How can I can I eliminate, reduce, avoid, or gain control over this stressor?

Now for the solution. I'm aware of my stressor, I know how I'm focusing on it to create stress, I know the worst thing that can happen from it, and I've shifted to what I'm grateful about it. I am now best mentally prepared and focused to find a positive solution. What's the solution? Well it depends on the stressor. I might need to eliminate it, reduce it, avoid it, or gain control in some other way. Trust your instincts now that you've shifted your focus. The idea is to move away from automatic negative response and to search and act on the best positive solution you can find for the circumstances.

Using the running theme of being late with my kids, I would find a way to reduce how late we are this time by staying calm and helping them get ready to go. Because I have now consciously realized that being late with them is not a big deal, I wouldn't allow myself to worry about my pride. I would just make a mental note to start getting ready earlier next time to be more on time.

6. How can I make my solution fun?

The final question is a paradigm shift for most of us. So often when we're searching for solutions to our challenges, we get too analytical and forget that most of our behaviors are driven by emotions. If we can find a way to make something fun, it not only reduces the stress of doing it, but also greatly increases our motivation for positive action. Try answering and following through on this question with sincerity and you'll see a major difference in your stress level.

Finalizing my example with my kids, I would add tickling them and hearing their laughter while helping them get ready. I would listen to a tape in our car that we all can sing along loudly to and have a good time on the way to our destination. What a difference! From angry and frustrated at being late to shifting my focus and attitude completely toward gratitude, a solution and fun.

The Sword—your offensive weapon against stress. Awareness through a stress early warning system and a positive attack with a six-question, focus-shifting set. This weapon won't be perfect at first. Don't expect it to be. Practice with it, hone your skills, and use it when stress builds in your life. Follow this advice and you will greatly cut away at the negative stress in your life.

The Shield

As I already explained, the Shield is a defensive weapon against stress. Its purpose is to reduce your need for the Sword and to strengthen your use of it when needed. In the traditional sense, these are lifestyle changes you can make to reduce your stress toward stressors and to strengthen your physical and mental capacity for handling stress. That's why I look at these four simple adjustments as your Shield against stress.

You can add all of these adjustments at once, one or two at a time, or just pick and choose a few to add to your stress-building arsenal. The choice is yours. Keep in mind however that the more you add, the greater your defense against stress will be and the stronger your Sword will perform when thrust into action.

Here are the four elements of your Shield:

1. Maximize your energy level.

2. Lean on each other.

3. Enjoy your free time.

4. Expand your comfort zones.

Let's look at these in detail one at a time.

1. Maximize your energy level.

This is the single most important element of your Shield. If you only plan on adding one of the four Shield elements or are picking one to work on first then choose this critical element. If you worked through your action plan from last module, you should be good to go in this area; but if you need some help for some reason, take your time and go back through last module as needed to ingrain its critical lessons into your positive habits.

2. Lean on each other.

Try not to be an island unto yourself. You're a human being and as such benefit greatly from the support of others. Create a support network of family and friends you can routinely share your challenges and stress-producing stressors with. Ask for their help in identifying when you slip into stress so that you can pull your Sword out and go to work. Also ask for their support in helping you build the best Shield you possibly can. Look to do the same for them as well. This was one of the greatest lessons I learned from my days at the Naval Academy and as a naval officer and aviator. You can't do it all yourself. You need others, and it's a sign of strength to ask for help.

3. Enjoy your free time.

Another great lesson I learned from Annapolis was to cherish my free time and to never take these precious moments of life for granted. Life is too short to always be serious. Laugh at yourself often, have fun as much as you can, and never take life too seriously. When was the last time you were having fun and suffered from negative stress at the same time? Never, I bet! They're two opposed behaviors.

This shift of consciously enjoying your free time will help you look to produce more of it in creative ways. Remember question six of your Sword? Make it fun! This simple shift will go a long way in strengthening your Shield.

4. Expand your comfort zones.

When you stay in the same comfortable box of experiences all the time, any stressor outside of that box will stand a good chance of producing negative stress. The more often you try new things, the more you stretch yourself and test, the greater your ability to handle new stressors will be. Get out of your box! Go to new restaurants, try new foods, talk to new people, try new hobbies, try a sport you never thought you could play, try new things in your job or your business, try something new and romantic with your spouse, try new things with your kids to stretch their box as well, whatever! The idea is get out of your comfort zone and stretch its limits. The more you try, the more mistakes you make and forgive yourself for, the less you will worry about what others think and the greater your Shield will be.

60-Second Power Summary

▶ Stress is a behavior.

▶ Positive stress: sense of control

▶ Negative stress: perceived lack of control

▶ Mind's focus creates stress

  ▷ You have complete control.

▶ Patience and continual success are keys to success in eliminating stress.

▶ Develop a more positive and stress-reducing attitude.

  ▷ Change and obstacles are constants in life.

  ▷ Focus on natural stressors as challenges instead of problems.

  ▷ Learn from your mistakes.

  ▷ Learn to forgive yourself.

▶ The Sword and Shield Technique.

  ▷ The Sword

    › Purpose: awareness and solution

    › Stress early warning system (awareness radar)

      1. What is the stressor causing my stress?

      2. How am I focusing on it to make me feel stressed?

      3. What is the worst thing that can happen?

      4. How am I or can I be grateful for this stressor?

      5. How can I can I eliminate, reduce, avoid, or gain control over this stressor?

      6. How can I make my solution fun?

  ▷ The Shield

    › Purpose: reduce your need for the Sword and strengthen your use of it when needed

      1. Maximize your energy level.

      2. Lean on each other.

      3. Enjoy your free time.

      4. Expand your comfort zones.

Put Your Knowledge Into Action

Your action plan for this module is to begin shifting your attitude about stressors in your life toward the positive and to begin training and developing your skills with the Sword and Shield.

First your attitude. Patience and continual success are the keys here. We're looking for small, minute improvements almost every day to give you the hundreds and thousands of percent improvement you desire. The best way to do this is simply reviewing the attitude tips I gave you toward your stressors on a frequent basis.

The first worksheet in this module is more of a checklist than a worksheet. The first part of it is a summary of the attitude-building tips to help you with your outlook toward the stressors you face daily. Simply copy this sheet, keep it handy and review the attitude tips for a few seconds as close to every day as you can. This shouldn't take more than 15 to 30 seconds of your time, but this simple effort should create a top of the mind awareness toward improving your attitude. That's all it takes to give you the critical half of a percent daily improvement. Try it for a few weeks and see if it helps.

The second part of your action plan is to practice wielding your Sword and to begin strengthening your Shield. The second part of worksheet one's checklist is a reminder about turning on your stress early warning system and a listing of the six stress-slashing questions of your Sword. This is another important reason to keep this checklist very handy. When you feel yourself slipping into stress, when your stress radar alarm begins to sound, simply pull out your Sword checklist and go through it. This isn't rocket science, so please don't let its simplicity fool you. Use this Sword technique for a few weeks, and let the results speak for themselves.

The Shield. The second worksheet in this module is a simple continual improvement log for adding and improving the four stress defensive lifestyle changes into your life. The log simply asks you if you performed the Shield element today, asks you to list why if you didn't, and asks how you can improve just a little tomorrow. Spending just one or two minutes on this log each night will guide you to continually strengthen your Shield toward stress. Again, try this for a few weeks and see if you notice any improvement in your control of stress and time.

Removing Stress from Your Life Worksheet 1

Improving Your Attitude

1. Remember patience and continual success.

2. Change and obstacles are constants in life.

3. Focus on natural stressors as challenges instead of problems.

4. It's okay to make mistakes!

5. Forgive yourself.

6. Test, make mistakes, forgive yourself, learn, and try again.

The Sword!

Turn on your stress early warning system—your stress radar!

1. What is the stressor causing my stress?

_____

_____

2. How am I focusing on it to make me feel stressed?

_____

_____

3. What is the worst thing that can happen?

_____

_____

4. How am I or can I be grateful for this stressor?

_____

_____

5. How can I can I eliminate, reduce, avoid, or gain control over this stressor?

_____

_____

6. How can I make my solution fun?

_____

_____

Removing Stress from Your Life Worksheet 2

The Shield Log

Date: _____

1. Did you get enough sleep (seven hours minimum)?   Yes   No
2. If "no" then why: _____

_____

_____

3. Did you maximize your diet and exercise?   Yes   No
4. If "no" then why: _____

_____

_____

5. Did you allow others to help you today?   Yes   No
6. If "no" then why: _____

_____

_____

7. Did you enjoy your free time today?   Yes   No
8. If "no" then why: _____

_____

_____

9. Did you expand your comfort zones today?   Yes   No
10. If "no" then why: _____

_____

_____

11. How can you improve tomorrow?

_____

_____

_____

_____

_____

Module

Controlling Your Values, Beliefs, and Character

Your values, beliefs and, character play an important part in your control of your time. According to Booker T. Washington, *"Character is power."* From growing up with my parents strong influence on my character; through four years at one of America's strongest value-based institutions—the U.S. Naval Academy; through an eight-year career around the world as a naval aviator and officer; through three years developing young men and women into leaders in college; and through my entire business career of teaching individuals and businesses how to be more successful, I have seen and experienced the power and incredible impact our values, beliefs, and especially our character have over our time.

How Your Values Impact Your Time

Values. Webster's Dictionary defines "value" as a "quality intrinsically desirable." All of us see values a little bit differently. Depending on our particular background we can see them as a foundation of all our actions, simply traits we would like to incorporate into our daily lives, or as deeply rooted religious principles. Even when we have similar feelings toward particular values as someone else, we may have slightly different definitions for them or view them from another angle.

This section will show you a unique way of looking at your values, a way that I've developed from my experiences and study over the last 30 years. If you see values a little differently, that's perfectly fine.

Similar to Webster's definition of values, being qualities that are intrinsically desirable, I believe that values are conditioned standards from desired emotions that give us a sense of right and wrong in our actions. There are three parts to this definition that I'll break down for you.

First, there are "desired emotions." I believe that values are emotions. Emotions are a particular blending of physiological chemicals and mental associations that create a particular feeling inside you when you're faced with a situation or are acting a certain way. When you act honestly, you feel a certain way. A very real chemical and mental process takes place when you act this way, and you remember this feeling as honesty through time. The same goes for integrity, courage, tolerance, respect, gratitude, passion, patience, commitment, fidelity, balance, love, justice, mercy, happiness, success, initiative and a litany of other values. Because each of these creates specific feelings inside of us when we act within our model of them, they are best classified as emotions.

By "desired" emotions, I mean a value is an emotion you want to experience or feel within you. This falls right in line with Webster's definition. Because you enjoy the feelings of these emotions when you act to create them, you conversely are repulsed and create negative chemicals and mental thoughts when you act against these values or emotions. These are the feelings and thoughts that someone who values honesty experiences when they cheat, lie, or steal. The same goes for someone valuing fidelity when they cheat on their spouse or loved one. Ditto for all other values.

Cheating, stealing, intolerance, disrespect, lying, and hate are all emotions as well. For most of us, these aren't values, but anti-values. The negative feelings we generate when we act emotionally are directly the opposite of what we want to experience. If someone were to actually have pleasurable feelings acting in these emotions and wanted to experience these feelings again, then they could actually hold cheating, lying, stealing, hate, etc. as values.

The second part of my definition of values is "conditioned standards." The reason we have positive chemicals and mental thoughts for a combined pleasurable feeling, the reason we desire a certain emotion, is because our culture and our upbringing have rewarded us when we acted a certain way and punished us when acted opposed. Our culture is the present world we live in. It's our family, our friends, our neighborhood, our schools, our churches, our government, our work places, and our media. They all play a role in educating us in what emotions we feel for our actions.

When I entered the United States Naval Academy, I was quickly taught my first day and conditioned over the next four years that a midshipman will not lie, cheat, steal, or tolerate those that do. The other military academies are very similar in their value base. So strong is this value system that whenever someone tries to test it by cheating or stealing, it quickly becomes national headline news.

Our upbringing also helps mold the standards of emotions we desire. It's a fusion of our experiences as children and all our past experiences to the present. It includes the influence of our parents, family members, guardians, and other influential people in our lives while we were growing up. It also includes all our experiences as an adult.

The final part of my definition of values is: "that give us a sense of right and wrong in our actions." I've established that values are desired emotions derived from standards set through our present culture and past experiences. We subconsciously create models for these emotions to compare all our actions to on a daily basis. From these emotions, we choose how to act when faced with daily activities or challenges. We know that if we act a certain way, we'll experience our desired emotion, giving us a sense of "right." We also know that if we act opposed to that way, we'll experience a negative emotion, giving us a sense of "wrong." Without ever realizing it, we hold these models up to our actions tens to hundreds of times every day.

Because values are subconscious models to help guide your actions, they directly influence your behaviors and that means they directly impact your time. The stronger your value system, in other words the more you are conditioned to want to experience positive emotions and avoid negative emotions associated with your actions, the greater the impact on your time. When your value system is in harmony with the culture you live, including your society and work, your actions create little to no friction from others around you. If you hold yourself to higher standards than those around you, it may well even generate respect and open doors of opportunity for your increased success.

The opposite is true as well. If you have a weak value system, you tend to be much more chaotic in your actions and choices. This leads to friction with those around you and can even mean a direct confrontation with your society's guiding value system—law. When you're values are not in harmony with those you love, your choices can lead to the destruction of relationships. When not in harmony at work, this can lead to losing your job. When not in harmony with your customers, this can lead to lost business. When not in harmony with society's law, this can lead to jail. Do you think any of these impact your time?

How Your Beliefs Rule Your Values

If your values are conditioned emotions you want to feel, then your beliefs are the rules or criteria that determine if your actions should generate the internal feeling of that emotion. Simply put, they are the "if-then" models or rules for your values, and their power is amazing.

Going back to the dictionary, Webster defines "belief" as a "conviction of the truth." This supports my model for beliefs' association with values. When you face a particular situation, your actions will lead to one of three paths for your values. When you subconsciously know your actions match or are approaching the criteria you have for a desired emotion, you experience "truth" and your body begins to experience the feeling of that emotion. When your actions are directly opposed to a value's criteria, then you begin to experience negative feelings. When your actions are neutral, neither matching nor opposing any value criteria, then you experience nothing at all.

Much like our values, our beliefs are conditioned by our culture and upbringing. And just because two people hold the same values, doesn't necessarily mean that their beliefs or criteria for those values are the same. Let's look at some examples.

Depending on your background and whom you associate with, honesty for you might mean that "white" lies and fully justifiable lies are okay. In this case, as long as you tell only "white" lies or feel that a lie was justifiable for some higher cause, then you will experience your emotion of honesty and truly feel you are an honest person. However, if your belief for honesty states that you must always tell the truth under all circumstances, then you will only experience the emotion of honesty when you are completely telling the truth at all times. In this case, if you bend the truth just a little bit or tell a "white" lie, you will experience negative feelings. This is the ever-present challenge in politics: not whether a politician or candidate holds the value of honesty, because they all do, but what their particular belief system is for this critical value.

Another example centers on the value of fidelity. Fidelity is being true to your spouse or partner. If you hold this value in your marriage and your belief for experiencing this emotion is that you love your spouse and no one else, then you could conceivably feel the emotion of fidelity even though you sleep around with others, so long as you only love your spouse. Conversely, your belief for fidelity may hold the criteria that you must never even look at another to experience this emotion. This is further proof that beliefs are extremely powerful around values. Especially in your most important relationships, it is every bit as important and maybe even more so to find out the beliefs another has for the values they hold. From now on, try to see values and beliefs as a tandem, creating the models for our actions.

Realize that you can change your beliefs or criteria for "truth" for any value you have. Why would you want to? Some of the value-belief combinations you currently have may be stealing your time and sabotaging your success. Let's look at an example to illustrate this point.

We're going to work on your value and belief system for success. Do you value success? The odds are that you do. Think about what it takes for you to feel successful. In other words, what criteria must be met before you can feel this emotion. Think of both business and family. Jot these criteria or rules down on paper if you can.

Based on your criteria, is it possible for you to meet them daily or almost daily? Or do you have to reach a far off place in the future before you will allow yourself to experience the emotion of success?

Let's say your criteria to experience the emotions associated with success are that you must make over $200,000 a year in income, you must have over $1,000,000 in cash and assets, you must be required to be at work only three days a week for only six hours each day, you must have three months of vacation time a year, you must never argue with your spouse, you must have children that never disagree with you, and you must have a model's body and an athlete's strength and energy. What do you think? Extremely high criteria for sure! If the case was that you must meet all of the above criteria in order to feel successful, how often do you think you would feel successful? Maybe a few times in you life, if ever at all.

Do you see a little of yourself in those overly zealous rules for success above? Many of us do. This is why many people who are rich, or are beautiful, or have power by society's standards, are unhappy and are often self-destructive. In your eyes, by your criteria for success, they're successful, but they have not met their own criteria. They are forever chasing fame, money, sex, power, or glory because they value success but require too much of themselves to experience it.

What's interesting is that this value of success, because it is a value, is something that we want to experience. It's a desired emotion. If you desire it, but have criteria for its fulfillment that you can't meet frequently, you have forged a double-edged sword. You want it greatly but won't allow yourself to have it often or ever at all. You have the power to change this!

Like tends to attract like. If you feel successful, you'll tend to look for things to continue to make you feel this way. Success begets success. So, consider restructuring your belief for success so that you can achieve it almost every day. This way you can feel successful and look for continued ways to experience it. This will keep your motivation high and keep you looking out for opportunities. A true time accelerator if I've ever heard of one.

Imagine if you shifted your criteria for success, your beliefs, so that you must try your best and grow at least a little almost every day, you must be willing to test and make mistakes, you must move forward toward your Clarity, and you must stick to the values you hold dear as best you can. Do you see a difference?

This belief set isn't a walk in the park. It still requires you to put forth positive effort everyday to feel successful. But the key is that it is achievable every single day. It makes it possible for you to experience success daily and build on it. This is a much better belief system to apply toward your increased control of time.

What about the rest of your values and beliefs for them?

Am I saying to feel more honest or tolerant, that you create very loose beliefs for these values so that you can experience them more often? Not at all! I'm saying look at the beliefs you have right now for the values you hold dear and examine if they're self-destructive. If they are, then consider adjusting your beliefs to be more realistic and attainable.

It's your choice. You can choose to accept the beliefs for your values as they've been programmed over your lifetime, or you can create and work on conditioning new ones. Neither way is more right than the other.

I just want you to realize that you have a choice, and your choice may affect your time. Should you desire to change a belief for a value, the Daily Corps Values tool at the end of this module will show you how.

Keep in mind that your values and beliefs are different than your Clarity and goals. Your values are emotions you desire and your beliefs are the criteria to experience them. Your Clarity and goals are visions and milestones of the future you want. Design your beliefs so that you can experience your desired emotions frequently. Avoid the mistake of building your criteria for your beliefs with goals and visions planned for years down the road. This can only lead to frustration and burnout.

How Your Character Is What Matters Most

Values are important. Beliefs are important. But you should know that your character is what matters most.

Webster's Dictionary defines "character" as "the attributes that make up and distinguish the individual." My view is just slightly different. I look at your character as the accumulation of acted upon values in your life. Values are the conditioned emotions you desire, and your beliefs are the rules or conditions for these values. So values are what you want to experience. Your character then is the sum total of what you actually do experience. Values and beliefs are in your mind. Your character is in your actions. And remember, it's your actions that give you power.

Your character can be measured on two different levels. The first is how the accumulation of your actions matches up to the values of your culture—your society, family, and friends. The second level of your character is your own internal measurement of your actions compared to your personal values and beliefs.

One level of measurement is not necessarily any more important than the other. Both affect your time. If your character doesn't match up to the expectations of your culture, then you'll experience friction with others around you—your family, friends, loved ones, co-workers, clients, and government. How much could this impact your time? Unless you're a hermit, a great deal.

The same goes for your character compared to your internal standards. Every time you act against your beliefs for your personal values, you generate negative feelings and accompanying physiological changes, including negative stress, ulcers, immune system breakdown, mood swings, depression, and anxiety. The more you act against your beliefs for your values, the greater the accumulation of these negative effects. How do you think this will affect your time?

Let's take a look at some examples.

You may value honesty and truly want to experience this emotion in your life on a frequent basis. If your actions match your culture's belief system for honesty, then you will harbor honesty as a character trait in their eyes. If your belief system for honesty is similar, you will internally have honesty as part of your personal character as well.

It is possible to have conflict with your character. Your own belief system for honesty may differ from that of your culture. This can result in others feeling you have an honest character while you feel your character is not very honest. This happens if your belief standards are more stringent than your culture's and you fail to meet them frequently. The opposite can occur as well. If your standards for honesty are looser than your culture's, then you may feel your character is honest but society may view you as dishonest. Again, politics are a great model for this.

A good second example is having success as part of your character.

If you match or surpass society's standards for success, then your character will have success as a part of it in their eyes. Regardless of how you see yourself, society will treat you as successful. If you match your own belief system for success, you will view your own character as successful as well. But if your standards are higher than your culture's and you don't live up to them, then you can feel your character is unsuccessful, regardless of society's view. This happens frequently to those that gain the national media spotlight. As a matter of fact, many so-called "stars" that are regarded with high esteem by society have low self-esteem because of their own view of their character.

Once again, your character is the accumulation of acted upon values. It's what you have done most that forges your character through time. The more you match your cultural beliefs for values, the greater your character is defined by these beliefs in others' eyes. The same goes for yourself with your personal view of your character. Your character allows for you to be human and make mistakes. You don't have to be perfect with values, just consistent. The greater your consistency, the stronger your character.

Your actions are what matter most. You may hold values and beliefs in your heart; but if you don't consistently act in alignment with them, then it means little to nothing. Your character, your actions are what impact your control of time. Keep in mind the two measurements of your character— your culture's and your own. Both impact your time but do so in very different ways.

Take Initiative!

Now that you have the basics on how values, beliefs, and character interact to affect our control of time, let us move on to a value I feel has incredible time-growing capability if you add it to your character. This value is initiative.

I have seen initiative have more impact on one's time than any other. What's funny is that very few of us incorporate this value into our character nearly as much as we could, and so most of us have just scraped the surface of the time-building benefits we could reap from it.

Simply put, initiative is about being proactive. It's about taking responsibility for your own life, understanding that your own actions and thoughts create your future, your destiny. It's not up to others. Others don't control you nearly as much as you think. Initiative is about you taking responsibility for your own success, your time, and your happiness.

There are two areas of initiative to consider incorporating into your character—initiative in your actions and initiative in your reactions.

The traditional way of looking at initiative is in your actions. This is where you take control, where you decide that action must come from you to effect change. With this as part of your character, you consistently look to do the right thing without being told or after being instructed only once. You don't look to pass the buck or depend on others to make something positive happen. It doesn't mean you don't ask clarifying questions when you need to know more or that you don't ask for help when you truly need it. It just means that you are never lazy and that you enjoy being aggressive in your actions. Responsibility and accountability become your personal trademarks.

This side of initiative was clearly planted my first day at the Naval Academy. After a full day of checking in, getting our heads shaved, learning how to salute and march, and taking our midshipman pledge of service, we were quickly introduced to a short 100-year-old article called "A Message to Garcia."

Written by Elbert Hubbard in 1899, this originally untitled magazine article focused on initiative. It related the story Lt. Andrew Rowan, U.S. Army, a West Point graduate, who was commissioned by President McKinley at the outbreak of the Spanish American War to hand deliver a message requesting military aide to rebel leader General Garcia. The only things relayed to Lt. Rowan were that the message was of vital importance, that General Garcia was located somewhere in the hostile mountain jungles of Cuba, and that time was short. Dropped off on the Cuban shoreline, Lt. Rowan took the initiative to carry out his vital task. Never looking for excuses or depending on others for the success of his charge, he found General Garcia, delivered the message, and returned on the opposite shoreline for pickup in only two weeks time. His was a true testimony to initiative in your actions.

Elbert Hubbard used this story in his article, eventually titled "A Message to Garcia," as a model to relate to employee initiative at the end of the 19th century. He summarized that those employees with initiative are the prize that every business fights to employ—the truly hard to find gems in the business world.

Hubbard's simple message struck a nerve in the business and military world across the globe. Like wildfire, it reproduced to 40 million copies, in all written languages at the time, within just 10 years! Every culture in the world seemed to cherish this underutilized value.

How "A Message to Garcia" spread was quite amazing. Having seen and been impressed with Mr. Hubbard's untitled magazine article, a United States railroad company asked for permission to copy the article onto 100,000 of their company brochures. Soon after, Russian railroad businessmen visiting railroad companies in America came across the brochures and took the idea back to Russia. The Russian military saw the article and made it required reading for their soldiers. Over the next few years, Russia went to war against Japan. Japanese soldiers found the article carried by Russian prisoners and had it translated to Japanese. It was soon mandatory reading for all Japanese military and government personnel. Through a continued series of events such as these, "A Message to Garcia" spread the word about initiative across the world in less than a decade.

During my four years at the Naval Academy, "A Message to Garcia" became synonymous with initiative, the terms interchangeable in our vocabulary. Responsibility, accountability, and aggressive action were ingrained into our character—initiative became a way of life, and its effect on our time was incredible.

I took this strong value through my naval career, and when I entered the business world, its effects were even more magnified. "A Message to Garcia" is just as important today as it was 100 years ago. Consistently studying those who are successful in business and in life in general, I've found that initiative is one of the key ingredients that separate those who have control of their time and their success and those who consistently wish for more.

The second area of initiative to consider incorporating into your character is in your reactions. As human beings, we have a natural tendency to be reactive. The key then to boost your control of time is to train yourself to react with values. Which values? Simply ones you feel are important to your life and that you want to make sure stay a part of your character.

Recall Victor Frankl, the Holocaust survivor who taught us in my Motivation Control module that you have the freedom to choose how you will react in any given situation. This reaction can be based out of fear or anger or it can be out of predetermined and conditioned values. The choice is yours. You can decide *right now* how you'd like to react to different situations; then train yourself to take initiative to make it happen.

After the Korean Conflict in the early 1950's many American prisoners refused to leave their Chinese captors after being freed. They had been brainwashed during their captivity and opted to live a life of communism over freedom.

Concerned by this, President Eisenhower felt that our servicemen were not prepared to handle this brainwashing and had no foundation to react with for these stressful circumstances. In 1955 he established the Code of Conduct to arm our servicemen with values for future conflicts. This code consisted of six simple and powerful articles establishing each soldier's, airman's, and sailor's loyalty to God, country, and his fellow prisoners should he ever be captured. Memorized by all military personnel, and reinforced for those entering combat, the Code of Conduct established a set of values to guide one's actions and reactions during the harshest of conditions.

The Code's first real test came during the Vietnam War, and it passed with flying colors. Prisoners during this conflict faced confinement, torture, and brainwashing on a scale that dwarfed the Korean Conflict. With values to help them react to their almost unbearable conditions, prisoners frequently pointed out in interviews following release from their capture that the Code of Conduct saved their lives.

Today, having been tested as recently as the Bosnian Conflict and the Gulf War, the Code of Conduct is a powerful testimony to the power of taking initiative in your reactions, reacting with predetermined values.

So what does the Code of Conduct have to do with you, in your personal life and in business? A lot. Not the code itself, but its message that reacting with values is a powerful form of initiative.

Everyday you face challenges in business and your personal time. You face things you didn't expect and are forced to react to. Things such as others lying, stealing, and cheating, unexpected stressors cropping up, employee issues, client issues, and family issues. How do you react to these? Are you consistent or do you act based simply on instinct and how you feel at the moment? If you want more control, reacting with values can make a big difference.

Daily Corps Values

Daily Corps Values is a Time Control tool that allows you to design your top values and beliefs for everyday living. It allows you to create a designated first line of battle for your daily decision-making. In a sense, it is a vehicle for you to take the initiative in your natural, daily reactions.

Notice the spelling I chose for this tool. I purposely chose "Corps" instead of a possible and expected "Core." Core means central, and I wanted something that better represented the power of this tool. So I modeled Corps after the United States Marine Corps.

I've developed a very strong admiration for the Marine Corps. It is an elite force, highly motivated and highly trained to handle it's main task of being the first into battle. That's the same way I viewed the set of chosen values and beliefs created by this tool that would guide one's actions and reactions through the trials of life. That's why I honored the title of this tool with Daily Corps Values.

Before you learn this tool, you need to understand the behavior-shifting power behind its effectiveness. Keep in mind that the power generated is great, but its creation is very easy. It is simply this: that knowledge internalized from frequent review gives birth to and nurtures positive behavioral change.

Studies by Dr. Deepak Chopra, a world-renowned expert on western medicine and physics and eastern consciousness, and Dr. Wayne Dyer, one of America's top psychology and consciousness leaders, show that knowledge inherently has organizing capability for your actions and for opportunities you come across for your success. You simply require awareness for the change you desire, with emotion ruling over logic. This in turn internalizes into your actions, behaviors, and outlook for opportunities. The process doesn't happen overnight and goes squarely against the "miracle pill" mentality of our present Western culture. As a matter of fact, trying harder for faster results produces stress and strain—both counterproductive to your success. Your power for positive change will grow slowly and surely through time, so long as you fertilize your knowledge with frequent review and emotion to strengthen your awareness.

This is exactly how you to gain success with your Clarity, your goals, and your Daily Motivation Questions. It's the basis for many of the worksheets throughout all of these Time Control modules. And it's the same guiding principle that will generate the power for controlling more of your time through your Daily Corps Values.

Creating and using your Daily Corps Values is a very simple five-step process. The steps are listed below:

1. Brainstorm values you want to experience every day.
2. Choose top three to five desired values.
3. Construct positive, daily-achievable beliefs for each.
4. Review at least five mornings a week.
5. Re-evaluate monthly and update as needed.

Let's take a look at these steps one at a time.

1. Brainstorm values you want to experience every day.

Using the worksheets with this module as a guide, take five minutes or so and brainstorm all of the values you would like to achieve daily. These are the values you want standing side by side with you when you face challenges throughout your day.

My personal Daily Corps Values are comprised of the values of love, gratitude, true happiness, passion, patience, and respect. Initiative is such an ingrained value in me that it's a part of my blood and breath. Because of this, I have chosen others I want to work on in my life. The only thing that really matters is what you want for the life you live. So brainstorm away, asking ideas from others you look up to in your life if you want and not worrying about how many or how few values you come up with.

2. *Choose the top three to five desired values.*

From your brainstormed list, choose the top three to five values you want to develop to be your front line of battle in your daily decision-making and reactions. Keep your list short, especially in the beginning stages of using this tool. Once again, we're working off the KISS Principle, keeping it short and simple for your success. Once you get comfortable with this tool, you can expand your number of values. Just because you don't choose a value from your list doesn't mean you don't desire it in your life. It simply means you don't choose to develop it at this time. This could be the case for values and beliefs that are already strongly ingrained inside you such as initiative with me. Or it could mean that you have decided to develop the value further in the future.

3. *Construct positive, daily-achievable beliefs for each.*

Now that you have chosen a set of values to help guide your daily actions and reactions, I want you to look at your belief criteria for each. Put your beliefs down on your worksheets using the given format "I feel (or experience)...when I..."

If you have never taken the time before now to try to put your beliefs for a value into words, it may seem a little awkward at first. Do your best. It doesn't have to be perfect.

The reason I'm having you write your beliefs beside your values is so that you can decide if your belief for a particular value is what you want. If you find that your belief for a particular value is unachievable or sabotaging your life in any way, such as the examples I went through before, then this is your chance to rewire your beliefs for those values. Simply write down the criteria you have currently or want for your chosen values.

To give you some guidance in how beliefs can be written, let me share my beliefs, my criteria for my chosen Daily Corps Values.

Love: I feel love when I give love and expect nothing in return.

Gratitude: I feel gratitude when I appreciate everything I have and know that God has blessed me with it all.

True Happiness: I feel true happiness when I remember joy is the natural state God has chosen for us and realize when I am not joyous then I am not living in true harmony with our Lord.

Passion:	I feel passion when I get the most out of every single day, living life to its fullest.
Patience:	I experience patience when I remember I have complete control of my reactions to all situations and apply this knowledge to all stimuli in my life —especially my family.
Respect:	I feel respect when I treat my wife, my boys and others with the respect their divinity deserves.

Hopefully these will give you good ideas as to how you can word your beliefs. Bottom line is don't worry about being perfect. Make your beliefs good, and you can always adjust them later.

4. Review at least five mornings a week.

Look at your Daily Corps Values at least five mornings every week. Reviewing them at the same time as your Clarity and goals is perfect. This process develops the principle of power explained earlier in this section. Remember, don't make this stressful. Simply look over your values and beliefs, knowing this is how you want to conduct yourself today. Through frequent review and emotion, you will begin a process of internalizing these values and beliefs into your actions, behavior and character. It won't happen overnight, but these results are assured if you are diligent, patient, and relaxed. Trust the process.

5. Re-evaluate monthly and update as needed.

Finally, look over your Daily Corps Values once a month or so and decide if you want to continue with what you have or make changes. As you develop this tool and as your life situations evolve, you will want to swap out values and make changes to your beliefs from time to time. No problem! This is your tool. Keep it updated for your benefit in time.

Daily Power Up Tool!

With the addition of your Daily Corps Values into your Time Control repertoire, you now have all of the tools necessary to completely focus your days and supercharge your time every single day for the rest of your life. You have available to you the four tools to use at least five mornings every week to create amazing stability and success in your time. These four tools are:

1. Your Daily Motivation Questions
2. Your Clarity
3. Your Daily Corps Values
4. Your Goals

This isn't the time to re-teach you these wonderful tools. If you have not implemented them into your life, now would be a great time to go back and review their appropriate modules. Going through your Daily Motivation Questions aligns your focus to positive motivation. Your Clarity is the future you desire in two to three years and should be the cornerstone for all of your daily actions. Your Daily Corps Values are your first line of battle for daily decisions to make sure you react with chosen values and beliefs. And your goals are the blinders you create to make sure you are living the path you desire.

Separately these four tools work to give you more control of your time. But using them together by way of a simple 15-minute combined review at least five mornings weekly will exponentially grow the powerful results each could produce alone. I call this four-tool synergy your Daily Power Up.

60-Second Power Summary

▶ Values
  ▷ Conditioned standards from desired emotions that give us a sense of right and wrong in our actions.

▶ Beliefs
  ▷ Value rules.
  ▷ People can hold the same values but have different beliefs for them.

▶ Character
  ▷ The accumulation of acted upon values in your life matters most.
  ▷ Cultural versus internal measurement.
  ▷ The greater your consistency, the stronger your character.

▶ Initiative
  ▷ Value that impacts time the most.
  ▷ Being proactive and taking responsibility for your success.
  ▷ Initiative in your actions.
    › "A Message to Garcia"
  ▷ Initiative in your reactions.

▶ Daily Corps Values
  1. Brainstorm values you want to experience everyday.
  2. Choose top three to five desired values.
  3. Construct positive, daily-achievable beliefs for each.
  4. Review at least five mornings a week.
  5. Re-evaluate monthly and update as needed.

▸ Daily Power Up!
1. Your Daily Motivation Questions.
2. Your Clarity.
3. Your Daily Corps Values.
4. Your Goals.

Put Your Knowledge Into Action

Go through the steps and worksheets for this powerful tool to create a set of values and corresponding, daily-achievable beliefs to guide your actions and reactions throughout your days. Take making this value and belief set seriously and then review it consistently (at least five mornings a week) without strain. Let time and continuous awareness work for you to slowly but surely mold your attitudes and behaviors into the character you desire.

Once you've completed your Daily Corps Values, combine it with your Daily Motivation Questions, your Clarity and your goals to create a Daily Power Up routine. If you haven't implemented any of these tools, go back to their appropriate module to review and complete the worksheets. Then commit to going through your Daily Power Up at least five mornings a week for the next three weeks. Evaluate for yourself if this tool, combining these four simple yet powerful tools, works to add more control, focus and motivation to your available time.

Daily Corps Values Worksheet (1 of 3)

1. Brainstorm values (emotions) you want to experience every day.

_____

_____

_____

_____

_____

_____

_____

_____

_____

_____

_____

_____

2. Choose top three to five desired values.

Value 1:

_____

Value 2:

_____

Value 3:

_____

Value 4:

_____

Value 5:

_____

Daily Corps Values Worksheets (2 of 3)

3. Write current beliefs or criteria for each chosen value.

Value 1:

I feel / experience _____

when I _____

_____

_____

Value 2:

I feel / experience _____

when I _____

_____

_____

Value 3:

I feel / experience _____

when I _____

_____

_____

Value 4:

I feel / experience _____

when I _____

_____

_____

Value 5:

I feel / experience _____

when I _____

_____

_____

Daily Corps Values Worksheets (3 of 3)

Adjust any time-stealing or self-defeating current beliefs to be daily-achievable, positive beliefs. Clean up your value/belief set.

Value 1:

I feel / experience _____

when I _____

_____

_____

Value 2:

I feel / experience _____

when I _____

_____

_____

Value 3:

I feel / experience _____

when I _____

_____

_____

Value 4:

I feel / experience _____

when I _____

_____

_____

Value 5:

I feel / experience _____

when I _____

_____

_____

4. Now review your Daily Corps Values at least five mornings every week!

MODULE

WINNING THE WAR AGAINST PROCRASTINATION

What Is Procrastination?

Procrastination is one of the most potent of the Killer 13 Time Wasters. It's a subtle behavior we've developed through life that is based on our decision-making. It's based on choices. Every day we're faced with making decisions—a choice in our actions. When we choose to put something off until later and continue to do so, we begin to walk the path of this dangerous behavior.

If you make a choice not to do something because it doesn't move you forward toward your Clarity or goals, you're not procrastinating. You're making an intelligent, time-saving decision. But if you choose to put something off that moves you toward your Clarity or goals or is unavoidably required (i.e. some paperwork and taxes), you're in danger of inflicting yourself with the negative effects of procrastination.

Have you ever put off important paperwork? Of course you have! We all have. Think back to a time when you put off completing or mailing in paperwork that was important to you. Simply by it's definition that it's important means that the paperwork should move you toward your Clarity when completed. Did you suffer any consequences by waiting to the last minute or missing a deadline? If you did, what were they and how did they impact your life?

As a college student and professor, I saw the consequences of putting assignments off to the last minute over and over again. The assignments were inherently important because they impacted a grade in a class. This in turn affected the vision of graduating and being in a position to choose one's path for future courses, scholarships, and job positions. You would be amazed (or maybe you wouldn't be) at how many students would wait until the last minute to work on assignments and papers—often pulling all-nighters, begging with poor excuses for more time from their professors, and suffering reduced grades from work that was well below their best effort. This same procrastinating pattern carried over into studying for exams and then became a life-long pattern, which has the potential to follow the students into their careers.

What's sad is that those who figured out the game and listened to their professors didn't really work any harder than those fellow students who procrastinated their assignments. They just worked smarter and were rewarded immensely for their initiative.

Case in point, one college student preparing to be a naval officer, had to work harder than most to get good grades. He discovered that turning in assignments early with good effort really paid off for him in the long run. He routinely turned in major papers to his professors at least two weeks before their deadlines. To a person, his professors were so impressed with his efforts to be early that they would go over his papers with him, showing him mistakes and where to make improvements. They then handed him back his papers, and he went back and reworked his papers, re-turning them in on the originally assigned deadline. With most of his fellow students' grades suffering from procrastination, he never failed to get lower than an "A" on a paper.

Another example of the costs of putting things off can be seen in business. My business is headquartered in Houston, Texas—one of America's top entrepreneurial markets. Recent reports from our Small Business Association show that more small businesses start up annually in Houston than in any other U.S. city. Unfortunately the vast majority of these businesses will go under. The latest statistics indicate that about nine out of 10 Houston startups will fail within five years.

Why so many? It's not that most of these businesses offer a poor product or service. It's that most business owners don't take marketing and innovation very seriously. These owners end up spending too much time working in their business rather than on it. Although they spend a ton of time working, inevitably their marketing and innovation procrastination costs them dearly. Taking procrastination by the horns and spending just a few minutes a day studying and testing new marketing concepts and innovations can make all the difference in the world between a business flourishing or dying with the pack.

Procrastinating behavior and its negative consequences can affect every facet of our lives. From the stress of having to pay penalties on late tax returns instead of receiving a refund check in late March or early April to the pain of lost social opportunities because we failed to ask someone we were attracted to out on date. Nothing is protected. As long as a choice is involved, the potential to suffer procrastination's effects exists.

Keep in mind that procrastination has been nicknamed the Thief of Time and the Silent Killer. It's easy to see why. Procrastination is one of the most powerful time wasters we face. So, like a thief, this behavior can steal your time that could otherwise be invested toward your Clarity and goals.

The name the Silent Killer is a little more interesting. Procrastinating behavior works subtly, slowly killing opportunities that could move you toward the future you desire. Developing through time into a negative habit, those trapped in procrastination's web become blinded to its devastation. More often than not, these people look for other excuses to explain their lack of success and fulfillment. Rather than see that their choices are killing their opportunities, they blame others or an apparent lack of time. Another victim soon falls to the Silent Killer.

A good way of looking at the accumulative effects of this Thief of Time and Silent Killer on your control of time is to view procrastination as the evil twin of Bit by Bit. As Bit by Bit adds up subtly and consistently to eventually grow your success to unbelievable exponential levels, procrastination does the same thing but on a negative level. Procrastination accumulates its negative effects slowly and consistently each time you avoid taking action. Eventually, if you don't change your behaviors, the lost opportunities and recourse on your life become exponential and wear heavy on your self-confidence and self-esteem to even want to succeed.

Putting all this into perspective, procrastination is a behavior based on the choices we make. Because it's a developed behavior and because it stems from making decisions, you have a choice when it comes to procrastinating.

What Causes Procrastination?

The root cause of procrastination isn't complex. In fact, it's very simple. It's fear. And this fear can be direct or very subtle.

Most of us are afraid of taking action. When we're faced with making a choice, the options we can choose from usually involve some form of action. When we fear what might happen from our actions, we begin to consider avoiding or delaying those options. We begin to slip into procrastinating behavior.

Why are we afraid of choosing certain actions? We are afraid of possible criticism. We are afraid of possible failure. We are afraid of possible success. And we are afraid of possible boredom.

Criticism is easy to see and is a direct form of fear. None of us likes to be criticized by others, especially others we care for. We are social beings, and it's important for us to fit in with our society. Because we care almost too much about what others think about us and how we perform, we magnify the possible effects of taking action. Just think back to high school or when you were participating in the dating game. Rather than face the pain of being criticized by others, many times we choose to avoid action or choices that might otherwise move us forward toward the vision we desire. We become frozen—trapped by procrastination.

The same goes for being afraid of failure, another direct form of fear. If we haven't developed a testing attitude and a positive outlook on challenges and so-called failures, then it's easy to develop a strong fear of failing. If failure is painful to you rather than just information to be applied toward future tests, then it becomes easy to slip into comfort zones and build strong walls preventing expansion. It becomes easy to choose to avoid actions that might lead to the possibility of failure. Once again, we become frozen and purposely blind to opportunities for success. We are held tightly by the grip of procrastination.

Being afraid of success is a very real but very subtle form of fear. Why would someone be afraid of succeeding? If someone is trying to succeed for the wrong reasons, if they are trying to succeed in something because of others and not themselves, then success becomes pressure-filled rather than joyous. Some of us may feel that if we succeed then we will be expected to continue succeeding, creating more pressure and more negative stress. If this is how you view success, then it becomes fearful. With fear involved in your choices, you will once again avoid actions that could lead to success, even self-sabotaging opportunities. Procrastination wins again.

Beware of this trap! The only pressure you have is the pressure you allow yourself to have. Remember that success is much easier than we give it credit for because so few people dare to take the simple action needed to achieve and maintain it. Your human behavior can be your absolute best, trusted ally or your worst enemy. It's completely up to you.

And finally, our fear of boredom, the subtlest form of fear. Many times we avoid doing something not because we fear criticism, failure, or success but just because we would prefer doing something more fun and less boring. If left unchecked, this form of fear can exponentially grow into a very powerful form of procrastination.

The bottom-line to keep in mind is that fear is painful to most of us. And if you remember back to the background for my Push-Pull Principle, our avoidance of pain is one of our strongest motivators according to the late 19th century psychologist Dr. Sigmund Freud. His Pain-Pleasure Principle states that our actions are primarily motivated by our avoidance of pain and our pursuit of pleasure. So when we harbor painful fear toward choices that could bring us criticism, failure, success, or even boredom, we are naturally inclined to avoid them. We naturally want to push them off to later or avoid doing them altogether. We procrastinate.

I've alluded to it before, but I want to stress again that perfectionism is one of the biggest forms of procrastination. Perfectionism is a subtle form of avoidance of action. Fearing anything less than perfect outcomes for their actions, those enslaved by perfectionism avoid action by overzealously planning for it. They have three of the four fears of action we have just discussed—criticism, failure, and success. But what separates them from others is that they disguise their procrastination through very detailed planning for the very action they are subconsciously avoiding.

Shifting Your Attitude

Procrastination is a behavior. It's one we've all been affected by to one degree or another. And its root cause is fear, where we avoid actions that might bring us some form of pain.

Now it's time to take control. The rest of this module is dedicated to arming you with attitude and behavior-shifting tools to win the war against the time-stealing, and opportunity-killing behaviors associated with procrastination.

Attitude and awareness are the simple, yet powerful, strategic principles we'll employ. In this section, let's continue building on the positive attitude we've been developing throughout this book. To severely weaken procrastination's grip on your control of time, make sure you work on developing three critical parts to your attitude—focus daily on your objectives, consistently take some form of action now, and face tasks and challenges head-on.

Let's take a look at each of these in a little detail.

1. Focus daily on your objectives.

This attitude attribute should be very familiar to you by now. Focusing on your objectives is nothing more than reviewing the Daily Power Up tool we developed in our last module. It involves reviewing your Daily Motivation Questions, your Clarity, your Daily Corps Values, and your goals at least five mornings every week.

The power you receive from adding this attribute to your attitude comes from awareness. By starting almost every morning off with a positive motivational focus, the vision of where you want to be in a few years, the values and beliefs you want to face your daily decisions with, and your future, desired milestones and objectives, you best arm yourself to look for positive actions and opportunities each day and greatly reduce any possible fear associated with them.

2. Consistently take some form of action now.

Work on consciously taking some form of positive action right away, right now, toward the tasks that are important to you. Rather than put something off until later and then falling into the trap of procrastination, look to quickly act on opportunities and tasks that move you toward your Clarity and goals.

Taking action doesn't mean you have to complete a task. It simply means moving it positively forward to some degree. As long as you're moving forward, it's easy to keep momentum generated toward your eventual success. Procrastination keeps you frozen in your fear to perpetuate its existence. Consistent and frequent progress to any degree will shatter procrastination.

Keep in mind that your action can be the obvious parts of a task or it can be simple yet important thought. Many times stepping back and thinking about innovative approaches to your task can be the best kind of action you can take.

Committing to a date for the next step in your task can also be good action. The thing to keep in mind here is that you must *commit* to a date. If you set a date for the next step in a task, you must act on that chosen date. If you just pick a future date and then postpone it once it finally arrives, you risk killing your momentum and falling into procrastinating behavior.

3. Face tasks and challenges head-on.

This attitude attribute is crucial in defeating procrastination. Since procrastination is built on a foundation of fear and avoidance, it is important to face your fears. By facing them, you will find that fears are often misplaced and are rarely as dangerous as they seem while we try to avoid them.

Fear tends to brood and feed on itself if you don't face its source. The longer you allow yourself to live in fear of something, the worse the potential consequences of your actions grow in your head. This pattern strengthens your avoidance of action and feeds your procrastinating behavior.

A great illustration of this is a friend of mine who has procrastinated going to the dentist for the last 10 years. She had painful experiences with dentists while growing up and developed a great fear of sitting in the dentist chair. Over the last decade, her fear has created horrible images in her head of what it would be like to go back to a dentist. She has literally lived hundreds to thousands of painful dental visits in her head as she strengthened her avoidance through the years. Recently when she had a pain in her teeth, she got sick to her stomach and went into a two-week depressive state knowing she had to go to a dentist to have it looked at. Until she decides to face her fear of dentists head-on, she will not be able to break her fearful avoidance and procrastination and will continue to suffer self-generated demons in her head.

It will take some time to add this attribute of facing tasks and challenges head-on, but just work on it a little at a time. Time will work for you, if you let it. Bit by bit. One step at a time. And your success is guaranteed. Don't worry about being perfect. Just be consistent at keeping this attitude attribute frequent in your awareness.

Permanent Procrastination Removal

Attitude and awareness are once again the strategies we're employing to win the war against procrastination. Having just given you three powerful attributes to begin conditioning into your attitude, you'll soon be armed with two awareness-developing weapons to wield against procrastination. Both of these tools work seamlessly together to keep you aware of the costs of procrastinating behavior and the rewards of incorporating the three positive-attitude properties you've just learned.

You will develop the habit of using these new weapons through a simple three-step process as listed below.

1. Apply Push-Pull Principle.
2. Apply Time Warp visualization tool.
3. Refer to Push-Pull and Time Warp as needed to condition and maintain change.

1. Apply Push-Pull Principle to procrastination.

You should be quite familiar with this tool by now. Remember, emotion rules over logic. The more painful you make your Push entries and the more pleasurable you make your Pull entries, the more powerfully and effective your behavior change will be.

So, to win the war against procrastination, go through a Push-Pull Principle worksheet to help you see and feel the costs of continuing your present procrastinating behavior and the rewards of shifting your behaviors and attitudes just a little bit toward positive action.

Brainstorm all of the pain procrastinating will cost you emotionally, financially, physically, socially, and spiritually if you continue as you have to date. What will it do to your self-confidence and self-esteem? What will it do to your savings, your debt, your salary, and your business' profits? What will it do to your health, your energy level, your ability to fight colds and disease, and your stress level? How will it affect your most important relationships? And how it will affect your personal relationship with your Creator? The only answers that matter are yours. Just be sure to have emotion in them.

Then brainstorm all of the pleasure you'll gain in your life once you begin to focus daily on your objectives, consistently take some for of action now, and face tasks and challenges head-on. Again you're looking for the emotional, financial, physical, social, and spiritual effects. If you positively shift your procrastinating behavior and begin living by these three action-producing attitude principles, what will it do to your self-confidence and self-esteem? How much more will you be able to save? How much will you be able to reduce your credit debt? How much more money could you make? How much more energy could you have? How many fewer colds?

How much less stress? How much more joyous could your most important relationships be? And how much closer and at peace could you be with your Creator?

2. Apply Time Warp visualization tool.

The second step in generating the critical awareness needed to help win your war against procrastination is through the power of visualization. Remember, your present focus and awareness create the filters to all of the stimuli around you. This in turn becomes your perception of reality and generates the motivation for your actions. Through visualization you can direct this focus and awareness and strongly influence your motivation for action—action that can shatter the bonds of procrastination.

The visualization you will use is called Time Warp. As its name implies, you're going to direct yourself through time, seeing the effects of both procrastinating behavior and action-centered behavior on your life. Having just completed your Push-Pull Principle for procrastination, you'll already have primed yourself to see the effects of these two very different paths for your choices.

You'll do this visualization in two steps. First, you'll go through worksheets designed to visually walk you through the negative effects procrastination has cost you in the past, is currently costing you right now, and will potentially cost you at different points in your future if left unchecked. You'll describe in detail how you think you'll look and feel in one year, five years, and 10 years from now if you don't change how you currently procrastinate. Then you'll do similar brainstorming and visualizing for the same future time periods except this time focusing on the positive effects of embracing action in your attitude.

What do you think this process will do to your awareness?

Realize that this process can be very emotional. As a matter of fact, the more emotional you let yourself become, the greater the positive effects of this tool on curbing your procrastination. Seeing the negative effects of procrastination in your past, present and potential future and coming face to face with who you will be if you don't change can be painful. That's the idea behind this part. I would much rather you shed light on all of the costs of procrastination in your life rather than hide from them. By seeing their devastating effects, you will no longer be blind to them. By feeling their pain, you can generate the drive to move away from it to positive action—away from procrastination permanently.

Don't fret over the pain you feel from the past or present. You can't change the past, but you can learn from it. Use this knowledge to prevent it from happening again in your future and use the pain to motivate yourself to your success.

Keep in mind that half of your Time Warp is spent seeing the wonderful possibilities of what shifting your behavior a little bit—toward action over avoidance—can bring you in your near, middle and far future. Be emotional in this as well, except this time letting yourself feel the joy, exhilaration, and pleasure of what consistent action can bring you. Let seeing your potential rewards motivate yourself to take action toward them.

Your Time Warp visualization will generate critical awareness and the pain and pleasure motivators that work together to move you away from procrastination and toward positive action. Everything you'll see for your future—the effects and how you'll look—are simply possibilities down two very different roads for your choices. You fully control this future. Remain aware, make your decision of what future you desire, and then take the necessary action to get there.

3. Refer to Push-Pull and Time Warp as needed to condition change.

Creating your Push-Pull Principle for procrastination and going through the Time Warp worksheets will have short-term benefits at best if that's all you do. The power of awareness and emotion are extremely strong weapons against procrastination, but they need frequency and repetition to succeed and change your behaviors. So, to truly gain and maintain the benefits of creating your Push-Pull and Time Warp, you want to go through your worksheets on a frequent, consistent basis.

I strongly recommend reviewing your worksheets with emotion for a few minutes, five mornings a week, for at least the next three weeks. After you begin to see a positive shift in your behavior and are able to maintain it for a few weeks, you can pull back from reviewing as often. Whatever you do, continue to review your worksheets at least twice a week. If at any time you find yourself drifting back to procrastinating behavior, simply go through the Time Warp visualization again and review your worksheets more frequently to strengthen your behavior. It's a balancing act. Work to continually maintain that balance of review and relaxation until you find the best combination for your situation and lifestyle.

Let time work for you in this behavior strengthening process. And don't make your reviewing stressful. Keep this process simple and it will pay huge dividends in your increased control of time. Remember, the whole idea behind reviewing your worksheets is to generate awareness to the pain of procrastination and the pleasure of taking positive action.

Keep in mind that the speed and permanency of change through this process depend on the amount of awareness you generate and your emotional level in your review. If you review a few times a week in the beginning then drift to once every couple of weeks, you can expect little change. If you breeze through your worksheets, practically speed reading through them with a logical mindset because you know what's written on them, again you can expect minimal change. Let yourself feel the pain of procrastinating you listed and let yourself feel the pleasure you brainstormed for taking action, and do so at least five mornings a week in the beginning and no less than twice a week once conditioned. Follow this recipe, and you are guaranteed success!

60-Second Power Summary

▶ Procrastination
  ◦ Behavior based on choices.
  ◦ Thief of Time.
  ◦ Silent Killer.
  ◦ Evil twin of Bit by Bit.

▶ Root of procrastination: fear
  ◦ Fear of criticism.
  ◦ Fear of failure.
  ◦ Fear of success.
  ◦ Fear of boredom.
  ◦ Perfectionism.

▶ Shifting Your Attitude
  1. Focus daily on your objectives.
  2. Consistently take some form of action now.
  3. Face tasks and challenges head-on.

▶ Permanent Procrastination Removal
  1. Apply Push-Pull Principle.
  2. Apply Time Warp visualization tool.
  3. Refer to Push-Pull and Time Warp as needed to condition and maintain change.

Put Your Knowledge Into Action

You should have a good idea of your action plan for this module. Work on developing your positive attitude and awareness to arm yourself against procrastination. First, write down the three attitude attributes for action we discussed on a note card. Remember, these are focus daily on your objectives, consistently take some for of action now, and face tasks and challenges head-on. Then, simply look at this list at least five mornings a week for the next three to four weeks. You can then pull back to a couple of mornings a week after that.

Also, go through the three-step process for procrastination removal. Go through your Push-Pull worksheet for procrastination and your Time

Warp visualization worksheets. As you go through this process, you might gain new insights into procrastination costs and action rewards. If you do, simply update your worksheets to reflect these insights.

Once you complete your worksheets, begin reviewing them at least five mornings a week for three weeks. If you notice significant improvement, you can then review them two to three days a week to maintain conditioning.

Keep in mind that if you begin to slip back into old procrastination habits, simply go through the Time Warp visualization again and increase your frequency of review to strengthen conditioning. Seek to continually find a balance for yourself.

By maintaining awareness infused with emotions of both the pain of procrastinating and the pleasure of action, your knowledge will metabolize itself into positive action and behaviors. Time will be on your side, and you will easily find yourself winning the war against procrastination.

Permanent Procrastination Removal Worksheet

(Push-Pull Principle)

I am totally committed to winning the war against procrastination and finding pleasure in taking action right away!

Push:

The *costs* if I continue to procrastinate at my current pace. (emotional, financial, physical, social, spiritual)

_____

_____

_____

_____

_____

_____

_____

_____

_____

Pull:

The *rewards* when I drastically reduce procrastination and find pleasure in taking action right away. (emotional, financial, physical, social, spiritual)

_____

_____

_____

_____

_____

_____

_____

_____

_____

Time Warp Procrastination Worksheet

Over the past year: What has your procrastinating specifically cost you emotionally, financially, physically, socially, or spiritually?

_____

_____

_____

_____

Over the past 10 years: What has your procrastinating specifically cost you emotionally, financially, physically, socially, or spiritually?

_____

_____

_____

_____

The Present: What is your procrastinating specifically costing you emotionally, financially, physically, socially, or spiritually right now?

_____

_____

_____

_____

Over the next year: What will your procrastinating specifically cost you emotionally, financially, physically, socially, or spiritually?

_____

_____

_____

_____

Face Yourself: Describe in detail how you will look and feel in *one year* if you continue procrastinating at your current pace.

_____

_____

_____

_____

Time Warp Procrastination Worksheet page 2

Over the next five years: What will your procrastinating specifically cost you emotionally, financially, physically, socially, or spiritually?

_____

_____

_____

_____

_____

Face Yourself: Describe in detail how you will look and feel in _five years_ if you continue procrastinating at your current pace.

_____

_____

_____

_____

_____

Over the next 10 years: What will your procrastinating specifically cost you emotionally, financially, physically, socially, or spiritually?

_____

_____

_____

_____

_____

Face Yourself: Describe in detail how you will look and feel in _10 years_ if you continue procrastinating at your current pace.

_____

_____

_____

_____

_____

Time Warp Consistent Action Worksheet

Over the next year: What will consistent action specifically reward you with emotionally, financially, physically, socially, or spiritually?

_____

_____

_____

_____

_____

Face Yourself: Describe in detail how you will look and feel in _one year_ if you take consistent action.

_____

_____

_____

_____

_____

Over the next five years: What will consistent action specifically reward you with emotionally, financially, physically, socially, or spiritually?

_____

_____

_____

_____

_____

Face Yourself: Describe in detail how you will look and feel in _five years_ if you take consistent action.

_____

_____

_____

_____

_____

Time Warp Consistent Action Worksheet page 2

Over the next 10 years: What will consistent action specifically reward you with emotionally, financially, physically, socially, or spiritually?

_____

_____

_____

_____

_____

_____

_____

_____

_____

_____

_____

Face Yourself: Describe in detail how you will look and feel in *10 years* if you take consistent action.

_____

_____

_____

_____

_____

_____

_____

_____

_____

_____

_____

_____

_____

MODULE

MOMENTS: THE SECRET OF LIFE

The Origin of Moments

In the fall of 1999, two unrelated media events sparked the creation of Time Control's Moments tool.

The first was an interview with former Dallas Cowboys' football star Deion Sanders. Having made a career of highlight reel interceptions and punt and kickoff returns for touchdowns, Deion reflected that he defined the success of his career by individual moments on the field. With all of the years of preparation for the NFL, with all of the countless hours of physical and mental conditioning, with all of the practices, with all of the hours of actual game time throughout his career, it was the individual big plays that defined Deion Sanders.

These individual defining moments could be summed up into just a handful of minutes. In his thousands of hours of living the game of football, Deion's success and fame were measured in mere moments. It is for these moments that he is paid millions of dollars a year.

When I heard the interview the Moments tool didn't hit me quite yet, but I began to think about how we measure our success and joy through time. I immediately thought of other sport stars and how their success and fame were measured the same as Deion Sanders's. Almost every sport's hero I could think of was defined by mere moments—the accumulation of short-lived big plays that made them famous.

Mark McGwire was perhaps the best sports example in my brainstorming. Mark McGwire, Major League Baseball's all time homerun leader, electrified a nation and rejuvenated a dying past time in 1998 when he not only eclipsed Roger Maris's 37-year longstanding 61 homerun single season record, he shattered it with an almost untouchable 70 homeruns.

Each homerun took only seconds to hit and just a moment or two to complete the running of the bases and a short celebration at home plate. Americans who never followed baseball began to watch and become more and more interested as the media followed his every step that season.

With each new homerun, with each monster swing closer to the record he took, special moments accumulated. McGwire's homerun swing to tie the record at 61 and his next to eclipse it were moments frozen in time for baseball history. The live national television coverage, the unbelievable amount of reporters and cameramen, the St. Louis hometown fans' intensity, and McGwire's classy sense of his place in history created a sense of magic for baseball that hadn't been felt in decades.

The true measurement of time for each of these events was only a few minutes. But their worth, their value to Mark McGwire, his family, teammates, and friends, Major League Baseball, the tens of thousands who were present, and the millions who watched live was priceless. Defining moments for Mark McGwire, Major League Baseball and America.

I thought this idea of defining moments was neat for sports stars but what about everybody else—what about in our own personal lives. I reflected on parts of my own past and tried to see if moments impacted me in the same way. They had. When I thought about my time in college at the United States Naval Academy, I saw it was moments that defined my experiences. Although I had spent four long years at Annapolis, all I could focus on in remembering my past was individual moments in time. The events that welled up in my memory only took a few minutes each—getting my head shaved my first day of arrival; overcoming individual physical, mental, and emotional challenges thrown at me my first year; experiences with friends and roommates; courting my wife; finally beating Army in football; receiving my diploma from the Vice President of the United States; and throwing my cover into the air with a thousand fellow graduates as the Blue Angels zoomed overhead during graduation.

I put this same focus toward my naval aviation career and had the same results. My eight years of aviation service was defined by moments. My success, my defining memories, my reputation were defined by the accumulation of individual minutes in time. Although I had spent years in training with countless hours of study and practice what stuck with me, what defined that time for me was the few exhilarating moments spent in my first flight, having my wife and parents pin on my Navy Wings of Gold, flying by myself for the first time, the handful of times I tracked Russian submarines, flying at the North Pole, missions in Bosnia, and dodging hurricanes and capturing drug smugglers in the Caribbean.

Following the Deion Sanders's interview and putting some thought into it I knew I was on to something that would help Time Control, but I felt I was still missing a piece of the puzzle. Then a week later I heard Faith Hill on the radio.

I was driving home one evening with my family and just randomly switching radio stations to find a good song. I seldom listened to country music stations at the time but just happened to lock on to one at the right time. Faith Hill's "The Secret of Life" was playing. It was an upbeat tune so I stuck with it. Then I began to actually listen to the words. The lyrics hit me like a bolt of lightning, and I got very excited. This was it! Hill's simple message was the missing piece of the puzzle I didn't even realize I was looking for.

Faith Hill's message was that the secret of life isn't complex or mysterious. It lies in the simple pleasures and rules of day-to-day life that we tend to overlook. As she sings in her song about two guys having a conversation in a bar, the secret of life is:

> *A good cup of coffee, keep your eye on the ball,*
> *a beautiful woman, Monday Night Football,*
> *Rolling Stones records, Mom's apple pies,*
> *gettin' up early, stayin' up late, try not to hurry,*
> *and to find the right woman.*

Obviously her list in the song doesn't apply to everyone, but her message does. Rather than trying to concentrate our lives on looking for a magical key to unlock the secret door of life, we should open our eyes to the wonders before us every day. They're different for each of us, but we all have them. Faith Hill's message is to be conscious of and grateful for the simple pleasures and truths in our lives.

By the time her song was over on my drive home I had completed my Moments tool. It only took a few minutes itself to create, but its impact felt so true and it complemented my other Time Control tools so well, that I knew it had significant value to our control of time.

The tool Moments says that our joy and enrichment in time are defined by our accumulation of individual, positive moments—both defining, significant moments and simple, everyday ones.

Your Moments: An Inventory

The Moments tool helps build your time through a continuous two-part process. The first part is taking an inventory of defining significant and simple moments for your past and present. The second is consciously trying to invest into your collection of moments every day.

Let's start with your inventory.

See how individual moments have defined your life. See just how many or how few significant moments you've had in your life to date and how many simple ones you may have taken for granted through the years. To do this, begin the process of regularly writing down the defining moments in your life, through a Moments journal. Use a blank journal, a notebook, loose sheets in a binder, your computer, or crayon and napkins—whatever works for you. Just make sure it's a medium you can keep and look back through in the future.

You can make this a personal journal that you just keep for yourself or you can create one with family or loved ones' contribution. Mine is a joint one with my wife with our little boys' help.

If you already keep a Gratitude journal, you can combine it with your Moments journal or you can keep separate journals. For my family and my personal situation, I find it easier and more beneficial to combine them. Keep in mind that your daily journal entries should be insightful and motivating. If doing them begins to create stress and feels like work, simply test a new way of writing down your gratitudes and moments. If you accidentally skip a few days or you need a short break from the routine, that's perfectly fine. Don't ever let this incredible tool become stressful.

Your Moments journal serves multiple purposes to help you in your journey to gain more control of your time. The first is it helps put time in a better perspective. Time is relative. When we're stressed and hurried, it flies unmercifully by us at breakneck speeds. In what feels like a blink of an eye, it can pass through days, months, even years, slipping opportunity after opportunity right by us. However, the opposite is true as well. When we're relaxed, grateful and observant of all that we've done and experienced in the past and aware of the wonderful possibilities that each day brings, then time seems to slow down and open its opportunities up before us. Remembering and writing down your past's defining moments and looking for new ones to log each day will put time in this better perspective for you.

The second purpose of your Moments journal is to keep you grateful. It will help you realize how rich your life has been to date and keep you from taking simple pleasures for granted. This can only help shift your mind's focus to be more positively motivated.

And the third purpose of your Moments journal is to act as a measuring stick for your Clarity. Each evening you'll be looking to record the defining moments of your day. Some will be the simple pleasures of the day, but others will be significant events. These defining significant events will be moments that move you toward the clear picture of your future, your Clarity. Because of your daily awareness and vigilance to record such events, you'll actually help motivate yourself to create them! Think of this journal as a Clarity progress chart and accelerator.

Now to put your Moments journal to beneficial use and begin creating that all-important moments inventory.

Set aside a small amount of time every evening when you are most relaxed to record your journal entries. Five minutes or so is all you need. Now that sounds familiar, doesn't it? For my family, we prefer doing our journal just before my young boys go to bed. You're human and your life doesn't revolve around your journal entry process. It's a tool to help you keep your behaviors working for you in time. Look for five nights out of each of your weeks to work on your Moments journal, and you'll reap the compounding rewards of time working for you.

When relaxed and ready to work on your journal, first think back through your life and record any significant defining moments that come to mind. Spend only a couple minutes doing this, listing only one or two events. Your goal is not to write everything, just what comes to mind in a few relaxed moments.

When you first start this process, you'll have a lifetime of possibilities to choose from. The possibilities will almost seem overwhelming. Don't worry! Just write a few. By going through this process a little every night you'll begin to chip away at your mountain of choices. Don't worry about being perfect, either. As you spend more and more time with your journal you may repeat writing down events that you've already recorded. That's fine. Rather than dig through your journal entries to see if you may have already written a past defining moment, creating stress and wasting time, just recognize that certain events are important enough for you to list more than once.

Don't worry about the order of your moments. Trying to write all of the significant moments in your life in their order of importance to you can create some stress. You'll end up not listing good moments that do come to mind because you haven't listed others that may hold more significance to you. Again, this process doesn't work if you make it stressful. Just write what comes to mind. You'll eventually get all of the important moments in your life as you continually go through this process.

When you list an event you can put as little or as much detail as you want with it. As long as when you look back through your journal and see your listed entry you recognize the importance it had in your life, you'll be good to go. If you find it enjoyable to write down the details surrounding an event and the impact it had on your life, go for it.

To help you get started, think back to your personal relationships for great moments—your family, your friends, past loves. Don't forget about moments in school, college, sports, hobbies, club events, work, business, church, and community service.

After brainstorming a few past significant moments, think for a minute on any simple defining moments from your past. These are the day-to-day pleasures since your childhood that bring a smile to your face and a warm memory to heart. What made you happy as a child? What about as you were growing older in high school? What did you used to enjoy that you've since taken for granted when you were a young adult? Continue this thinking process to present day. Again, you'll face a large group of possibilities. Just choose one or two, not worrying about any order of importance or time.

This is very similar to the process for a Gratitude journal except rather than focusing on the present you're allowing yourself to go through your entire life.

Lastly, look at today. Write down any significant and simple moments that come to mind from today. That's it!

Through the entire five-or-so-minute nightly process, you should come up with one or two past significant events, one or two past simple moments, and any significant or simple moments that defined today for you. Remember, don't let this become stressful. Make this fun and something you look forward to every night. The rewards will be worth it!

Your Moments Bank Account

The Moments tool helps build your time through a continuous two-part process. The daily inventory process you just learned is the first part, creating critical awareness for the power of significant and simple moments in your life. The second part comes from consciously trying to invest into your collection of moments every day.

To do this, think of your collection of moments as a bank account. Like a regular bank account, you can make deposits to your Moments account. You do this by creating defining moments through your day. Every time you create or experience a positive moment you add to your account's total worth. Although not in any specific measurable way, significant moments are worth more than simple ones. Because they carry more weight in your life, each makes a greater impact on your account balance than simpler moments. However, simple daily moments are much more easily abundant in your life. You can create and find life's hidden pleasures and joys every day if you choose. So don't lose the opportunity to let simple moments greatly increase your account balance through the compounding power of time.

Also, like a real bank account, your Moments account earns interest. Every time you recall past moments with fondness you remember the richness of your life and wealth of time well spent. By not taking past significant and simple moments for granted you earn interest on your Moments account. You do this every time you write in your Moments journal and every time you spend a few minutes reviewing past entries. The end result is shifting your time to an increased positive perspective!

So what do you do with the wealth you accumulate in your Moment's account? Unlike a normal bank account, you cannot make any withdrawals from your Moments account, but its value does hold great worth for you. Your account balance serves as a measure of the worth of your life and your time. The greater your balance, the better your perspective on time and your control of yourself within it. The more you're aware of this wealth, the more you'll realize the incredible opportunities you have each and every day of your life.

Take Charge of Your Wealth: Moment Investing

Begin creating the continuous habit of trying to invest into your collection of moments every day. Become your own moment advisor for your bank account. Every day, consciously look to create significant and simple moments for you to record in your nightly inventory. In your morning review of your Clarity and goals, see if there are any significant actions you can take to move closer to your future vision and milestones. Then look for the moment opportunities in your day to make them happen.

If a day or so passes without you being able to make significant strides forward, don't sweat it. The idea is to consistently and consciously look for opportunities for significant moments. You won't get them every day, but trying will open doors you never imagined and quickly make you a wealthy person through your Moments bank account.

Every day, remain aware for the simple moments you can experience as well. They're everywhere, and just keeping you eyes open will massively help you from taking these important simple pleasures for granted.

Look to add to your Moments bank account every day. It's not hard; it's just a matter of increasing your awareness. Your increased awareness will act like a money magnet for your account. By looking for significant and simple moments every day, you'll put the power of continual success and Bit by Bit to work for you. Time and all of its rewards will now seem to work for you rather than against you. This is true Time Control!

60-Second Power Summary

▸ Our joy and enrichment in time are defined by our accumulation of individual, positive moments.

    ▹ Defining, significant moments.

    ▹ Simple, everyday moments.

▸ Moments Journal

    ▹ Puts time in a better perspective.

    ▹ Keeps you grateful.

    ▹ Acts as a measuring stick for your Clarity.

    ▹ Five minutes, five nights a week.

    ▹ One or two past significant events.

    ▹ One or two past simple moments.

    ▹ Any significant or simple moments that defined today.

▸ Invest into your collection of moments every day

    ▹ Moments Bank Account.

    ▹ Increase awareness

Put Your Knowledge Into Action

Your action plan for this module is pretty self-evident. Obtain a Moments journal within the next few days and commit to going through the Moments tool process of inventory and investment for the next three weeks. Shoot for at least five nightly sessions each week. After your three-week trial, evaluate if this nightly process is making a difference in your perspective on time and helping you make strides toward your Clarity. Then decide if you want to make this tool a permanent part of your Time Control arsenal.

Module

Maximizing Any Experience

How many times have you gone through an experience and afterwards, with 20/20 hindsight, wished you had gone through it differently?

▸ **After an important meeting at work.**
Have you ever wanted to go back in time and change your preparation, your delivery, what you wore, or the just the location and atmosphere?

▸ **After an important phone call, whether it was business or personal.**
Have you ever wished you could have said something different or been more prepared or been more aggressive?

▸ **After a sales event.**
If given the chance to say or do something other than what you did or if you could have been better prepared for the prospect or focused more on the prospect's wants and needs over your own, would you do it differently?

▸ **After a routine day at your job or in your business.**
Looking back, have you ever wished you would have spent your hours differently, wasting less time and focusing more effectively?

▸ **At home, after a typical family evening or your weekend or a vacation.**
Have you ever wished you spent your time in a better way, with less stress or arguments or wasted time? Have you ever wished you spent less time in front of the television?

▶ **Or just after a simple night's sleep.**
Do ever wish you were more comfortable and less stressed or
had eaten or drank less before going to bed? Do you ever
wake up the next morning, wishing you had watched a little
less television the night before or spent a little less time on
your computer or worked a little less? How many times have
you mentally beat yourself up for not going to bed earlier?

To go back in time. To do it again. To do it differently. Unfortunately,
there is no magic key to go back in time and change things for the better.
But the next best thing is—Maximizing!

Maximizing for Your Success

The armchair quarterback; the backseat driver—there's something
positive and constructive to be said about these.

When you can sit back and look at events or experiences from a distance, removed from the stress and distractions involved, you see things in
a completely different light. You tend to look at the bigger picture and can
see the forest through the trees. And you can pick up subtle details that
you have a tendency to lose when caught up in the action.

This is the essence of Maximizing. To play armchair quarterback with
yourself but to do so ahead of time so you can make changes that make a
positive difference. To control your experiences, to control your time, to
the very best of your ability.

The reason why we wish we could go back so often in time and do things
differently is because of our human behaviors. When we are overworked,
overstressed, overwhelmed, or just acting on autopilot and taking an event
for granted, we very rarely step back to see the big picture and important
details. We tend to get caught up in the action and sometimes hung up on
trivial details and just get by. Afterwards when we have the time to replay
the experience in our heads and review what we did or said, we realize
there were things we should have done differently. That's when we wish we
could go back in time!

A simple tool can prevent this, make the difference, and can break
your behavioral pattern before an event and give you the power to see the
big picture and play armchair quarterback ahead of time. This simple tool
is Maximizing and only takes a few minutes to do—a few minutes that can
make all the difference in the world!

Maximizing is about taking control over things you have influence
over prior to an event or experience. Obviously you can't control everything that happens during an event. Other people's choices and reactions
and external factors such as the environment are outside your sphere of

direct influence. But you do have complete control over how you prepare, how you act and what you say.

More often than not, when you want to go back in time and change an event, it has to do with your actions. Preparing better ahead of time, saying something different, doing something different. All your actions are in your sphere of control. All able to be Maximized.

The Maximizing Tool

The concept of Maximizing is extremely easy to pick up. First, before an event or experience that you want Maximized, simply ask yourself how prepared you think you are both mentally and physically for the event. You'll go through the details in your head and take a subjective measurement similar to the one you use to measure your motivation.

Then you'll ask yourself what you can do to make the event a little better ahead of time. You'll repeat asking this question over and over until you've exhausted your beneficial possibilities, listing your answers each time. When complete, you'll have a laundry list of actions to maximize the event ahead of time. You'll then choose which actions you want and take action. Maximizing the event for your increased success in time!

By measuring your preparedness for an event ahead of time and forcing yourself to think of little ways to make yourself better and better prepared, you get to play armchair quarterback ahead of time. You pull yourself back and look at the big picture with a chance to make positive changes. Something we fail to do more times than not.

Maximizing almost sounds too easy. It really is kindergarten in its complexity—and it doesn't take much time. Be careful, though. Simple tools are many times the most powerful things we can do to make a positive difference in our lives. Because they are simple we tend to overlook them. In our blinded maturity we often forget the basics. If it's not complex, we often feel it's not worthy of our consideration. It's beneath us. But what would a multi-million dollar athlete be without the basics? Soon looking for another team to play for! What would a business be without marketing and customer service basics? Out of business! And what would a sailor, soldier, or an aviator be without the basics? Dead!

Let's Practice!

The best way to ingrain the habit of putting Maximizing to work for you is to go through examples and get you to practice. Go ahead and make several copies of the worksheet for this module.

Let's look at the layout of the worksheet. As seen in *Worksheet example 1a*, it's a scale from 0 to 100, similar to the motivation measurement scale. This scale is best seen vertically, though, with 0 on the bottom and 100 at the top.

Maximizing Worksheet

```
100
  |
 90
  |
 80
  |
 70
  |
 60
  |
 50
  |
 40
  |
 30
  |
 20
  |
 10
  |
  0
```

Worksheet example 1a

On the scale, 0 represents that you are utterly and completely unprepared both mentally and physically for an event. By mentally unprepared, I mean you have no knowledge or training for the event's subject, you have no plan of action for the event, you haven't rehearsed what you're going to do or say during the event, and you're not motivated.

By physically unprepared, I mean you've made no preparations in your own or others' personal physical conditioning or appearance. This is your physical training for an event, but it also includes your clothes and personal grooming. Being physically unprepared also means you made no positive adjustments to the environment of the event. The event's environment involves the location of the event, the layout of the room or event area, background music and noises, smells, temperature, décor, drinks, snacks, handouts, and presentation multimedia.

Conversely, a 100 on the scale represents that you've done every single positive thing possible to bring the outcome of the event to a successful end. You're mentally prepared to the absolute best of your ability, with a very strong knowledge of the event's subject. You have a well-thought-out plan of action, have comfortably rehearsed what you're going to do or say during the event, and are very motivated.

A 100 also means you're physically prepared, with solid preparations in your own and others' personal physical conditioning and appearance. Your clothing and personal grooming are top-notch for the particular event. You've also made the best positive adjustments to the event's environment. You've chosen the best location, the best room or area layout, the best background music, the best aromatic smells, the best temperature, the best décor, the best drinks and food, the best handout design, and the best presentation multimedia for those that apply.

Being at a 0 is hard to imagine. You'd have to be taken completely by surprise or have no regard for the event to approach this side of the scale. A 100 may also be equally hard to hit, demanding an almost perfectionist attitude to reach.

Remembering that perfectionism is more times than not wasteful to the outcome of your time, you don't need to be a 100 to be effective. You simply need to consider approaching it for a particular event, determine what individual steps are within your power to take to get close, then choose what steps you are actually willing to commit to in order to Maximize the event's outcome.

I'm going to go through 11 examples that cover many of the basic situations you might run into both at work and home.

Example 1: Studying This Module

This first example is absolutely relevant to this very moment. Normally, you'll want to Maximize an event before you start if you can, but for this example we'll see what you can do to improve studying this module for the rest of your session today.

Taking into account your mental clarity and present motivation level, your physical comfort, your location, your sleep level, and all other external environmental factors, ask yourself how prepared you are for absorbing the beneficial information in this module. Mark your level on the worksheet scale.

You probably marked somewhere between 0 and 100. The difference you have between where you marked and 100 is how much room you have to Maximize and improve your control of the outcome.

For example, let's say you chose 60. It's marked on *Worksheet example 1b* for illustration.

Now comes the fun part—the heart and soul of Maximizing. Ask yourself, what you can do to move yourself a little closer to 100. In other words, what would it take for you to move from a 60 to a 65 or 70, just a small improvement?

You've got all kinds of choices. Just try to include both mental and physical improvements in your brainstorming.

Let's say you chose to increase your motivation level by performing a few simple Power Breaths. Doing these would probably clear your mind and help you focus, moving you to a 65. If you choose to do them outside they could even move you to a 70.

```
Maximizing Worksheet
 100
  |
 90
  |
 80
  |
 70
  |
 60   —Present level
  |
 50
  |
 40
  |
 30
  |
 20
  |
 10
  |
  0
```

Worksheet Example 1b

```
Maximizing Worksheet
  100
   |
  90
   |
  80
   |
  70   —Power Breaths done outside
          in fresh air
   |
  60   —Present level
   |
  50
   |
  40
```

Worksheet example 1c

Mark this on your worksheet as seen in *Worksheet example 1c*. If you chose something else, go ahead and mark what you came up with instead.

Now continue to ask yourself what can you do to make studying this module a little better and a little better and so on. Keep marking these incremental improvements on your worksheet until you've exhausted your possible positive improvements. Spend five or so minutes doing this and don't worry about being perfect or missing possible ideas.

Keep in mind that the order of these improvements isn't important. If you have a great brainstorming session and come up with more incremental ideas than you have room to list at small five to 10 point increments to 100, don't worry about it. Just list the other possible action ideas somewhere neat on your worksheet.

Remember the purpose of the worksheet with it's measurement scale and incremental improvement listings is just to get you take stock in where you are in your current preparation for an event and to brainstorm small, easy to do improvements for you to choose from to Maximize your control of the event. Don't make this hard. The worksheet is a guide, and its structure or rules shouldn't restrict you from listing good possible action ideas.

Below is the continuation of my brainstorming for this example and how I marked the improvements on my worksheet.

Mental improvements to improve focus and motivation:
  - *Perform a few Power Breaths (outside, if I can)*
  - *Listen to motivational music*

Physical and environmental improvements include:
  - *Adjust or change clothing to be more comfortable*
  - *Play good background music*
  - *Remove or reduce distracting noises*

```
Maximizing Worksheet
  100 —Remove or reduce
         distracting noises
   |
  90  —Play good background music
   |  —Listen to motivational music
  80  —Adjust or change clothing to
         be more comfortable
   |
  70  —Power Breaths done outside
         in fresh air
   |
  60  —Present level
   |
  50
   |
  40
```

Worksheet example 1d

Once your worksheet is complete, you're ready for action—the most important part of Maximizing. Going through the process of creating your Maximizing worksheet for an event means absolutely nothing and is a complete waste of time unless you commit to acting on some or all of your brainstormed incremental improvements! Decide which of your listed incremental improvements you're willing to do and act on them before or during your event. Obviously, the more you're able to do, the greater the impact of you Maximizing the event to your advantage.

For this example, I had some improvements that I felt would improve my studying this module by five points and others that had a little greater impact at 10 points each. All things being equal on timing, I try to do the actions that give me the greatest impact first.

Right now, pause from studying this module further until you take action on your brainstormings or my suggestions above to Maximize studying this module. See if it makes a positive difference when you return and helps you absorb this material at a higher level.

Example 2: Getting Ready for Work

For this example, on the scale from 0 to 100 where would you say you are on a typical workday on getting up, getting ready for work and making the commute to your job?

Let's assume you find getting up a challenge, often find yourself hurried to get out the door and are stressed on your commute. This would typically be about a 30 on the scale.

After marking this on the worksheet (see *Worksheet example 2*), I begin the simple brainstorming process of asking what can I do to make this event a little better. I try to think of mental improvements to increase my motivation and positive attitude and physical improvements to increase my energy and comfort. I simply mark each increment on the worksheet as I brainstorm, again not worrying about order.

Maximizing Worksheet

100 —Eat a healthy breakfast
| —Make house temperature more comfortable
90   —Listen to improvement tapes during commute
| —Listen to motivational music
80   —Review , Daily Power Up!

|
70   —Prepare for the morning the night before
| —Exercise for a few minutes (stretch, walk, jog, push-ups, sit-ups, etc.)
60
| —Get up earlier for personal quiet time
50
| —Go to bed earlier (eliminate sleep debt)
40
|
30   —Present level
|
20

Worksheet example 2

Now simply commit to where you want to be in the morning and take the appropriate actions to get there! Don't take your mornings for granted and diminish their importance to the entire rest of your day.

Maximize them!

Example 3: Performing Your Job

For this example, where on the performance scale would you say you are on a typical workday for performing your job or running your business?

Depending on how much you love or dislike your work, your present level could be all over the scale. For this example, though, I'm going to assume you like your job but know you could improve or be more motivated in your performance. We'll start with a level 50.

Worksheet example 3 is my completed worksheet after brainstorming.

Again simply commit to where you want to be in your work performance and take the appropriate actions to get there!

Maximizing Worksheet

```
100  —Daily perform Bit by Bit to improve job skills
 |   —Adjust temperature, airflow, and lighting to comfort
 90  —Perform Power Breaths and  Power Screams throughout day
 |
 80  —Reduce distractions and time wasters
 |
 70  —Play good background music
 |   —Listen to motivational music
 60  —Review Daily Power Up!
 |
 50  —Present level
 |
 40
```

Worksheet example 3

Example 4: Running or Participating in a Meeting

By now, I'm sure you're getting the idea of how Maximizing works. Simply determine where your performance level is for an event ahead of time, brainstorm simple incremental improvements, and then commit to action. No problem!

I still want you to see how Maximizing works for other areas of your life, but I also don't want to be too repetitive. So, for the remaining examples, I will simply show you my completed worksheets to give you some ideas.

My completed worksheet for running a meeting is seen in *Worksheet example 4a*. This can apply to an informational, decision-making, or sales meeting.

```
Maximizing Worksheet
  100 —Follow agenda
   |    —Start and end on time
   90  —Improve meeting environment (temperature, lighting, layout)
   |
   80  —Improve presentation multimedia
   |    —Create better handouts
   70  —Create and distribute an agenda
   |
   60  —Determine purpose and desired outcome of meeting
   |
   50  —present level
   |
   40
```

Worksheet example 4a

My completed worksheet for participating in a meeting is seen below. I'm assuming I'm not very motivated for the meeting to begin with.

```
Maximizing Worksheet
  100 —Actively participate in meeting
   |
   90  —Take notes during meeting
   |    —Get good night's sleep before meeting
   80
   |    —Don't eat big meal before meeting
   70  —Listen to motivational music before meeting
   |
   60  —Perform Power Breaths and Power Scream before meeting
   |
   50  —Study and prepare for my part of meeting
   |
   40  —Obtain meeting agenda at least one day in advance
   |
   30  —present level
   |
   20
```

Worksheet example 4b

Example 5: Studying, Writing, or Thinking

Whether you are studying for school, training, or personal development, whether you are writing for school, business, or pleasure, or whether you are looking for quiet time for thinking, mediation, or reflection, the following worksheet will give you good ideas to Maximize your time.

Maximizing Worksheet
100 —Light candles or incense for motivating aroma
| —Perform frequent Power Breaths
90   —Adjust temperature and airflow
|
80   —Play good background music
| —Listen to motivational music ahead of time
70   —Change into comfortable clothes
|
60   —Reduce distractions and time wasters
|
50   —present level
|
40

Worksheet example 5

Example 6: Relaxing at Home

Coming home from work and relaxing for the evening can be one of life's hidden great pleasures. But how many times a week do you go to bed and wonder what happened to the night? Why you don't feel like you relaxed and why you feel like you "wasted" an evening? Maximizing your evening ahead of time can help you gain back control of this important time.

Maximizing Worksheet
100 —Be selfish with at least 30 minutes of personal time
| —Exercise for evening energy
90
| —Get proper sleep for evening energy
80
| —Don't eat a heavy, bloating dinner
70   —Review family/personal Clarity and goals and take action
|
60   —Review Daily Motivation Questions on way home
|
50   —Listen to motivational music on way home
| —Perform Power Breaths and Power Screams
40   —present level
|
30

Worksheet example 6

Example 7: Going on Vacation

Going on vacation is something we all look forward to, but how many of your vacation experiences have ended in stress and frustration? Many times we're more exhausted from vacation than we are from our jobs! Has this ever happened to you?

The following worksheet can give you a few ideas to Maximize this time to your advantage.

Maximizing Worksheet
100 —Exercise patience and flexibility
 |
 90 —Review family/personal Clarity and goals daily
 |
 80 —Review Daily Motivation Questions throughout vacation
 | —Make sure vacation events are aligned with Clarity and goals
 70
 |
 60 —Present level
 |
 50

Worksheet example 7

Example 8: Spending Time with Someone Special

Spending time with those you love and care about is probably the greatest gift of life and the very best use of your precious time. By Maximizing your time with those you love, you not only prevent taking these moments for granted but you also take your level of joy and commitment to another level.

Below is a worksheet with ideas to help Maximize this time to you and your loved ones' advantage.

Maximizing Worksheet
100 —Look for ways to serve those you love
 | (Your time and attention are your most valuable gifts)
 90 —Get proper exercise
 | —Get proper sleep
 80 —Review family/personal Clarity and goals right before
 |
 70 —Review Daily Motivation Questions right before
 |
 60 —present level
 |
 50

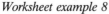

Worksheet example 8

Example 9: Performing House Chores

House chores, whether cleaning your home or washing the dishes, are the necessary evils of life. If you look upon them with drudgery and disdain, you'll take longer to do them and consider the time wasted. Find ways to Maximize this time, however, and you'll not only perform your work faster but you'll also be able to enjoy it.

Maximizing Worksheet
```
100 —Perform Power Screams while working
 |  —Perform Power Breaths while working
 90 —Make a game out of the work (be creative!)
 |
 80 —Get someone to help and talk to while working
 |
 70 —Dress comfortably
 |  —Review Clarity and goals while working
 60
 |  —Review Daily Motivation Questions while working
 50
 |  —Play motivating music while working
 40
 |
 30 —present level
 |
 20
```

Worksheet example 9

Example 10: Exercising

Exercising plays a huge role in helping you gain control of your time. It helps you build stores of energy to put toward effective uses throughout your day. But most importantly, it makes sure you have enough fuel left in your energy tank to give your best to those you love when you come home from work. How many times have you come home from work with only enough energy to eat dinner and crash on the couch in front of the tube? How many times have you told your kids that you're too tired to play with them? Exercise is an important key to help!

Usually we blow off exercising to some lame excuse because we aren't motivated and we don't find it much fun. If you get in the habit of Maximizing your exercise, you can help insure you'll exercise more often and enjoy the process much more.

```
Maximizing Worksheet
   100 —Warm up slowly and thoroughly
    |  —Listen to motivational music
   90
    |  —Choose exercise I enjoy
   80
    |  —Get an exercise partner
   70
    |  —Review Clarity and goals
   60 —Review Daily Motivation Questions
    |  —Choose peak time of day
   50
    |
   40 —Get proper equipment and clothing
    |
   30 —present level
    |
   20
```

Worksheet example 10

Example 11: Getting a Restful Night's Sleep

My last example is in an area you know I feel is critical to your control of time—getting a good night's sleep. For most of us, the main reason we don't get a good night's sleep is because we fail to Maximize its importance to everything we'll do the next day. Let the following worksheet help guide you to Maximizing your sleep for your best control of your time!

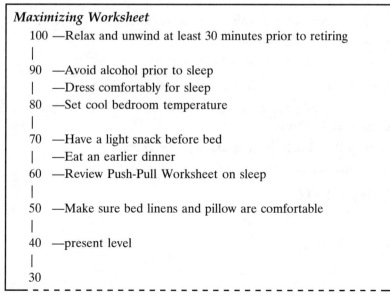

```
Maximizing Worksheet
   100 —Relax and unwind at least 30 minutes prior to retiring
    |
   90  —Avoid alcohol prior to sleep
    |  —Dress comfortably for sleep
   80  —Set cool bedroom temperature
    |
   70  —Have a light snack before bed
    |  —Eat an earlier dinner
   60  —Review Push-Pull Worksheet on sleep
    |
   50  —Make sure bed linens and pillow are comfortable
    |
   40  —present level
    |
   30
```

Worksheet example 11

The Key to Maximizing: Testing

You've seen plenty of examples in how to apply the power of Maximizing to your business and work lives. Focus for a moment on how to maximize Maximizing. The key to this is simple. Having an experimental and testing attitude is the key to successful long-term Maximizing.

When you're going through the Maximizing process for events you do on a frequent or moderate basis such as the 11 examples above, be sure to note how effective your chosen incremental action steps actually are in improving your control and desired outcomes. Some of your chosen action steps from your brainstormed worksheet will have tremendous positive impact. Others will seem to have little to no effect for the time taken to act on them. Take mental or written notes on this.

The next time you try to Maximize that event be sure to include the action steps that made a difference and weigh their impact accordingly on the scale. Don't include those action steps that didn't seem to pull their weight for your invested time. Instead try to think of new incremental actions that you can try.

Continue this "keep and try" attitude every new time you Maximize a frequent event. By doing this, you'll continually apply the Continual Success Improvement Formula to Maximizing—getting better and better and better at the event each time. What do you think this will do to your success in time?

Keep what works, eliminate what doesn't, try new things, and maximize your Maximizing!

60-Second Power Summary

▶ Maximizing
  ▷ Taking control over things you have influence over prior to an event or experience.
  ▷ Armchair quarterback ahead of time.
▶ Start with a subjective measurement of your event.
▶ Repeatedly ask yourself what can you do to make the event a little better ahead of time.
▶ Laundry list of actions to maximize the event
  ▷ Choose actions.
▶ Testing is the key.

Put Your Knowledge into Action

Make as many copies of the Maximizing worksheet included with this module as you need and begin applying Maximizing to the events of your life. Use the examples to help guide you, but don't feel you have to follow my brainstorming. Your situation and your tastes are probably different than mine. Brainstorm what works, is comfortable, and is doable for you. Commit to what level of performance you want for the event, and then take action! Action is your key to success.

Focus on making this a positive habit over the next three to four weeks.

You don't have to apply Maximizing to every part of your life. Start at a comfortable pace and add more events as you become proficient with this powerful tool.

Apply Bit by Bit to your success in using Maximizing. Focus on just spending a few minutes brainstorming your worksheet for an event. Five minutes or so works great! Putting a time limit on your brainstorming keeps you from being stuck in the time waster of perfectionism. It also keeps you from making an excuse that you don't have time to Maximize.

Maximizing Worksheet

100
_____
|
_____
90
_____
|
_____
80
_____
|
_____
70
_____
|
_____
60
_____
|
_____
50
_____
|
_____
40
_____
|
_____
30
_____
|
_____
20
_____
|
_____
10
_____
|
_____
0
_____

CONCLUDING ACTION PLAN

If you're reading this after working through all 13 modules and their respective behavior-shifting action plans, you're in an extremely enviable position. At the very, very least you should see a time control increase of two to four more profitable, productive, and enjoyable hours to each of your days. You've probably experienced more, much more.

If You Read Quickly through This Book

If you read quickly through this book without working through the action plans, it's time to go back step-by-step, module-by-module. You have the knowledge; let's take it to true, time-building power. Go back through each module, reviewing its material and acting on its action plan to restructure your behaviors for the extra time you desire. Reading through this book once straight through to get an overview of its material, style, tools and action plans is perfectly fine as long as you now *commit* to returning to Module 1 with your sleeves rolled up for some work.

You're at a crossroads and it's time to make a choice. You can just settle on the intellectual stimulation you gained by reading through this book or you can choose to have more knowledge and more *power* in your life by returning to the modules one at a time.

Where Do You Go from Here?

So you've completed your module action plans and have already gained significant control of your time. What do you do next? Simple. Your concluding Time Control plan is to maintain your behavioral gains and continue your growth.

For starters, continue applying the behavioral tools you've learned to maintain your gains and leverage your time on a continuous basis. The main time-building tools you've learned are:

- Clarity
- The Continual Success Improvement Formula
- Bit by Bit
- The War Board
- Proper Sleep
- Behavioral-based Goals
- Reducing Distractions and Time Wasters
- Body Motivation Tools
- Daily Motivation Questions
- The Six % Solution for Increased Energy
- The Sword and Shield Technique
- Daily Corps Values
- Push-Pull Principle and Time Warp for Procrastination
- Moments
- Maximizing

Although you've learned and tested each of these Time Control tools, you don't have to apply all of them for the rest of your life. You're human, and some of the tools may not fit your lifestyle or situation. Just make a commitment to yourself to continue applying the Time Control tools you've learned that gave you the biggest impact and best resonate with your life at both work and home.

Don't ever sweat slipping back into old behaviors that steal your time. If this ever happens, simply recognize that you're a human being and not a machine. Then go back and rework through a particular module that covers that behavior for a month to strengthen or rebuild your positive habits in that area.

The second part of your concluding Time Control action plan is to never stop growing. Make this a lifelong process and make it fun. Your continued growth can be in any area of your life that you want to improve and can be at any pace you choose, so long as you maintain some form of momentum. Apply continual success, Bit by Bit, and the War Board as needed toward future self-help or business books you read, tapes you listen to, or seminars you attend. These tools should make the future tools and techniques you learn even better.

Gain control of yourself,
And you can fully control your time.
Control your time,
And you control your destiny. (SM)

Index

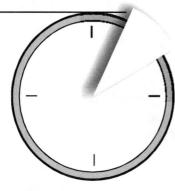

ABOUT THE AUTHOR

Vince Panella is the founder of Success-Centered Time Management. He has taught his Time Control program to thousands of companies and hundreds of thousands of people in 25 countries since 1982, beginning at the age of 14. He is a graduate of the U.S. Naval Academy, a former naval officer and aviator, a former university professor, and presently an international author, speaker, trainer, and success coach. Vince currently lives in Houston, Texas with his wife and two sons.

Visit Vince's Web site, *www.timecontrol.cc*, to take your Time Control training to even higher levels of success!

▶ Subscribe to free weekly Time Control e-newsletter
▶ Join the Time Control Training Room
  ▷ The Internet's most *effective* and *comprehensive* time-building course
  ▷ Over 30 Time Control modules
  ▷ Over 600 pages of downloadable text
  ▷ Over 50 behavior-shifting, downloadable worksheets
  ▷ 30 motivating hours of streaming audio/video slide shows of Vince coaching you through each module step by step